THE DANCING
DRUIDS

THE DANCING
DRUIDS

GLADYS MITCHELL

St. Martin's Press
New York

Library of Congress Cataloging in Publication Data

Mitchell, Gladys, 1901-
    The dancing druids.

    I. Title.
PR6025.I832D36   1986   823'.912   86-13792
ISBN 0-312-18207-4

First published in Great Britain by Michael Joseph Ltd. in 1948.
Published in 1975 by Severn House.

First U.S. Edition

10 9 8 7 6 5 4 3 2 1

To

THE NINE STONES OF WINTERBORNE ABBAS
which suggested the story

'And he ordered the stone figure to be taken up, and placed in his room near to his bed; and as often as he looked at it he wept and said, "O that I could bring thee back to life again . . .!" '

The Brothers Grimm—FAITHFUL JOHN

★

and to

MY DEAR ELIZABETH STAMP
for whom it was written

'Fain would I, Chloris, ere I die,
Bequeath you such a legacy,
As you might say, when I am gone,
"None has the like!" My heart alone
Were the best gift I could bestow;
But that's already yours, you know.'

Anonymous—17th century

Chapter One

★

'The young man set out with this letter, but missed his way, and came in the evening to a dark wood.'
THE BROTHERS GRIMM (*The Giant with the Three Golden Hairs*)

A HANDSOME young man in dirty white running-vest and shorts paused for a moment at the crossroads of a little market town in the south-west of England and then trotted on past the obelisk which commemorated the end of the Boer War. He turned down a narrow street and encountered a child of eight or nine years of age.

'Soppy runner!' said the child. The young man checked, smiled, glanced behind him, and then nodded as he thrust the damp hair from his brow and looked down at his bramble-scratched shins.

'I believe you,' he cordially responded. He then ran on again, heading south for the sea, and, immediately he had disappeared, round a bend came a straggle of eight or ten other young men who seemed in pursuit of the first.

With an instinct to support, as he thought, the weaker side, the child pointed to an alley which ran eastward, under a Tudor arch, and cried excitedly (for he was unused to telling lies, and found the experience exhilarating):

'That way! He run that way! I seen him go by!'

With one exception, the pursuers swung off to the left and vanished beneath the archway. The last of the group, however, ran blindly on, a long, thin, black-haired youth with a long, thin, freckled face, deep-set, intelligent eyes and a Spartan, kingly jowl.

He was, in point of fact, descended from kings, and occa-

sionally, although not often (for most of the kingliness had
been educated out of him) he reacted to the call of his blood.
He settled down very easily, however, after one of these in-
frequent, atavistic outbreaks, to the easy mediocrity of
democratic behaviour, and was behaving democratically now,
for it was not a desire for princely solitude which had caused
him to run in the right direction while all his companions took
the wrong one. It was that he had a fair knowledge of the
countryside and also of the psychology of the hare, who
happened to be his cousin, and this knowledge he was prepared
to place at the disposal of his team of hounds.

In the direction towards which he was heading there was
an ancient hill-fort. From the top of it he proposed to survey
the countryside, locate the hare, and, unless they were too far
off, give the view halloo to the hounds.

This altruistic scheme was doomed to disappointment.
Encouraged by what they regarded as a heaven-sent bit of
information, the hounds streamed away to the east, and found
themselves involved in a kind of suburb of the town from
which nothing was visible but houses, more alleys, some mean
factories and a tributary of the river. Undismayed, they ran
on, until good luck brought them on to a major road which,
acting on the directions of a signpost, they followed in what
was roughly the right direction—that is, in the direction taken
by their quarry; in other words, to the resort called Welsea
Beaches.

Meanwhile the solitary hound, whose name was O'Hara,
ran on until he came out past the cattle market and the station,
and on to a road which forked south-east on one prong and
south-west on the other, past what had been, in early history,
a third-century Roman amphitheatre. The high, grassy banks
of this ancient monument would afford, he thought, a preliminary view of the road which his cousin might have taken,
so he turned aside through an iron gate and ran on to the stiff
green grass. In three leaps which did credit to the iron muscles
of his thin, long legs, he was up on the mound which surrounded the open space of the amphitheatre, and was looking
about him.

Men were scything the grass below him, and he paused to consider their work. Before the Romans came, the amphitheatre had been a place of assembly of a different kind, a place of worship, a Neolithic or early Bronze Age meeting-place, a place of sanctuary, sacrifice (or coronation, maybe), mysterious, holy, horrible, and something of its departed glory clung about it as bright and soluble clouds will cling round the afternoon sun.

O'Hara lifted his eyes from the three men with their scythes, and, walking along the top of the mound, he looked ahead of him to where the road forked west and south and the railway kept a course as straight as a yard-stick towards the sea. He could see no sign of the hare.

'Gone to ground; foxing us, perhaps,' thought O'Hara; for it was what he himself would have done in his cousin's place. 'He's going to throw us off his track and then run round us. But I'll spot him all right from the fort.'

He descended the bank where the old Roman gateway had been, ran out from the enclosure through the modern iron swing-gate, and then took the road to his right, away from the railway. He crossed a hump-backed bridge, and for a quarter of a mile he followed the main road. After that he swung further to the right, and trotted along a narrow, sandy lane. At the main-road end of it were houses, ·but further on, past these, the road narrowed into a track, which, appearing to lead to a bell-barrow, turned southwards in a half-mile semi-circle, and led, instead, to the hill-fort, grim and gloomy, and shadowed by heavy cloud, which he had chosen as the real objective from which to survey his route and spot the hare.

The track became a footpath ascending the hill. Soon it was very steep. O'Hara could do no more than drop into a walk as the slope of the hill grew shorter, for the gradient sharpened abruptly into something resembling a cliff-face, or a test hill in the Tourist Trophy race.

He saw a shepherd with his flock and dog on the western shoulder of the hill, but when these had gone, the hillside was deserted and desolate, and the young man, pausing a moment to look about him, instinctively shrugged from his shoulders

the weight of its lonely vastness. Around him he saw nothing
but the sky and the towering hill-top, and, between the two
and defying them, the scowling mounds and ditches of
primitive man's defence against his enemies.

O'Hara climbed the fifty-foot banking and walked along the
outer walls of the fort. From the top of these Cyclopean battlements he looked abroad over miles of rolling country. Below
him was a bell-barrow, to his right the deep, dark ditches of
the inner defences. Ahead of him, miles away, he could see the
surrounding hills, and, between and among them, the little
winding roads, like strings of dirty tape, along one of which he
thought his Cousin Gascoigne must be running. But although
he gazed long and carefully, he could still see no sign of his
cousin, and, glancing once more towards the inner earthworks
of the castle, it occurred to him how strange it was that, on a
fair afternoon, the fort should remain so gloomy. So unpleasantly persistent did this thought become (as did the one
which followed it of how lonely the situation was) that he was
obliged, in self-defence, to project his mind very strongly on to
the object of his search, the valiant hare, who seemed to have
disappeared (another uncomfortable thought from which he
soon recoiled) without leaving a clue to guide the pursuers.

'Hang it!' thought O'Hara, forcing himself to return to the
circumstances of logic. 'He must have cut off towards the golf
course and gone to Horston! Why didn't I think of that before!
I shouldn't spot him from here!'

He had a last look for the hounds, and picked them out
away to the east. Only a hawk-eyed person would have seen
them at all, and only one who knew what to look for would
have recognized them for what they were, for they were almost
blurred by distance into forming part of the landscape. The
sight of them put an end to his morbid fancies, and, not too
well satisfied (for, although he had now worked out another
route which the solitary hare might have taken, he had no
proof that Gascoigne was really, after all, on the Horston
road), O'Hara turned in his tracks, reached the ancient
entrance to the fort between monumental bastions of earth
(now well grassed on top of the chalk), and descended to a

stony little path which circumscribed the hill-fort instead of
mounting it. He struck off to the south, then bore eastward.
Suddenly he obtained a glimpse of a runner in white making
for a gap in the hills, and not more than three hundred yards
ahead.

'Wonder what's happened?' thought O'Hara. 'Gerry ought
to be further on than that! However, it looks as though I've
got him!'

The track, having dropped from the hundred-foot contour
to something nearer sea-level, degenerated into a ditch.
O'Hara, running too confidently, turned his ankle on loose
pebbles, but still limped on until he reached a secondary road,
which broke out of the ditch and went alongside a small,
shallow brook.

His ankle hurt sharply at first, but gradually settled to a dull
pain which, without being unbearable, considerably slowed
him up. In spite of this, he still had hopes of catching up with
the hare.

'He'll go wrong after Horston,' he thought. 'He'll take the
wrong way across the golf course. I'll get up to him, or, anyway,
head him off, somewhere this side of Little Welsea. It'll be a
close call, but I know it round there and he doesn't.'

The road beneath his feet grew firmer, the pain in his ankle
slightly less. He would have liked to sit down on the grassy
verge and rub his foot, but he did not want to lose time, and
he felt, too, that so long as he kept on the move, the ankle
would stand no chance of stiffening.

His pace was not more than a jog-trot, and he was limping
along until he could see where the sandy road terminated,
when he met a man in a car. The road they were in was so
narrow that the car pulled up and O'Hara dropped into a
walk. The man in the car leaned out. He was a middle-aged,
shrewd-eyed fellow with a brisk voice.

'Like a lift?' he asked. 'I see you're limping a bit.'

'It's nothing,' O'Hara replied. 'Thanks, all the same, but I
think I can manage all right. There's plenty of grass alongside
the main road ahead. Perhaps I'll be better on that.'

'I see,' said the man. 'What is it—a cross-country run?'

'More or less. Hare and hounds. We don't use scent, that's all.'

'Is the hare a tall fellow with fair hair?'

'Yes,' said O'Hara, beginning to feel impatient, and prevented by his native courtesy from showing it.

'Take the footpath immediately opposite when you get on to the main road, then. That's the way he took. I saw him turn off. I'm afraid you won't catch him, all the same. He was going very strongly when I passed him.'

'I thought he'd make for the golf course,' said O'Hara, who could not see why his cousin should have taken the way the man said.

'I don't know, I'm sure, about that, but this fellow was taking the footpath I'm telling you of. I stopped to see him go by, and waited about a quarter of an hour to see whether there were any more behind him, but no more turned up, so on I came. You're a bit late, aren't you?'

'Better late than never,' said O'Hara.

The man eyed him doubtfully.

'*Very* late, aren't you?' he said, in a curiously impressive tone of voice.

'I don't think so,' O'Hara replied. 'But I'd better get on if I'm to catch him. Thanks very much for the tip!'

He broke into a lumbering trot, annoyed to find that his ankle had stiffened after all. When he reached the main road and glanced back he could still see the car. The man was standing in the road gazing after him, interested, no doubt, to see whether his advice would be followed.

Strong in this innocent assumption, O'Hara soon came in sight of the railway, and, following the footpath, crossed the main line by a footbridge. If the hare had passed that way, there was no other track he could have taken, but O'Hara, feeling dubiously that he had been sent on a wild-goose chase, found himself in another sandy lane. Two hundred yards along it he entered a wood, or, rather, not a natural wood but a plantation. It was gloomy, and, to his Celtic imagination, slightly frightening. Although the trees were young the atmosphere was heavy with a kind of mental thunder, as though ancient wrong had been done there and the land remembered it.

It was difficult to combat the suggestion of evil, and O'Hara, much oppressed by this, lengthened his stride and so quickened his pace that soon he was through the plantation and almost up to the house to which it belonged.

The détour he had made had added five miles already to the distance roughly estimated by the runners. An hour of precious time had gone, and the light was waning. O'Hara was now in a part of the country he did not know at all thoroughly, and this he found disconcerting, for, before embarking upon this ambitious heading-off of the hare, he had had, as he imagined, the landscape mapped out in his mind.

'I wonder what place this is?' he thought. 'And how far Gerry really has led us up the garden? I think that fellow must have been wrong. Still, I'm in for it now. I can't go back all that way. All the same, I wish I'd had another look at the map. This house . . . what a beastly place! And yet . . . what's wrong with it?'

He slowed to look at it. The house stared back at him so oddly, sulkily and uncomfortably that he stopped, as though to meet a challenge. Then, with some idea of asking his way— for it seemed foolish to feel frightened by a house—he began to limp up to the gates.

These were wide open. There was no lodge, and yet this seemed to be the main entrance. A broad but weed-grown drive led straight as an arrow to the front door, which was like the door of a church except that it had an incongruous nineteenth-century porch to shield it from the weather. A stained and almost indecipherable notice just inside the gateway, and attached to a lichened post, said, with enviable curtness:

KEEP OUT.

Nothing was further from O'Hara's thoughts by this time than to go in, and he remained gazing, in the fascination of horror, at the house. It was eerily still, and he thought at first that it might be uninhabited, for the blank and staring windows seemed to be without curtains and the place had a deserted, ghostly look, as though no human being ever went near it. It led, O'Hara fancied, a life of its own, apart from human life and antagonistic to it. It was not at this house that he would ask to be directed on his way.

Just as he was thinking thus, an old man, wheeling a barrow, came round the side of the house and, in doing so, broke the spell. O'Hara grinned to himself in contempt of his own foolish thoughts, and entered the grounds. At sight of him, however, the old man dropped the handles of the barrow, waved him off, and then scuttled into some bushes at the side of the building, rather in the manner of a surprised hen taking cover from a boisterous puppy.

'Well, I'm damned!' said O'Hara aloud; and turned back towards the road.

The blue mist was dimming the woods, and he thought, as he ran, of the hotel to which he was going; of the pleasures of a bath and a change of clothes—for the team had sent baggage on ahead of them and some were staying the night and would remain over Sunday in the seaside town, spending the morning swimming and the afternoon perhaps sailing on the bay. He groaned, half-humorously, and tried to quicken his pace.

'Lucky if I get to Welsea in time for breakfast!' he thought, as he eyed the deepening evening.

The road made a right-angle bend to pass by the side of the house. Four trees stood in a clearing among some rhododendron and holly bushes. There were an elm, a beech, an oak and a hornbeam. The trees were dead. Their stark branches, paper-grey, stuck out like the ribs of skeletons. They might have been gibbets, thought O'Hara, each with its dead man hanging and keeping the sheep by moonlight. The late afternoon was chilly. The young man shivered and ran on.

The road crossed a little stone bridge, and led past the lodge of the house, which was situated, curiously, at what seemed a secondary entrance. Behind the house was a paddock, but beyond it, and as far as O'Hara could see, the countryside, lonely and vast in the dusk which was now descending, stretched like an unmapped continent, uninviting, hilly, and sad.

His ankle was stiffening badly and hurt a good deal. His only object now was to reach his destination, and that as soon as he could. He was certain, by this time, that he had been misdirected, and he cursed himself for having taken any notice of the information given by the man in the car.

Of the golf-course, to which at one time his thoughts had been directed, there was now no promise, for he had left it far away to the west. Beside him there loomed a hill; beyond him there rose another. The road had the horrid unendingness of a dream of frustration and longing, but there seemed nothing to do except follow it to its end, and hope to find a village or a farm at which he could ask the way. Even a lift would not be out of the question. He was doing his ankle no good by keeping on his feet for so long.

Suddenly from the clouds which had rested on the hills and of which he had become increasingly conscious as they blotted out the last of the daylight, great drops of rain began to fall.

'That's the last straw,' thought O'Hara. 'I don't mind getting wet, and I don't much mind being lost, but the two together are too much. Why the devil did I listen to that fellow? I might have been in Welsea by now!'

As he indulged in these thoughts the road began to drop fairly steeply and to become much narrower. Far from being perturbed by these signs, he felt a sense of relief.

'A farm,' he thought. 'They can put me upon my way.' The road now entered a gloomy route between hedges, and trailed out into a wood. O'Hara decreased his pace and dropped into a walk. The rain came down fairly fast but he was saved from the worst of the downpour by the overhanging trees.

At last the road bent to the left and he saw some buildings. Behind them the trees were thick, and a round-roofed hut of military pattern seemed to shoulder its way in amongst them. A little beyond it was a cottage, but this was in ruins. In the dusk O'Hara had been about to knock when he saw that the cottage had no door.

'Oh, well, where's the farm?' he thought; and, as though to answer the question, further on, and among the trees, a light sprang up.

Chapter Two

★

'. . . *but all was dark, and he could find no clue to this strange*
business.'

Ibid. (*Peter the Goatherd*)

THE house from which the light shone was about twenty
yards back from the road. The room from which the
light came was empty. So much O'Hara could see at
once as he galloped up the drive and glanced in at the uncurtained window before he knocked at the door.

There was a long pause. Then he could hear someone
moving about upstairs. He knocked again, a little more
confidently this time. Footsteps descended, and the door was
opened. No light was switched on in the hall and the occupant
of the house carried no candle. It was a woman who stood
there. She opened the door wide and stood well back from it.

'Who is it?' she asked. O'Hara deduced from her voice that
she was fairly young.

'I beg your pardon for troubling you,' he replied, 'but I'm
out on a cross-country run and I've lost my way.'

'Which way do you want?' she enquired.

'Welsea Beaches or Abbots Ingham would do.'

'You're a long way from either.'

'How far?'

'Ten miles, by the nearest road, from Welsea.'

'As much as that? Oh, Lord! Well, I suppose . . .'

'You'd better go through the farm,' she went on ,'and up
and over the Seven Acre. Then you go left by the Barrows and
up past the Druids. I'm afraid you'll never find your way in
the dark, and I . . . and I don't see how I can come with you
to show you the road. You'll strike it quite soon past the

Druids. I've got a sick man in the house. I ought to send for the doctor . . . I don't quite know what to do. It's getting so late.'

'I'm sorry,' said O'Hara. 'Is he bad?'

'It's getting so late,' she repeated. 'And I'm afraid it's a hospital case. I don't know what to do.' She retreated and began to close the front door.

'Where does the doctor live? Perhaps I could go?' said O'Hara. 'And it isn't so awfully late.'

'Oh, no, no, thank you. You'd never find it in the dark. And I couldn't trouble you. That isn't what you're here for.' A new note had entered her voice.

'Well, look here, then, would you care to let me have a look at him? I'm not a doctor, of course, but it might be better than nothing.'

'You're a medical student? Oh, but . . .' Her voice sounded frightened.

'Oh, no, I'm not a medical student,' said O'Hara. 'I know a bit about massage and First Aid, and that sort of thing. That's all.'

'I'm afraid it's infectious,' she said hastily, 'and I couldn't expose you to the risk. Please go. I'm sorry I can't help you. That's your way, look, through the cartshed and over the hill. Or—wait a minute! Perhaps you could go in the car. Come with me. I'll soon find out.'

'But . . .' O'Hara began to protest. The woman would not let him continue. It seemed that she had made up her mind.

'Please come,' she said. She came out into the porch and caught his arm, but shrank away at once at the touch of the naked skin. 'Oh, you're . . . Oh, you're . . .'

'I'm in running togs,' he said, smiling. He could discern her face, pale in the darkness, but merely as a paper-like blur.

'Of course. It's this way.' She clutched his bare arm and almost hustled him down the path and through the gate. 'Watch your step. I mean, it's rough and rather muddy out here. And hurry, please! I really mustn't leave him more than a minute!'

They went side by side along the road and then through the open cartshed which seemed to straddle it. Beyond the cartshed were barns, and to the right of these were what O'Hara took to be stables, for he could hear the movements of horses and could smell their odour.

At the end of the stable block was another large barn. It seemed as though the woman had not expected to find it locked, for she exclaimed something under her breath and began to hammer at the door.

'Let me,' said O'Hara. He set his shoulder to the door and gave it a shove, but it did not budge, nor even rattle. 'It's locked, I'm afraid. Haven't you the key?'

'Yes. Indoors,' she said. 'Wait here. I'll go and get it.'

O'Hara began to feel chilly. He swung his arms and stamped his feet, and hoped that soon the key would be forthcoming. The woman was gone about ten minutes, which seemed an unduly long time, considering that the house was less than fifty yards off.

He was beginning to wish that he had never stopped at the house at all when he heard the sound of voices and saw the gleam of an electric torch. The woman was returning. With her she had a tallish man, and it was he who was carrying the torch. He shone it on to O'Hara, allowing the light to travel slowly over the young man's long, thin body, over his grimy shorts and sweat-stained running-vest, over his long, thin legs, and at last to his face.

'Not at all a bad notion,' he said to the woman. Then he turned the light on to the lock and fitted a key. He pushed the door open with his shoulder. It swung inward, and as the man shone the torch into the darkness O'Hara could see the gleaming coachwork of a car.

'Keep back,' said the man. 'I'll bring her out, and then you'll have to help me with *him*. You're very late, aren't you?'

He climbed into the driver's seat and backed the car out without troubling to wait for an answer. He got out, opened the door of the car, and invited O'Hara to get in.

'Might as well take a seat. We'll be a few minutes.' he said. 'Wrapping him up, you know. It wouldn't do for him to get cold.' He concluded these words with a very sinister chuckle.

'There are rugs,' said the woman to O'Hara, 'if *you're* cold.
We'll be as quick as we can. I'm sorry. I didn't know . . .'

'Make yourself at home,' said the man. He chuckled again.
'It's the whale of a notion. Gets us out of a very nasty mess.'

Rather astonished, O'Hara listened to their retreating footsteps. The whole business seemed to him more than a trifle
mysterious.

'I hope the fellow hasn't got bubonic plague,' he thought.
'Why did the woman say she was alone when this chap was
there all the time? There's something fishy going on. I wish
to the Lord I'd never stopped here. Oh, well, I'm in for it now!'

Thankful for the rugs, he wrapped one round his body and
one round his long legs, and reclined against the upholstery
of the car. He felt sleepy, and, becoming warm, began to doze.
The sound of footsteps brought him wide awake again.

'Now then, cully,' said the man's voice, 'you'd better come
along and help me lift him. Here, I've brought you a coat.'

O'Hara discarded the rugs, opened the door of the car and
groped his way out. His arms were thrust roughly and strongly
into the sleeves of an overcoat. It was full big for him, and,
although he was an unusually tall and long-armed young man,
the sleeves came almost to his knuckles. 'Now, then, let's get a
move on,' the man added. He led the way back through the
cartshed, and O'Hara followed.

He was taken by a gravel path to the side of the house,
where the man pushed open a door which led into a narrow
passage. At the end of the passage was a staircase and at the
top of the staircase, which was lighted by a blue-shaded lamp
of tiny size and very feeble glimmer, was a bedroom. The
bedroom door had been lifted off its hinges and was flat on
the floor.

'I thought we might need it,' said the man. He led the way
into the bedroom, and flashed his torch on to a camp bed.
Lying on it, in a face-downwards position, was an enormously
broad figure so wrapped and entwined in blankets that it
resembled nothing so much as a gross and ape-like mummy.
Even the head was completely hidden, so that nothing of the
face or even the hair could be seen. Great motoring gloves

covered the hands and had been tied round the wrists with tape. So much O'Hara could see, but nothing more, and that he saw only as his guide flashed the torch.

'Now,' said the man, 'as you see, he's a pretty tidy weight to lift and carry, so if you find him too heavy you'll need to give me plenty of warning, so that we can set him down gently. I think I've fixed him all right, but we don't want to bruise him or anything. You take his legs, and don't be hasty. The stairs are steep and I don't want to break my neck. Rather a joke if I did, but I should have to miss the laugh, and that would be rather a pity.'

The weight of their burden was not short of fifteen or sixteen stones. O'Hara was a powerful fellow and in excellent training, but he could scarcely stagger down the stairs. His companion appeared in like case, for he grunted and groaned as they descended, and, in the hall, had to beg for a respite whilst they put the sick man down. A hot-water bottle which was evidently wrapped up in the blankets had been burning O'Hara's wrist, and his ankle was now very stiff. The extra weight on it was very nearly unbearable.

'Ready again?' said the man. 'Then up-se-daisy!'

The journey in the dark to the yard seemed endless, and even when it was over there was the difficulty of getting the sick man into the back of the car. At last they managed to place him along the back seat, and O'Hara ducked in after him.

'Hold on to him, now,' said the man, 'and on no account let him fall off!'

O'Hara grunted, liking the business less and less, and the man climbed into the driver's seat and slowly drove off up the hill. How he managed to find his way, much less to pick a track on the cart-ruts they seemed to be following, O'Hara had no idea, for the car was not lighted at all, either inside or out. It crawled along in what was now the thick darkness of a misty and moonless night, and, except for the occasional swish of the branches from an untrimmed hedge against the window, O'Hara would not have known that they were not bucketing their way across a desert.

There was no conversation. He himself had all he could do to keep the mummy-like invalid on the back seat as the car slowly jolted and swung. The driver, he assumed, had all his work cut out to find the way and to keep the car on its track for not once did they drive on a road.

The further they went, the less and less O'Hara liked what was going on. He could not desert the sick man, and yet there was something so corpse-like about the inert and swaddled body that he began to feel a horror of it similar to the horror he had felt for the house with the four dead trees.

He found himself holding his breath and trying to hear the sound of the invalid's breathing. There was no sound at all, so far as he could determine, but he thought perhaps the noise of the car was enough to blanket other sounds.

Suddenly the car pulled up, and O'Hara was flung sideways. The driver put his head out.

'You there, Willie?' he called. There was no answer. The driver pulled in his head again with an oath. 'What's the matter with everyone?' he added.

At the notion that they were to meet someone else in this curious spot, O'Hara decided that he had had enough of the affair. He was crouched on the floor to hold the invalid in place, and from this position he put his head to the man's chest to hear his breathing. He could hear nothing, although the car had stopped.

'I say!' he cried. 'I think this chap's worse! I believe he's dead!'

Upon these words, he slipped out of the enormous, borrowed overcoat, opened the door of the car as it began to crawl forward, crouched on the step and then fell gently on to soft, wet turf.

'What the devil are you doing?' cried the driver, as the door swung to. O'Hara did not reply. He was too busy rolling down a hill. The grass of the hillside was soaking, and rain was now falling fast. The car, he knew, had pulled up. He got to his feet and ran.

'What's the matter there, Con?' cried a new voice behind him. There was nothing strange to an Irishman in hearing another man addressed as Con, in England the name of a girl. O'Hara took no notice, intent only on getting away.

Shouts pursued him. He limped and stumbled, but soon out-distanced the sounds. He could tell he was on a path. It felt like a cart-track. His chief hope was that it did not lead back to the farm. He crashed against a stile and bruised his shins. Thankfully, he climbed over. Ahead of him he could see the lights of houses. There was another stile to cross, and then he was on a high-road. Regardless of his stiff ankle, he now began to run as fast as he could. He was dogged all the time by the nightmare feeling that he made no progress at all. He redoubled his efforts, and at last came in sight of the friendly lights of a pub.

Encouraged, he flung himself onward, and reached the welcoming glow. Oblivious of the spectacle he must by this time present (for, besides being muddy, he was also soaked to the skin) he pushed open the door and went in. A group of men regarded him stolidly for a minute or two. Then the barman said wonderingly:

'Bless ee, young fellow, 'ave ee bin killin' a pig?'

Chapter Three

*. . . and rode so quickly that he did not even see the golden road,
but went with his horse straight over it.'*

Ibid. (*The Water of Life*)

O'HARA glanced down at his shorts, once white, now very grimy. Apart from the mud, however, from waist to knee on the left side he was an unpleasant mess of dark blood washed brownish by the rain.

'Good Lord!' he said. 'I helped to carry a man . . .! Here, give me a drink!'

'Been mixed up in an accident, I doubt?' said the barman, eyeing the bottles dubiously. 'What be goin' to have?'

'Whisky—a double,' said O'Hara. He unpinned a pound note from inside the breast of his running-vest and placed it upon the counter. 'I helped to lift the fellow on to the back seat of somebody's car to get him to hospital,' he added. The implied suggestion that he had been mixed up in a road crash seemed the best explanation of his plight.

'Must have been in a bad way to bleed on you like that,' said one of the men at the bar. O'Hara nodded, and took the end seat on a bench.

'He was pretty bad,' he said briefly. 'I didn't see the accident, though.' He hoped there would be no further questions, and, having drunk his whisky in three gulps, he asked whether it was possible to telephone to the Royal Hotel at Welsea. He then rang up his cousin, the hare, presuming rightly that he would have finished the course.

'I say, Gerry,' he said. 'I'm in rather a spot. Could you possibly send somebody with a car and an overcoat to the Spotted Lion, Upper Deepening? That's where I seem to be.

No, I'm all right. Yes, more when we meet. Too long to tell you over the 'phone. No, I'm not injured. Turned my ankle, that's all.'

'Well, you *are* an old ass!' said his cousin cheerfully. 'Bad luck, though, all the same. All right, I'll come myself. We've reached the strawberry ices, and I don't mind missing the speeches if I have to. Jolly glad you rang through. We couldn't think what had happened!'

O'Hara went back to the bar and ordered a pint of beer and some bread and cheese. The curiosity of the customers and the barman appeared to be sated. They were discussing League football. O'Hara had just finished his very belated meal when the handsome Gascoigne walked in, carrying over his arm an overcoat and a pair of grey flannel trousers.

'I've got Featherstone's bus outside,' said Gascoigne. 'Feathers wants to get back to Town to-night, so I promised I wouldn't be long. I suppose you've seen nothing of Firman? He said he probably shouldn't be able to finish. I expect he got a train at Cann's Crossing and went to his uncle's. He said he probably should if his gammy leg gave up. How bad is your ankle? Can you manage to hop to the car?'

While his cousin drove him into Welsea, O'Hara recounted his adventure. Gascoigne made no comment except to say:

'It's odd they told you the fellow had an infectious illness if he'd really met with an accident. And why give him hot water bottles? Although that might have been their idea of treatment for shock. And—I don't know! Oh, well, you missed a jolly close finish.'

'You got in first, I suppose?'

'By about a hundred yards. Had to put my head down and sprint like the devil to make it. Eaves nearly caught me. He's very persistent, that bloke. Says he shall try for the marathon next season. I wouldn't be surprised if he won.'

'I'm glad *you* won,' said O'Hara. 'Can I get any dinner, do you think?'

'Sure. I took care of that before I came away. And they're giving us some quite decent port, unless it's all been finished before we get there.'

They arrived when the dinner was nearly over, but food was procured for O'Hara, and the port was all that Gascoigne had promised. O'Hara was the butt of a number of crude jokes because of his late appearance, and he made such responses as seemed necessary, but his adventure was in the forefront of his mind. The party broke up at last, and he went rather thankfully to bed.

The cousins had booked a twin-bedded room, and at just after midnight O'Hara was able to give his cousin a complete account of his afternoon and evening.

A comparison of times, distances and places produced, not greatly to O'Hara's surprise, the unassailable fact that the runner he had seen from the vantage point of the prehistoric fort could not possibly have been Gascoigne. It remained to be seen whether it could have been Firman.

After considerable discussion, Gascoigne closed the matter in the early hours of the morning by saying drowsily:

'Look here, then, I suggest we sleep on it, and, if you feel the same 'orrid doubts in the morning, we'll go out and have a look-see. But I expect you saw Firman. I suppose he was packing up the run. Nothing very odd about that.'

'Nothing odd at all. Where does his uncle live?'

'I don't know exactly. Somewhere around these parts, from what he said when he told us he might not finish.'

'Oh, well, I don't suppose it matters. By the way, I haven't any clothes except my running togs. I sloshed them about in the bath a bit when I'd taken them off, but they don't look too good even now, and probably won't be dry first thing in the morning. Of course, there's my soup and fish, but I can hardly career about the countryside on a fine Sunday morning in braided bags and a dinner jacket. We weren't proposing to spend the night here, you know.'

'Oh, that's all right! I've collared Bodger's tweeds. He's near enough your height . . . a bit broader in the beam, but that won't matter. He went off by car in his evening clothes, very tight. I'd have had to send the things on to him, any old way, so you might as well wear 'em first. And I've borrowed Smithson's for myself. He took Bodger with him.'

'You are the very pineapple of politeness,' said O'Hara gratefully. 'But what will Bodger say when he's sobered up?'

'Oh, he won't mind at all. Well, let's sleep on it, shall we? And then we'll go over to the farm, or whatever it is, after breakfast. Good thing it will be Sunday. People will be the less suspicious of a couple of ignorant hikers.'

O'Hara was soon asleep, but Gascoigne lay awake for some time, thinking over the story his cousin had told him. The more he thought about it, the more unaccountable became the conversation and actions of the persons involved, and the less he liked the thought of O'Hara's adventure.

'A good thing for him he slid out of it when he did,' was the final conclusion he reached before falling asleep.

They breakfasted at nine, and by ten were out on the road. The borrowed tweeds fitted O'Hara well enough, the morning was crisp and sunny, and the cousins, who had no car, stepped briskly along the road which led north from Welsea Beaches. It was well past opening time when they reached the Spotted Lion at Upper Deepening, so they went in and called for beer.

'Now, then,' said Gascoigne. 'Where do we go from here?'

'It was dark, you know,' said O'Hara, 'and I don't remember any landmarks, but at any rate, we ought to keep straight along this road for quite two hundred yards, and then we turn off to the right across a stile.'

The road sloped uphill. The stile was gained. Regarding it doubtfully, O'Hara refused to commit himself to a definite statement that it was the right stile, but said he thought it must be.

'It's queer,' he said. 'It all looks so ordinary by daylight. I feel as though I'd dreamed the whole thing now. You don't think I had *delirium tremens*, or a mental blackout, do you?'

'Don't weaken,' said Gascoigne, grinning. 'There must be a right of way, anyhow, if there's a stile, so we shan't be trespassing.' He climbed over, followed reluctantly by his cousin.

The footpath was a very rough track which led upwards to a five-barred gate. Beyond the gate were two disc barrows on the side of the hill, and, further over, a circle of standing stones.

'That's where it was,' said O'Hara suddenly. He pointed towards the stones. 'That's where I got out of the car. Let's look for tracks. Would a car leave tracks on this turf? Anyway, it certainly does seem fishy. Where could one take a car from here?'

Gascoigne led the way to the circle of standing stones. None of the stones was more than seven feet high. Some were very much shorter. One was nothing more than a small boulder almost hidden in the grass. The ditch which would have surrounded the stones when they were used as a prehistoric temple was almost wholly ploughed out, but traces of it could be seen by those who knew what to look for, and Gascoigne was soon pacing a circular track about twenty yards distant from the stones, of which there were nine.

'You know,' he said, returning to O'Hara, who was looking for tracks of the car, 'the best thing for us to do, I fancy, is to go to the local hospital. Hospitals always make Sunday a visiting day. If he did not arrive at the hospital we've got something definite to go on, and then, I suppose, we shall have to stir up strife.'

'But can we? I can't see us going to the police and telling them that a man ought to have arrived in hospital and hasn't turned up,' said O'Hara. 'What reason could we give for butting in?'

'The best of reasons—the one you gave me yourself. Why did that woman say it was infectious illness when all the time the fellow was bleeding?—possibly bleeding to death?'

'I know. That *is* the point. Look here, then, I'll tell you what. Let's walk over the hill and make sure I can identify the farmhouse. Then, possibly, we could spy out the lie of the land, and, after we've been to the hospital, we could then perhaps go to the police. All the same, I'm not very keen. It

isn't our business. I mean, they didn't attempt to coerce me.
I helped them of my own free will. Besides, who's going to
believe me?'

Gascoigne gazed at his cousin. 'Nonsense, man! What are
you afraid of?' he asked.

'Being a nosey parker, I suppose. Come on, then. It ought
to be this way. We never came out on to a road. I know that
all right. I could hardly hold that poor blighter on to the seat.'

They returned to the path and followed it over rough grass
until they came to a barn.

'This isn't the place,' said O'Hara. 'It was further off, and
the house was quite a fair size.'

They went through a gate and the path changed into a cart-
track beside a field. There was still another gate at the top,
but, once through this, the track turned sharply to the left and
sloped steeply down to a large collection of buildings grouped
round a house among trees.

'This is the place,' said O'Hara, 'but it seems such a short
distance. . . . I mean, we drove miles, I should have
thought.'

At the foot of the hill they swung left again through a gateway which led to an open cartshed. Beyond the cartshed was
the house. A narrow road climbed a hill to the east of the
farmyard, but was soon lost to sight among the trees. Beyond
the house, the lane, from which O'Hara had seen the light in
the empty room, sagged sandily past the ruined cottages and
into the woods.

'This is the place, then?' murmured Gascoigne, and gazed
in great surprise at the house. Its windows were uncurtained,
its appearance was that of dissolution and decay, and it
seemed to have been tenantless for some time. The front door
swung back as he put up his hand to knock, and disclosed a
mildewed, stained, dilapidated hall, a picture frame hanging
by one cord and part of an old mangle lying at the foot of the
stairs.

He stepped aside to look in at the nearest window. He
beckoned O'Hara to join him.

'I'm going in,' he whispered. 'This is a very rum go. You

stand by in case anybody comes who thinks we've no business in here.'

'No, I'll go first,' said O'Hara. 'I'd like to see it by daylight. I can hardly make any comparisons, though, because I saw so little last night.'

He was not gone very long. The side-door had been bolted on the inside, but he found his way to the bedroom by way of the front stairs, and explored the rest of the house before he returned to his cousin.

'Nothing,' he said, very briefly. 'But the bedroom floor and the stairs have recently been scrubbed, I think. *You* go in and have a look.'

Gascoigne contented himself with the most cursory inspection of the house. It was the front room downstairs to which he devoted most attention. There were ashes in the grate which he took care not to disturb, and a circle of lighter film showed against the dust on the mantelpiece.

'An oil lamp; the light you saw shining from the house,' he said. 'I wonder why they lit it? A signal to someone, I suppose.'

'Did you go upstairs?' asked O'Hara.

'Yes. The room and the stairs have been scrubbed all right. Well, now for the hospital. We'd better get back to that pub and ask where it is. If the fellow isn't there, I certainly think you ought to go to the police. In fact, I think you'll have to.'

'Yes, I think I must. The empty house settles that.'

'Well, I hope to heaven he *is* at the hospital, that's all, and then that will let you out.'

'Yes, so do I. Good Lord! There's old Firman in a car! Come on! He can give us a lift. Wonder what he's up to round here? I expect he saw us go in.'

The car waited for them.

'Why, Firman, you old ass!' shouted Gascoigne, climbing in beside the driver. 'Why on earth didn't you join us last evening?' O'Hara, surprised by the bonhomous nature of this greeting, for his cousin, so far as he knew, was not well acquainted with this particular member of their club and did not much like what he knew of him, waited for Firman's reply.

'I didn't want to be roasted about not finishing,' responded Firman, a round-shouldered man with eyes too old for his face. 'My bones began to creak at the three-mile mark, so I packed up and went to my uncle's house in Cuchester. What are you two doing, roaming so far off your beat? I should have thought bright lads like you would have been putting in a pleasant morning by the sea, and giving the girls a treat.'

'We're just out for a stroll,' said Gascoigne, before O'Hara could answer. 'Give us a lift to the nearest nice pub, and we'll buy you a drink, old man.'

'I'll give you a lift,' said Firman, 'but I can't stop, even for a drink. My uncle has his lunch at half-past twelve, and as I'm his heir I can't afford to keep lunch waiting.' He looked at his watch. 'Hop in, and I'll drop you at the *Bell-Wether*. That's the best pub around here. Mention my name, and they'll let you have anything you like and as much as ever you want.'

The cousins accepted the lift but did not take advantage of the advice. Over their drinks they asked the barman to direct them to the local hospital.

'Which do you want—the Cottage or the County?' enquired the man.

'Both, then,' Gascoigne replied. 'A pal of ours was in a car crash last night. We only heard this morning, and we thought we'd go and look him up. Heard he'd busted a leg and a couple of ribs.'

The barman gave them the information they needed, and they caught a bus into Welsea, lunched, and then visited the hospitals. No patient except, at the County hospital, a six-year-old child who had swallowed a spool of silk, had been admitted within the past twenty-four hours.

'So what?' said O'Hara. 'Oh, damn it, I *don't* want to go to the police!'

'Well, look, then,' said Gascoigne suddenly. 'I'll tell you what! There's a fellow my mother used to know when she was a girl . . . a chap called Ferdinand Lestrange. He's a K.C., and what he doesn't know about the law is certainly not worth knowing. Let's put it up to him. He proposed to my mother once, so I feel I know him, although actually I've never met him in my life. Still, I know where he lives when he's not in London, and that's not so very far from here. We could go to-morrow. Of course, if *he* says go to the police, we'll have to go. Now let's forget the whole thing and go and have a look at the sea.'

'Did you say Lestrange?'

'I did. He's got a quaint old mother—a psychiatrist or something. You must have heard of her. She's famous.'

'Is *her* name Lestrange?'

'Only partly. Beatrrice Adela Lestrange Bradley. She still believes in Freud—1856 and all that. Still, I believe she's ninety.'

'We'll date her up,' said O'Hara.

Chapter Four

★

*'But the wizard king was not at home, and his grandmother sat at
the door in her easy chair.'*
                          Ibid. (*The Giant with the Three Golden Hairs*)

NEITHER Mrs. Bradley nor her son Ferdinand had very
much spare time; neither was their scanty leisure
coincident. It happened, however, that a new grandchild had been born, and Mrs. Bradley had attended the
christening; thus she was at her son's house, three miles from
Cuchester, when two handsome boys turned up to see
Ferdinand and to ask his advice.

'I suppose I throw them out?' suggested Mrs. Bradley's
young and competent secretary, Laura Menzies, when, having
been apprised by the butler of the presence of Gascoigne and
O'Hara, she had confronted Mrs. Bradley with the news. 'It
seems a pity. They're easy on the eye and ear, and come from
what the *cognoscenti* call Oxford College.'

'Admit them,' said Mrs. Bradley, leering horribly at her
grandchild who happened to be lying in her lap.

'But doesn't our native honesty compel us to explain that
Sir Ferdinand is in London defending the public-spirited
murderer of six G.I. brides?' demanded Laura.

'True, child. But do not stress the fact of his absence just at
first. Do I know these boys?'

'*I* don't . . . at least, I didn't until they introduced themselves. They are Irish, I should think, from their names. Let's
see.' She closed her eyes, opened them, and recited, 'Mr.
Patrick Michael Brian Maurice Bennett Sean O'Hara. Mr.
Gerald Fitzgerald Gascoigne. And very nice, too. As a Scot, I
appreciate aristocratic nomenclature, and they've got it in
gobs.'

The baby blew a series of congratulatory bubbles and Mrs. Bradley swabbed these away with absentminded efficiency. A moment later the two tall young men, one as black as Saturn, the other fair as Apollo, were shown into the room by the butler in accordance with Laura's instructions.

They looked apprehensively at the baby, critically at Laura, and with evident interest at Mrs. Bradley, who scarcely did justice to the ninety years with which she had been credited.

'Sit down and speak freely,' said she, handing the baby to Laura much in the manner of the Duchess in *Alice* handing over her sneezing child. 'Be bold. Confess—for only the walls have ears.'

'We came,' said Gascoigne gravely, 'to . . . to put a hypothetical case, as it were, to Sir Ferdinand Lestrange. I . . . er . . . that is, my mother used to know him. It's . . . well, it's Michael's . . . my cousin's . . . story, really. Go on, Mike. Speak up.'

'Begorra!' said Mrs. Bradley, fascinated by the lordly Hibernians and anxious to do them honour by employing what she affected to believe was their idiom. 'Arrah, now, be aisy, wouldn't ye?'

This last remark, apparently addressed to the baby, achieved its object. The young men laughed, with some constraint but to their own relief. Laura rang the bell, passed the buck (in her own words) by giving the baby to the nurse who answered the summons, and seated herself at the table with notebook and pencil.

'Go on, please,' she said, 'but make it snappy. We have to catch the three o'clock train.'

'Well,' began Gascoigne, 'as I say, it's really Mike's story, and, to tell you the truth'—he turned to Mrs. Bradley again— 'it isn't too easy to explain.'

'I see,' Mrs. Bradley observed. 'You haven't, by any chance, committed murder, I suppose?'

'No,' said O'Hara, coming in boldly at this. 'But I'm wondering whether, perhaps, I'm an accessory after the fact.'

'Interesting,' remarked the elderly lady. 'Well, go on. Don't leave out any details, however unimpressive they may seem, and don't cut a long story short, whatever you do. The three o'clock train doesn't matter.'

'Step high, wide and handsome,' agreed Laura, licking her pencil and looking expectantly at them.

'Well, it was like this,' said O'Hara. He told the story of the hare and hounds cross-country run, and of his experiences at the lonely farm. 'And I'm now quite certain that the man was dead,' he concluded, 'and from the fact that he was said to be suffering from something infectious, but actually bled all over me, I'm wondering whether there wasn't something rather peculiar, in fact, something rather nasty, about the business, and, if there was, well—I'm involved, I suppose. I'd rather like to know what to do.'

'It might be better if my son did not advise you. Not, at the least, face to face. I will put the facts before him myself, if you desire it, and, if you will give me an address to which my secretary, Miss Menzies, can write, I will let you know his unofficial views.'

'I say, that's awfully good of you,' said O'Hara. 'You see, when we found that the fellow had not been admitted to hospital . . .'

'I do see. Now, there are just one or two points which my son may want to have clear. First of all, tell me, how many of you were running across country that day?'

'Eleven, including Gerald. He was the hare.'

'Had you only one hare?'

'Yes, only one.'

'So there were nine others besides your two selves, and all nine of these were hounds. Was anybody missing from the reunion at the end of the day?'

'No, we were all there. I got in late, of course, but . . . Oh, one fellow didn't finish. A bloke called Firman. He'd told us he probably wouldn't, though. We met him next day while we were messing about at the farmhouse. He turned up in a car and gave us a lift. That was—well, just a bit queer. That he should have been there, I mean. But I don't suppose there was anything in it, you know.'

'Was there any untoward incident, other than Mr. O'Hara's extraordinary adventure, on the day of the race?' Mrs. Bradley asked, turning to Gascoigne.

'Not that I heard of. But I didn't see any of the others during the run. At least, not to speak to. We were pretty close at the finish, but I was running my hardest then, and wouldn't have had much breath to spare for gossip.' He paused for a moment, laughed, and very soon added, 'But there was plenty of chance at dinner for the men to swop stories, and I didn't hear of anything unexpected.'

'There *was* that fellow, though, that I took to be you,' said O'Hara.

'Oh, but that must have been Firman, as we said. You must have spotted him after he'd decided to give up.'

'Yes, I know. Still, it doesn't altogether fit in with the rest of his story. His uncle doesn't live in that direction, and he *was* hanging round that farm in his car next day.'

'And it couldn't have been any of the others, because they were all in a bunch for the whole of the run. We know that.'

'Who *were* these others? Were they all particular friends of yours? And were they members of your University?' Mrs. Bradley enquired.

'It's nothing to do with the Varsity,' Gascoigne explained. 'It's an athletic club. They don't bar anyone so long as he can run a bit and pays his subscription and isn't a bounder. I expect you know the sort of thing. We joined while school was evacuated during the war, and now turn out when we can.'

'Ah,' said Mrs. Bradley, scanning the plaintiffs narrowly, and ignoring most of their remarks, 'and what interpretation are we to put upon the word "bounder," I wonder?'

The cousins exchanged glances; then Gascoigne said:

'Rotter, I suppose. I don't know quite how one's . . .' he smiled . . . 'one's aunts would interpret the word. I meant that anybody can join, and they keep him in unless they find they don't like him, and then they bung him out. That's all there is to it. Unless you're a bounder you're welcome for as long as you like.'

'Does it ever happen that a member is asked to resign?'

'Hardly ever, but they did give a miss last year to a fellow who pinched money from the dressing-rooms. It's awkward, you see, if the fellows can't leave their loose change in their trousers' pockets. Then there was a chap just before the war who was blackballed for dirty running.'

'It was more dirty temper than dirty running, I think,' put in O'Hara. 'At least, that's what I was told. He used to spike fellows round the bend behind the water jump—very malicious, I believe. Two other clubs complained to the secretary, and chaps don't complain about that sort of thing for nothing. I mean, anybody is liable to get spiked if there's manoeuvring for position going on, especially in a tight race and with a big field. Fellows get boxed in, you know—it's all tactics in the longer races unless you've got the legs of the rest of them, and even then you've got to keep your wits about you. But with this chap it was a bit nasty, apparently, so he came off the books. Can't have bad blood between one club and another. Ruins the whole thing. The committee were quite right to sack him.'

'Does the club wear a uniform?'

'Not for cross-country running. We turn out in any old shorts and vests. We wear club colours for athletics matches in the summer when one can keep nice and clean. Ours is an apple green band on a white running-vest, and we wear white shorts.'

'Very tasty, very sweet,' observed Laura, who was following the narrative with great interest.

'If it had been an orange band, I suppose you two wouldn't have joined,' Mrs. Bradley remarked. 'Was your secretary one of the hounds in this cross-country run on Saturday?'

'Oh, yes, He's dead keen, you know. A fellow called Shoesmith, a bank-clerk. Very decent.'

'Can you give my secretary his address?'

Laura took down the address, and then Mrs. Bradley continued:

'I had better take you point by point through your story. Let us begin at the beginning. You took a different direction from the rest of the hounds at Cuchester, I believe, Mr. O'Hara?'

'Yes. They turned off to the left through the town, and I kept straight on to the amphitheatre and then went up to the fort.'

'You believed you would more easily catch up with your cousin that way?'

'I hoped to be able to spot him, and give the others the tip, but I wasn't lucky.'

'This man with the car seems interesting. Were you surprised when he stopped you?'

'Yes and no. I mean that strangers do take an interest in cross-country running, and they do quite often offer gratuitous advice. Sometimes, of course, it's useful, and we have no rule against accepting it.'

'I was interested in the form of words he used. Granted the circumstances, they seem rather striking.'

'I didn't notice anything in particular.'

'Did you not? You used almost the same words when you reported the conversation you had with the woman at the door of this mysterious farm. You remember? About being late? It was the repetition of that remark by the woman which made what the man said significant. And now why do you suppose the man took you in the car?'

'To hold the body on the back seat, I imagine, and to help lift it out when we got to wherever it was that we were making for.'

'Couldn't the woman have held the body on the seat? After all, the driver was expecting to meet someone else up there on the hill. He called out to someone, you said.'

'Yes. He called to someone named Con. And I suppose the woman *could* have held the body, although it was frightfully heavy. Still, she could have managed. I suppose there was some reason why she had to remain at the farm.'

'Yes, I think you are right. It might be useful to know what that reason was, might it not? Now, you left the car when you heard the driver call out to this man he was to meet, and you gained the impression that the car had travelled a long way from the farm. Yet when you went back there on Sunday morning, you discovered that it was not so very far, after all. What do you make of that now?'

'I don't know what to make of it, except that it was to give me the impression I got—that the distance we had travelled was considerable. And that's fishy, too.'

'*The Engineer's Thumb*,' said Laura, an encyclopædia of the Sherlock Holmes stories.

'Yes, but why?' asked Mrs. Bradley. 'Why should he want to deceive you about the distance? It may equally well have been that the driver knew he had time to spare between leaving the farm and contacting this man Con. He had to get you away from the farm, I think, as soon as he could, for he must have realized that the first man had made a mistake and had sent him the wrong assistant. The woman was left behind, I have little doubt, to warn the right man when he turned up.'

'You think the fellow in the car near the hill-fort had been sent to direct someone on to the farm, then?' demanded Gascoigne.

'It seems likely,' Mrs. Bradley answered. 'On the face of it— but we have not much evidence yet—it seems as though he mistook Mr. O'Hara for another of the runners. You said just now, Mr. O'Hara, that you saw another runner in front of you and supposed him to be Mr. Gascoigne. But it is now shown, by Mr. Gascoigne's own account of the matter, that this lone runner could not have been he. The inference is that it was Mr. Firman—unless, of course, it was somebody quite unconnected with the club. I suppose it is not impossible that a solitary enthusiast should have been running over this county on Saturday afternoon?'

'Not impossible, but rather unlikely,' said Gascoigne.

'And more than a bit of coincidence, surely?' suggested O'Hara.

'Well,' said Mrs. Bradley, 'we will see what can be done to ease Mr. O'Hara's mind.'

'It's eased already,' said O'Hara.

'Bless their hearts!' said Laura sentimentally, for she was at the age when she felt like a mother to all boys two years her junior. 'How much of the yarn do you think was true?'

'I think we may proceed on the assumption that it is all true,' her employer replied.

'What do you think Sir Ferdinand will say?'

'It all depends upon what you and I find out in the meantime, child.'

'Oh, we are going to look into it, are we? I rather hoped we were. The first job, I take it, is to clear this spiked-shoes person out of the way . . . you know, the one who was sacked from the club for dirty running. It couldn't have been he, so we'd better prove that it wasn't.'

'An intelligent suggestion,' Mrs. Bradley replied, 'but perhaps not quite the first thing on our list.'

'What about the pickpocket, then?'

'The pickpocket?'

'Well, I thought that if we could look into the antecedents of the two obviously criminal members of the club . . . people who *didn't* commit murder . . . if it *is* murder . . . and argue from cause to effect——'

' "And so grow to a point," ' said Mrs. Bradley, grinning. 'I think it might take some time, and I feel it might also be wasted labour, child. I believe it might be better to discover the antecedents of the young man named Firman.'

'Oh, rather! Yes, of course! We certainly ought to check up on *him*,' agreed Laura, with some excitement. 'Well, how do we begin? What is my first assignment?'

'To proceed to the bathroom and wash the inkspots from the ends of your eyebrows,' Mrs. Bradley responded. 'Then I think you might eat your lunch. I heard the gong some three minutes ago. Which of the young men did you prefer?'

'Oh, Adonis, I think,' said Laura, after a brief pause for thought.

'Mr. Gascoigne?'

'Yes. Which did you?'

'I like nearly all young men,' said Mrs. Bradley sincerely.

'They are almost always delightful. I also like all very young women . . . or very nearly all.'

'Present company excepted from the whole of that statement!' said Laura. 'By the way, I call the saturnine one . . . O'Hara . . . a "dark Celt." Kipling knew them, didn't he? There's something different about that lad from the other. Wouldn't you say that "dark Celt" somewhere tips him off? . . . And yet you could scarcely mistrust him!'

'He has, at any rate, stepped into a dark adventure, child. Do you know, I have a fancy for this business. It promises to be of extraordinary interest. The nature of the countryside, the dead man kept warm by the application of hot-water bottles, the mysterious journey taken by the car, the decidedly sinister touch of the circle of standing stones, the badly-frightened woman who declared untruthfully that she was alone in the house except for an invalid suffering from an infectious disease, the plot (as I see it) to murder Mr. O'Hara . . .'

'*What!*' shouted Laura, in horrified delight.

' . . . these are deep matters, child, which cry out for our attention. There is a smack of minor Elizabethan drama about them which I find highly absorbing.'

Laura regarded her narrowly.

'You *do* believe what those boys told us, don't you?' she enquired. Mrs. Bradley cackled, and prodded her in the ribs with a bony forefinger.

'We shall see what I believe,' she responded. 'Go and wash, there's a good child. After lunch we will take George and the car, and go to this farm and invent spells and recite charms. Did you know that the Neolithic inhabitants of this island had the name for being cannibals?'

'In a strictly religious sense, of course,' said Laura. 'You don't mean that the people who murdered this heavy man were cannibals, do you? Because, if so, I'm dashed if I'm coming with you. I don't mind the risk of being killed, but I'm jolly well not going to be eaten. Of course,' she added thoughtfully, 'it would tend to solve a murderer's chief difficulty, wouldn't it? I never thought of that before.'

'It would only do so if the murderer had the attributes and appurtenances of the elderly gentleman in *Through the Looking Glass*, child.'

'Eh? Oh, you mean Old Father William?'

'Yes. He finished the goose with the bones and the beak . . . Ah, well, let us see what cook has done about lunch.'

'I'm not sure that I'm hungry,' said Laura.

Chapter Five

★

'All the day long she flew about in the form of an owl, or crept about the country like a cat, but at night she always became an old woman again.'

Ibid. (*Jorinda and Jorindel*)

M RS. BRADLEY had one characteristic in particular which her young and lively secretary was child enough to appreciate. It was that when she planned a thing the plan was carried out without delay. Too many older people, Laura Menzies had always thought, put forth fascinating ideas and made rash and delightful promises, only to drive their youthful protégées demented by loitering, gossiping, or remembering duties which had to be performed, until the dust and ashes of frustration and disappointment completely covered the bright gold of the pleasure in store.

Mrs. Bradley was free from this regrettable fault. When she planned an outing it 'stayed planned' as Laura had once gratefully and inaccurately observed. Therefore it was with pleasant feelings of excitement and interest that Laura ordered the car after lunch, convinced that when Mrs. Bradley said 'five to two on the gravel,' she meant just that.

At five to two, therefore, Mrs. Bradley's car appeared at the front of the house, and by two o'clock Mrs. Bradley, accompanied by Laura, and with the chauffeur, George, at the wheel, was out on the Cuchester Road.

'We are not going quite as far as the farm in this,' said Mrs. Bradley. 'Some of our investigations would be better conducted on foot. Have you brought the map?'

'Yes, of course. I've also brought your revolver.'

'Tut, child. It's daylight, and we shall be home before dark.'

'I feel safer with it,' said Laura doggedly. 'I don't like all these corpses and hot-water bottles. Besides, I'm a pretty good

shot, and I wouldn't mind trying my skill. So if any ugly
blighters come into my line of vision I shall know what to do,
that's all. One can always plead self-defence.'

She stretched out her five foot ten of abundant muscle, bone
and firm flesh, and grinned contentedly.

The car, travelling south and a point towards the east, came
opposite the Early Iron Age fortress from whose mighty
battlements O'Hara had tried to follow the movements of
Gascoigne the hare.

'And now,' said Mrs. Bradley, as George pulled up on the
turf, 'George shall take the car round to where Mr. O'Hara
says that he met this man who directed him wrongly, and we
will pick up the car again when we have followed the route
which Mr. O'Hara says he took before he met with this man.'

'Ah, checking up on O'Hara's story,' said Laura, approv-
ingly. 'Intelligent, if I may say so. And I'd like to say that we
ought to check Gascoigne's, too.'

'You may say what you please, child,' said Mrs Bradley
with her usual good-humour. 'Those are, I should say, the
obvious things for us to do.'

'Yes, we must explore all avenues,' agreed Laura. 'You
know, I feel I'm going to enjoy this business. There's a smack
of Edgar Allan Poe about it which rather appeals to my sense
of the bizarre and the macabre.'

'I didn't know you had one,' said her employer. Laura
grinned, and then added, with her usual cheerfulness:

'Anyway, it's a grand afternoon and it's glorious country,
and I like to have something to do. Somewhere to aim for, I
mean. I say, though, it's steep up here! And talk about the
wind on the heath!'

They avoided, however, the steepest and shortest slope, and
followed the rough path which ended in a wooden gate beside
which was a notice. This proved to be indecipherable, so,
unable to take advantage of any warning or invitation it might
once have conveyed, they opened the gate and passed through.

To their left a narrow track led them up to the entrance of
the fortress, two great banks of earth, turfed over now, but
reinforced underneath with enormous blocks of hewn stone.

'We must come here again,' said Laura, as they mounted a high bank and began to circumambulate the citadel. They were moving to their left, round the northern circuit of the embankments, past a ditch which was fifty feet deep. To their left stretched the fields and lay the sheepfolds of a lesser and more homely civilization. Farther off was a symmetrical round barrow, and in front of them, everywhere that they faced, were hills, but hills higher and kindlier than the shadowed and doom-laden mound on which they stood.

'By Jove, you know, it makes you think,' said Laura.

'This way, *I* think,' said Mrs. Bradley. She crossed a bridge of earth at the western end of the ditch. Laura followed, and soon they had cut through the middle of the inner sanctuary of the fortress. They passed the ruins of a Roman temple, by-passed the heights on which the cattle of the Iron Age had pastured in time of war, and regained the track which ringed the fortress. Soon they were in the ditch where O'Hara had turned his ankle. From this they reached the sandy lane where O'Hara had been stopped by the man in the car.

'Well, O'Hara told the truth so far, wouldn't you say?' enquired Laura, leaning against a gate. 'And there's George. Geo—orge!'

She waved, and George drove towards them.

'There has certainly been a car up here, madam,' he said, 'and only one. I made a sketch of the tyre-tracks in case you should want to identify them anywhere else.'

'Excellent, George,' said Mrs. Bradley, handing him back his drawing. 'And very useful. Miss Menzies and I are going to continue our walk. You have directions for finding the farm. You had better keep about half a mile away from it, or, if anything, rather more. You don't want to seem interested in it in any way whatsoever. There are plenty of things to admire. Be careful to excite no suspicion.'

'Very good, madam.' He reversed the car towards the main road, and turned it expertly at a gateway.

'Now, then,' said Laura, 'on we go! Come on, and I'll walk your legs off!'

'Done!' said Mrs. Bradley, accepting the challenge in deed

as well as in word. She set such a cracking pace up the sandy lane that even Laura, always in training, had to lengthen an already Amazonian stride in order to keep up with her.

The countryside was delightful, and Laura enjoying the prospect of bluish downs, the green of the sloping fields and the miles of open country, had forgotten the object of the walk until the road began to darken and they found themselves passing a strange house with an inhospitable legend.

'Keep out,' said Laura, slowing up and reading aloud these unsociable words. 'I wonder where the old chap has gone with the barrow? You know, this place looks a bit like a lunatic asylum to me. One of those grim places you read about in Victorian novels. What do *you* think?'

'I don't think at all at present. I merely observe and note,' said Mrs. Bradley. 'This is undoubtedly the Elizabethan manor which has the four dead trees in the park, for, as we turn the corner, there they are! Mr. O'Hara has not, so far, misled us.' Her tone expressed something more than satisfaction.

'It *is* a queer-looking place,' said Laura, gazing in fascination at the trees. 'How did that notice affect you, by the way? Personally, I have an almost uncontrollable desire to turn in my tracks and Go In.'

'We have not much time to spare,' said Mrs. Bradley, setting out briskly again. Soon they had left the grim gibbets of the four dead trees. The woods began to show bluish away to the south, and, at last, Mrs. Bradley leading, she and Laura entered a deep, dark tunnel of trees in a small, silent, circular wood, and were at the farm.

Opposite the ruined cottage Mrs. Bradley stopped, and Laura came up and caught her arm. From a chimney of the farmhouse smoke was coming.

'I say!' muttered Laura. 'I don't like this very much! Did you expect to find the place occupied, after what those lads told us the other day?'

Mrs. Bradley did not answer, and the two of them moved forward with great caution. They crept up the front garden path and peered in at the window. The room was empty, but

flickering flames were being thrown out by a small and lively
fire.

'Well, I don't know what *you* think,' muttered Laura, gluing
her nose to the glass, 'but I should say that fire's not been
lighted very long. You know, this is what I should call
rummy—very rummy. Those lads said the place was empty.
Could it have been sold between Sunday and to-day? Or—oh,
of course, they *did* find the ashes of a fire in this same
grate——'

Mrs. Bradley drew her enthusiastic secretary away from the
window, and they moved quietly round to the side door of the
house. This was ajar. To Laura's surprise, Mrs. Bradley
walked in and called loudly:

'Is anybody about?'

There was the sound of footsteps on the uncarpeted stairs,
and an elderly woman came down.

'Did you want anything?' she asked.

'Can you direct us to the nearest garage?' Mrs. Bradley
enquired. 'We've had to leave the car up the road and are
strangers to the neighbourhood.'

'I don't know whether I can help you,' replied the woman.
'How far away is your car?'

'Oh, a mile or so,' Mrs. Bradley vaguely replied. 'Somewhere over there.' She waved a skinny claw in a north-easterly
direction.

'I'm afraid I can't help you. I'm only here to air the
house. It's been let because of the film people down at
Cottam's.'

'Really? Oh, well, thank you.' Mrs. Bradley touched Laura's
arm. 'We had better go back and try that other little lane, my
dear. I don't envy you if you're staying the night here,' she
added, turning to the woman. 'It seems very lonely, doesn't it?
We happened to see the smoke from your chimney. I am so
sorry to have troubled you.'

'Oh, I don't live here,' said the woman. 'I'm only here to
oblige. The gentleman sent a postcard to ask me to air the
house. I live at Little Dorsett, over yonder, up the hill.
There's a short cut. It isn't very far. You could walk it in

half an hour. I'll put you on the road if you like, but I mustn't be long, else my old man will be shouting after me.'

She took off her apron, hung it on the end of the banisters, smoothed her hair with a working-woman's blunt-fingered hand, and then went with Laura to the gate.

'I shall be slower than you will,' said Mrs. Bradley to the woman, 'so I'll follow behind, and meet you as you come back. You go on, Laura, will you?'

Laura nodded intelligently and urged the woman along at a pace which was almost a trot. Mrs. Bradley loitered behind them, and, as soon as they had turned into the wood, she darted back to the house, went in, and hastened into the room in which the fire was burning.

For what purpose it had been lighted she could not determine. There was nothing to show that it had not been lighted to air the house, as the woman had said. There was no sign that documents had been burnt on it. A stout poker lay in the hearth. Thoughtfully impounding this, and holding it in a gloved hand, Mrs. Bradley searched the rest of the house.

It was getting too dark to see much, so, trusting that no one would see the glow of it, she switched on her torch. There was nothing to be discovered on the ground floor, so she mounted the stairs, retaining the poker as a weapon.

Just as she reached the bedroom described by O'Hara, she thought she heard sounds from below. She opened the door of an enormous built-in cupboard and stepped inside.

'Nellie!' cried a man's voice. 'Nellie! Where the plague have ee got to, woman?'

Mrs. Bradley awaited with interest the next part of the proceedings. She could hear doors being opened and shut, and, as the footsteps grew fainter and the man went towards the kitchen, she emerged, and, switching on her torch again, made a rapid survey of the floor. Except that, unlike the downstair floors, this one had been scrubbed recently, there was nothing remarkable about it.

The remaining bedrooms were dusty, cobweb-tapestried to an almost incredible degree, unfurnished and undisturbed.

Mrs. Bradley was leaving the last of them when an angry bellow came up the well of the stairs.

'Oh, there ee be, Nellie, confound ee! Why the devil don't ee answer when I calls you?'

Mrs. Bradley slipped into the corridor and came on noiseless feet to the head of the stairs. There was a slight recess in the wall. She flattened herself into this and waited for the man to ascend. She still held the poker. She hoped he would not bring a light, but was ready to knock it out of his hand if he did.

He had no torch. She could hear him stumbling up the stairs.

'Nellie!' he bellowed. Mrs. Bradley allowed him to walk past her. Then she slid out of her alcove and descended the stairs. She replaced the poker on the hearth from which she had taken it, came out to the side door and ensconced herself in the shadows. She waited. The man came downstairs as soon as he had searched the upstair rooms.

'Nellie!' he called desperately. 'It do be you, don't it? Answer me, girl! Where be ee?'

Mrs. Bradley let him get half-way down the kitchen passage, and then she gave an eldritch screech of laughter. She heard a startled oath, and then the sound of a panic-stricken voice shouting:

'Nellie! Nellie! For God's sake! It do be 'aunted after all! Where *be* ee, girl? Why the old Nick don't ee answer?'

Mrs. Bradley sped down the weed-grown drive and ran for dear life along the lane in the direction the others had taken. Then she slowed down, and, by the time the woman reappeared, Mrs. Bradley was patiently toiling up the long, rutted slope of the hill.

'She've got long legs, your grand-daughter,' said the woman. 'But you keep all on up along here, and you'll pick her up in good time.'

Mrs. Bradley thanked her, and toiled on. Half-way up the hill, Laura emerged with conspiratorial caution from a bush, and, crossing the hill, they made a détour, aided by the map, and reached George and the car without passing the farmhouse again.

'I'm sorry you had to come so far after us,' said Laura, 'but I felt bound to go on a bit after she left me in case she turned round and spotted me, and began to suspect us of something. I was worried about you, though I hope you had time to snoop round? It didn't seem to take you very long.'

'I did nicely, thank you, child. The bedroom floor had been scrubbed, as those young men told us. I think I'll have a word with the County Police when we get back.'

'Will they think a scrubbed floor enough to go on?'

'Time will show, child. It is the question of the heavy man's failure to arrive at the hospital which will interest them. There was a man in the house, by the way. I am reasonably certain that he is the woman's husband, and that they are there to get the house aired or for some innocent and similar reason. When the new tenants are installed we may be able to find another excuse to call. Meanwhile, there are more profitable fields to explore. Did you get very wet in that hedge?'

'Soaking,' said Laura complacently. 'Did the man in the farmhouse see or hear you?'

'He both saw me and heard me, child. I gave an eldritch cry, like Tam Lin's fairy queen, and I am afraid I may have conveyed to him the impression that the house is haunted. It seemed, from what he said, that there is a tale of a ghost. If there is, it might be as well to find out the details. There is scope for many strange things in a house which has the reputation of being haunted.'

'I'd like to have seen the bloke's face when you screeched in his ear,' observed Laura.

'I did *not* screech in his ear,' said Mrs. Bradley. 'But you might screech in George's, and tell him I want my dinner.'

Chapter Six

★

' "*Heaven rest his soul!* . . . *He has lain these ten years in a house that he'll never leave.*" '

Ibid. (*Peter the Goatherd*)

'I WANT you,' said Mrs. Bradley, fastening her brilliant black eyes upon those of the Chief Constable, 'to have your young men look up all the cases in which people have disappeared during the past few weeks.'

'Past twenty years, you mean,' said the Chief Constable. 'We don't go in much for disappearances in these parts except disappearances under ground in the usual regrettable course of events, you know.'

'When was the last disappearance of the kind I mean?'

'In 1939, I think, just after war had broken out—or just before. I can't remember.'

'None since?'

'None that have been brought to my notice.'

'And before 1939?'

'I'd have to look up the reports.'

'I wish you would. What happened in the 1939 case?'

'Officially we're still looking for the fellow. He disappeared in what the Irish call "the dark of the moon," and has never been heard of again.'

'It was a man, then?'

'Yes, I believe it is mostly men who disappear. Debts, or bigamy, or get tired of their homes, I suppose. Crime, sometimes, of course . . . suicide . . . drowning. It was rather odd about this chap, though, because, so far as we could tell, he didn't come under any of the known headings. As a matter of fact, we didn't even know he'd disappeared until the following year, when some relatives in London wanted to billet themselves on him during the blitz. He couldn't be found, so they asked us to try to trace him. We had no luck, and as there was nothing against him, so far as we knew, we gave it up.'

'How old a man was he?'

'Twenty-seven, I believe. Youngish, anyhow.'

'Didn't you think he might have joined the Army?'

'He had a bad heart, it turned out. According to his doctor, there wasn't the slightest chance of his having been accepted for any of the Services, or of his having been able to do much good, even for A.R.P.'

'Why did nobody mention his disappearance sooner? A year seems a very long time.'

'Since the death of his father in 1932, he seems to have lived by himself. He was an artist and a bit of an archæologist. The people who were enquiring for him were his uncle and aunt. They had quarrelled with his father and had lost touch with the son, but when the fun began in London, of course, they wanted somewhere to go, and thought of this nephew, only to find his place deserted.'

'Was there no clue at all to his disappearance?'

'Never a one. I never knew such a case. We began our enquiry according to routine, but beyond establishing the fact that he'd left word with the tradespeople that he wouldn't want anything delivered after some date or other in March— that was the March of 1939, of course—we got nowhere. As there was nothing criminal about the case, we weren't particularly worried . . . after all, a man has the right to shut shop and clear out of his home if he wants to . . . but there was just one odd thing. The uncle said that his nephew had written to them at the time of Munich, and, after a few facetious remarks about gas-masks, had stated soberly that he was certain war was coming, and that if they ever wanted a refuge he was perfectly willing to put them up at his cottage.

'The uncle even produced the letter. We still have it, and, as it happened, the grocer the fellow used to deal with had kept the note telling him to ease off sending supplies. When we compared the two, though, there was no doubt that they had been written by different people. We got the uncle to write a piece for us, and put the handwriting experts on to all three scripts. There was no doubt that all three had been written by different people. We then recorded the finger-prints on the various documents, and also those in the empty cottage. There were the young man's prints, of course, all over the furniture, and it seemed, from the comparisons we were able to make, that the letter sent to the uncle was genuine and had come from the nephew. There were other prints in the cottage, but none which corresponded to any of the prints on the scrap of paper sent to the grocer or to those made, at our request, by the uncle and aunt. We got no further.'

'Dear me!' said Mrs. Bradley. 'And what happened to the uncle and aunt? Did they return to London?'

'No. They were given billets in the village of Little Dorsett, and, for all I know, are still there.'

'What is their name?'

'Allwright. William and Caroline Allwright.'

'Had the nephew the same surname?'

'Yes. The uncle was his father's brother.'

'Oh, yes, of course.'

'But he used to sign his pictures with the name Toro. Thought they'd sell better under a foreign label, probably.'

'Did they sell well?'

'He made some sort of living. According to the uncle he had inherited very little from his father, but used to manage to keep the wolf from the door. I saw one or two of his pictures in the cottage, but I've no idea whether they were any good.'

'Why didn't the uncle and aunt take over the cottage? Why have gone to another village?'

'The aunt was an invalid. There's a doctor at Little Dorsett, and they thought she ought to be within easy reach of one. The blitz had upset her nerves and brought on heart attacks, I believe.'

'Where was the nephew's cottage?'

'A couple of miles outside the village of Easey. Do you know it? The cottage was in a lane off the Salisbury road.'

'A lonely situation?'

'Yes, although it was very near the main road. A group of trees screen it from that side, and the nearest house is half a mile away. Are you thinking he was abducted?'

'I am wondering whether he was murdered,' said Mrs. Bradley. 'I shall be very glad to have the reports of any other disappearances.'

She recounted to the Chief Constable the strange story she had had from young O'Hara. It was then the Chief Constable's turn to ask the questions.

'You've consulted your son and he thinks we ought to take it up? Well, so do I, but where do we begin? The young fellow couldn't say for certain that the man was dead, you say?'

'Nor that his companions were *not* taking him to hospital. On the other hand, the man, if he was not dead, was either badly hurt or was suffering from severe hæmorrhage, and, that being the case, it seems strange that neither of the local hospitals was asked to admit him. Besides, it seems likely, from Mr. O'Hara's account, that the driver of the car simply drove round about the farm.'

'It does seem strange. Yes, that's right enough. Can your young man describe the fellow whom he helped to carry the sick man to the car?'

'Not sufficiently to serve any useful purpose, I am afraid. It was rather dark, you know.'

'Did he notice the number of the car?'

'Apparently it was too dark for him to notice anything particularly. The only thing he feels certain about is that the car did not come out on to a road.'

'Well, look here, I'll get Superintendent Thomas on to it. It all sounds a bit queer. And we'll have another go at the Toro-Allwright business, although I feel rather helpless over that.'

'Will your Superintendent Thomas frighten these people? I would not like Mr. O'Hara to come to any harm. He may not have seen much of *them*, but they may be able to recognize *him*. Cannot you act unofficially and with great discretion? I tell you frankly that I don't like the look of this case. Oh, and by the way, suppose that it should turn out to be murder, how will that affect an innocent accessory? In other words, how will it affect young Mr. O'Hara?'

'I don't see that it will, necessarily, affect him at all. He won't be of much use if he didn't see the sick man's face—that is, if we find a dead body . . . By the way, how did O'Hara come to lose his way?'

'He was misdirected by a man in a car.' Mrs. Bradley described the circumstances, and then added, 'And of this incident there are, it seems to me, three possible explanations: the man may have been mistaken in the direction he had seen Mr. Gascoigne take; he may have seen a Mr. Firman, who gave up the run and went off to his uncle's; and he may have been posted to waylay and mislead either Mr. Gascoigne or Mr. O'Hara, or, of course, this Mr. Firman. My own view is that he mistook Mr. O'Hara for Mr. Firman, but I have no real evidence for this.'

'On what do you base this idea, then?'

'It seems that if it *was* Mr. Firman whom Mr. O'Hara saw, he was not on his way to his uncle's.'

'I'd better just interview all three of these young fellows, perhaps,' said the Chief Constable, thoughtfully. 'It wouldn't do any harm. I shan't give anything away. I'll say a bull got loose because somebody left a gate open on that Saturday afternoon, or something of that kind, and just find out where · they went and check their stories.'

'I certainly wouldn't give anything away,' said Mrs. Bradley seriously,' particularly to this Mr. Firman, who turned up at the farm on the Sunday morning,'

'Taking a solemn view, aren't you? Do you suspect this young Firman of being concerned in the affair?'

'Perhaps. Look before you leap has always been a motto of mine.'

'Not when you used to go ski-ing in the old days,' said the Chief Constable with a reminiscent chuckle. 'I've heard from my father. . . . Oh, well, I hope you're *not* right about this business. We don't want a case of murder around these parts. We're not accustomed to murders here.'

'But perhaps you specialize in disappearances?' suggested Mrs. Bradley.

'I'll look up our records and see. You've spoilt my morning,' replied the Chief Constable.

The records, which came to Mrs. Bradley two days later, were interesting and remarkable. Two other disappearances had been brought to the notice of the County Police, and neither person had ever been found. A man named Battle had disappeared from the village of Newcombe Soulbury during the September of 1930, and another called Bulstrode had been reported missing, believed drowned, in the autumn of 1921, from a lonely little place on the coast called Slepe Rock.

'Hm! Arithmetical progression,' said Laura Menzies, to whom Mrs. Bradley had handed the Chief Constable's letter. 'And at intervals of nine years. A bit instructive, that.'

'How so?' Mrs. Bradley enquired.

'Oh, I don't know. Carefully spaced intervals and the number nine ought to have some significance, don't you think? I wish there were a record for 1912, don't you?'

'In an arithmetical progression . . .' began Mrs. Bradley, knitting her black brows. She paused.

'And I wish we could see into the future—say into 1957,' continued Laura, taking advantage of the pause.

'Do you? I do not. We have enough here to help us, I think. I expect the police will check the disappearances, under dates, of people in the adjoining counties, and——'

'And we could buy all the Ordnance Maps of England and Wales and mark them off,' said Laura, with enthusiasm. 'Isn't it a tallish order, though?' she added, as the magnitude of the otherwise delightful task came home to her.

'That remains to be seen,' Mrs. Bradley replied. 'Jot down the details of these four disappearances we have already . . .'

'That means counting this last one, and, somehow, I feel, it's different from the rest. Still . . . oh, I don't know . . .'

Mrs. Bradley left her at work and sent for George, the chauffeur.

'George,' she said, giving him a slip of paper, 'I want you to drive to these three places and report to me upon the lie of the land.'

'Very good, madam,' replied the sober, stocky, smart and respectable man. 'What particular aspect of the lie of the land would you be requiring?'

'I don't know, George. And I don't want to put ideas into your head. Just the general lie of the land, let us say, and please don't question the inhabitants. I want you to let me have your views in a completely unbiassed form.'

'Very good, madam.' He glanced at the list he was holding. 'It will take me all of half a day, madam, to get round these three places. They're all inside the County boundary, but some of the roads are narrow and all are winding.'

'Time is of no particular object, George, at present.'

'Very good, madam. I shall do my very best.'

He returned that evening to present his findings and a written report.

'The 1939 address, madam, is a small Tudor cottage about two miles beyond the village of Easey. It is situated behind a small copse, is occupied but is up for sale. It is in a remote spot, in spite of being only two miles out of the village. There is one road leading to it. The subsoil seems to be gravel, and there is a small river—a branch of the Frome—nearby. The village boasts an ancient church of Norman origin with fourteenth-century additions, some good Queen Anne and early Georgian houses, another Elizabethan (or earlier) Tudor cottage now used as a blacksmith's forge which is reputed to be haunted, a small general shop-cum-post-office, and two public houses, a small one called the *Kicking Wether* and a larger and more modern one called the *Storbright Arms*. Beyond the cottage, which is on a by-road, is the main road to Salisbury.'

'Splendid, George.'

'I have a more detailed report, madam.' He handed it over. Of the other two addresses, the 1930 one is about a mile and a half to two miles out of the village of Newcombe Soulbury on the road to Yeovil, and the 1921 address is just on this side of Slepe Rock, eight miles south-west (roughly speaking, madam) of Hopham. At Newcombe Soulbury the house consists of two adjoining cottages converted into one and embodying what looks to me like an artist's studio. I didn't attempt to examine the building closely, madam, as it appeared to be occupied, but one noticed the conversion of the upper floor with a very large north window. The garden was untended and the curtains were drawn across the downstair windows. The subsoil, as one would expect to find in that locality, is mostly chalk. The house is half-way up a very steep hill, and is situated at least a mile and a half from the railway station at Newcombe Soulbury.'

'This is marvellous, George! Exactly what I wanted.'

'The 1921 address, madam, I was unable to locate with exact certainty, failing enquiry of the local inhabitants. My guess is that it has been pulled down and a refreshment shack put up on or near the site. It is very near the sea. At Slepe Rock itself a mushroom sort of hotel has been built with a pull-in for motor coaches and a small car park on the opposite side of the road. The refreshment shack would be incorporated in this enterprise. Slepe Rock, I believe, madam, has only been exploited to any extent since about the year 1935. It was just getting into its stride, as it were, when the war broke out. Before 1935 I should say that the house stood in one of the loneliest places in England, madam. It is in a dip among four or five very large turf-covered hills of the Downs type, and the road which leads down past it to the cove is still not much more than a track. It looks a real old smugglers' hole to me, madam.'

'You've done wonders, George. Thank you very much. The common factor stands out in almost militant fashion, does it not?'

'The lonely situations of the respective addresses, madam?'

'Exactly, George. It is what I hoped for and partly expected. The plot thickens. And now I wonder whether you would like the day off to-morrow? I am going to London and shan't need you.'

'Thank you, madam, but, if quite convenient, I should be obliged if you would permit me to drive you to London, for the reason that I would then be able to take my mother to a music hall.'

'I didn't know music halls were your cup of tea, George, but I'm delighted to hear that they are!'

'They are not, as a matter of fact, in the ordinary way, madam, although I enjoy them occasionally. The fact is, madam, that my mother, I have recently discovered, is nourishing a passion for Mr. Max Miller, and chooses to believe that he picks her out as the special recipient of his shafts of wit. Mr. Miller, although you may not be aware of the fact, madam, has a good-natured way of appearing to address himself to the more hysterical female portion of his audience in order to rally and admonish them. This my mother greatly appreciates.'

'Why does she want you with her?'

'Well, madam, she does not follow all the more modern references, but she keeps them in mind and I am in request to explain them to her as soon as the performance is over.'

'Isn't that rather difficult?'

'I should select the adjective "embarrassing," madam. It is not always an enviable task to explain Mr. Miller's more Athenian epigrams in a crowded Underground train.'

In London Mrs. Bradley made a lightning round of visits and an important telephone call. Her visits, in chronological order, were to her son in his chambers, to the British Museum, to the London Library, to the geological section of the Victoria and Albert Museum, and to a famous archæologist of her acquaintance. She then rang up O'Hara.

'I am exceedingly grateful to you for introducing me to a most fascinating affair,' she said. 'I have interviewed my son, and also the Chief Constable, and you need have no fear of being arrested as an accessory after the fact of murder. It is not certain yet, in fact, that a murder has been committed.

However, the affair is now in the hands of the Chief Constable and the County Police. From time to time I will let you know what progress, if any at all, is made in the enquiry. . . . You would like to help if help is required? . . . and your cousin, too? Excellent!'

'Are they still interested?' asked Laura, who was in the room during the conversation over the telephone.

'Oh, yes, I think so. And now I must set to work, child.'

'Golly! What on earth have you been doing all day, then?' Mrs. Bradley grinned.

'I think I must study George's reports with relation to the Ordnance Survey, child. Then, to-morrow I think I shall visit the scenes of these disappearances. It will be very interesting to compare them.'

'May I come with you?'

'I should not think of going without you.'

'You do think these people have been murdered, don't you? We ought to try to trace what connection they have with one another, oughtn't we?'

'Your acumen is only matched by your innocent assumption that a theory is as good as a fact,' said Mrs. Bradley, poking her secretary in the ribs.

'Well, one must begin somewhere,' argued Laura, 'and lots of theories are preferable to facts—notably that the human race has progressed since Neolithic times and that England is a Christian country. Besides, theories, as it were, should be based upon facts in much the same way as a desirable residence rests upon its foundations.' She squinted complacently down her nose as she put forward these striking premises.

'Nevertheless, as you rightly point out, the foundations have to come first and must be of solid construction,' said Mrs. Bradley. 'So far, we have no reason for assuming that there is anything to connect the disappearances of three widely-separated persons except for the interesting (but not necessarily significant) fact that an interval of, roughly, nine years elapsed between disappearances one and two, two and three, and, now, between three and four.'

'Well, anyway, let's get hold of a map, and see if we can

deduce where this fat blighter came from,' said Laura. 'Once we know that, we know all.'

'How so?' Mrs. Bradley enquired.

'Well, we've only to question the local inhabitants to arrive at a complete history. You know what villages are. And once we know why we know who. Isn't that so?'

'Sometimes,' Mrs. Bradley cautiously replied. 'But, even if the villagers tell us all they know . . . which it is not very likely that they will, as we are strangers . . . I am not at all sure that we shall be so very much further forward. You see, the lonely situation of these houses from which the men seem to have disappeared, makes it unlikely that any of the villagers knew anything of the disappearances until some time after these had occurred. And the time factor in such cases is often of great importance.'

'Oh,' said Laura, somewhat dashed by this elementary reasoning, 'I see what you mean. Still, it won't do any harm to pore over the map for a bit. Will you do the poring, or shall I?'

'Oh, you do it, child.'

'Right. Thanks. I like mucking about with maps. Now I shall want . . . let's see . . . yes, I'd better have a transparent ruler, a protractor, compasses, a piece of thread marked in inches to wriggle along the winding roads and rivers, dividers, a set-square, some little flags stuck on pins . . .' She went happily to work to collect these, pausing only to add, 'And we ought to include Little Dorsett, I suppose, as we've had two references to it. Isn't that where that woman at the farm said she came from? And if the Allwrights are living there as well . . .'

'We must certainly include Little Dorsett,' Mrs. Bradley agreed.

Chapter Seven

★

'Thus the spell was broken, and all who had been turned into stones awoke, and took their proper forms.'

Ibid. (*The Queen Bee*)

ONCE she had assembled her tools, Laura went to work, and some simple measurements and a complicated table of statistics produced satisfactory results. Laura, at any rate, was pleased with them, and at ten-thirty made known her findings.

'What do you think?' she demanded, looking up from her self-imposed task of twiddling a pair of compasses on the middle of the one-inch map. 'Significant, I should call it, shouldn't you?'

'I hardly know,' replied Mrs. Bradley. 'Should I?'

'Rather! You wait until I tell you! . . . Oh, there's one thing I want to do, by the way, before we third-degree any villagers, and that is to go to that circle of standing stones above the farmyard. When can we go?'

'To-morrow morning, if you wish, child.'

'Oh, good! It had better be as early as possible, then, I think. We must leave plenty of time to do the villages properly after breakfast. What about leaving here at five for the circle of stones?'

'As you wish,' said Mrs. Bradley, grinning. 'I will call you myself.'

She did this at four, and by five they were in the car with Laura driving. It was a clear grey morning with no hint of autumn in the air and not a great deal in the trees. Study of the map had taught Laura, in addition to other matters, that it was possible to drive to within three-quarters of a mile of the circle of standing stones without going past O'Hara's mysterious farm.

The woods around the house where they were staying gave place very soon to the main road to Cuchester. Laura turned off from this about a mile to the south of the first village through which it ran, and the car mounted a long hill before it entered a narrow belt of trees on the further side.

After this the road became open, treeless and straight, and then, to avoid a high hill which was crowned by a Neolithic fort known locally as Mabb's Mound, it took itself off southeast, but still in a line as straight as a ruler could have made, past a farm, a long barrow, and a road which petered out up a hill and ended in moorland at the top.

Soon the car found another high-road, and, by keeping to this for some miles, Laura passed through a long and beautiful village, skirted the park of a large house surrounded by trees, dropped cautiously down the steepest gradient in the county, and by-passed the town of Cuchester.

Three or four miles beyond Cuchester she made the détour which would bring her round to the west of O'Hara's farm, and, beyond the discovery that the road had a very loose surface and in places was only fit for a sheep walk, she learned nothing that she had not known before.

She parked the car in a gateway on to a field, and then she and Mrs. Bradley set out for the circle of stones. A footpath which was crossed by two stiles led up and over the hill, for the stones were not quite at the summit.

Laura and Mrs. Bradley were walking round to inspect each stone when over the hill came two men. Mrs. Bradley called good morning as they came near, and one of them left the path and walked over towards the stone circle.

'Interesting,' said Mrs. Bradley, indicating the stones as though they had sprung up like mushrooms during the night.

'Ah, they be very interesting,' said the man. 'Calls 'em the Druids, we do, though I dunno for why. The Dancin' Druids some calls 'em, and one gentleman from London, he comes up along over 'ere once every year and he watches for to see if they dances.'

'And has he ever been fortunate enough to see them dance?' Mrs. Bradley enquired.

'Well,' said the man. 'I dunno as to that, I'm sure. Last year 'e swore as 'e *did* see summat, and this year e's talked of bringin' a film company over to see if they can't make a picture. But *I* dunno! They never danced during the war, I *do* know that, for I used to be on Observer Corps duty up 'ere, with nothing much to look at except them stones. Stood firm enough when *I* looked at 'em, that I'll swear.'

'The Dancing Druids,' said Mrs. Bradley, when the two men had gone on. 'Not an uncommon superstition.'

'Isn't it?' Laura enquired. 'A *most* uncommon one, I should have thought.'

'It is certainly an odd one,' Mrs. Bradley went on, 'but, in Cornwall, legend connects such circles as this one with girls turned into stone for impious behaviour—notably for dancing on a Sunday. The "Whispering Knights" of Little Rollright on the border of Oxfordshire are likewise believed to dance.* It is a striking survival, I believe, of the importance attached in early times to dancing as a religious exercise. There is also, of course, the fascinating paradox that dancing, although voiceless, is a language.† The ballet proves that.'

'I see,' said Laura. 'Well, I don't much want to be present when these dance. Do you really think anybody would be idiot enough, though, to believe that they do?'

'Place yourself here at twelve on a night of full moon and scudding cloud; when there is mist below in the valleys and the living silence of the windless dark all around you, and I am not at all sure that you yourself would not be idiot enough to believe that they danced,' said Mrs. Bradley.

She made a lengthy survey of the circle, looking carefully at every stone in turn, and also closely examining the ground around it. She seemed satisfied at last, and pronounced that it was more than breakfast time.

Laura, glancing at her wristwatch, was surprised to find

* I am indebted, for this and much other fascinating information, to *Prehistoric England*, by Grahame Clark.—G. M.
† Gilbert Keith Chesterton—*The Club of Queer Trades*.

that it was past nine o'clock. They returned to the car by the way they had come, and reached home at just after half-past ten.

'A little late to begin exploring, I think,' said Mrs. Bradley, to Laura's disappointment. 'To-morrow might be better than to-day.'

'Oh, but there's plenty of time!' said Laura, setting to work upon her breakfast.

'There is more still to-morrow,' Mrs. Bradley replied; and from this decision not to visit the villages that day she refused to be moved.

'What shall we do, then?' asked Laura.

'I shall knit,' Mrs. Bradley replied, producing, as soon as breakfast was cleared away, the shapeless and repulsive length of jetsam which it was her custom to dignify by the name of knitting. 'You may do anything you please, but don't be in later than midnight because we shall need to be up in good time in the morning.'

Armed with a *carte blanche*, Laura spent what remained of the morning in solitary confinement (as she herself expressed it) completely surrounded by maps. After lunch, looking complacent, important and secretive, she asked whether she might borrow the car.

'Provided you will borrow George as well,' Mrs. Bradley replied. 'I distrust that expression on your face. You are going to get into mischief, and George will extricate you. I have implicit confidence in him.'

'Oh, I don't mind George,' said Laura. 'In fact, we can take turns at driving, and he can mind the car if I leave it in funny places.'

Mrs. Bradley asked no questions, and, at just after two, Laura and George set out.

'You know, George,' said Laura, settling herself in the seat beside that of the driver, 'I think sometimes that it's a mistake, in a way, to work with anybody as clever as Mrs. Bradley.'

'Do you, miss?' George enquired, negotiating the double gates with care and skill.

'Yes. It saps one's intellect. One finds that one ceases to use one's own brains at all. One merely relies upon hers.'

'One could do worse, miss.'

'True. Yet sometimes I think I shall be glad to be married to my comparatively moronic spouse and resume my place in the aristocracy of the non-boneheaded. I used to be quite intelligent, and against a brainless husband I ought to show up pretty well.'

'May I enquire, miss,' said George respectfully, but with an expression of slight concern upon his broad and sensible face, 'what this all might be leading up to?'

'Well,' said Laura, 'to put all the cards on the table, I've got an idea.'

'Oh, dear, miss!' said George, who had had experience before of some of Laura's ideas and felt that they got her into trouble.

'Yes, I thought you'd say that,' said Laura, with great satisfaction. 'But this one, George, is different. Only, I shall need a bit of co-operation. Are you on?'

'Moderately speaking, miss, certainly. But if you'll allow me to say so——'

'Oh, Mrs. Bradley would be the first to admire this great thought that I'm going to place before you, only, you see, I want to surprise her with the *fait accompli*. Now what I want you to do is this: I want you to take me in the car to where we parked early this morning, and then I want you to meet me at that place called Slepe Rock. Can do?'

'Meaning that you are proposing to walk from the Nine Stones to the sea, miss?'

'Meaning just that, George.'

'But it's a matter of seventeen miles, miss!'

'I don't think it is, except by road,' said Laura. 'Anyway, I'm going to find out. There's no path marked on the map, but I've a hunch that there used to be an old trackway over

the Downs. If I can locate it—or, rather, if I can find out how
it used to run—I believe I can cut off about eleven of those
seventeen miles. What do you say to that?'

'And suppose you lose your way, miss, up on the Downs?—or
suppose you find you're on private land?—or in the middle of
a field with a bull in it?'

'Oh, George, don't be so discouraging! You run me along
to the Nine Stones, and I'll meet you at Slepe Rock as sure as
eggs are eggs.'

'Addled, I wouldn't be surprised, miss,' said George, with
great tolerance and good-humour. 'But just as you say.'

The lovely September afternoon was almost too warm for
walking, but Laura, full of her project, set off without any
misgivings as soon as she had left George. She did not wait to
see him turn the car, but climbed the hill at a rapid rate and
came out by the stone circle to get her bearings.

It was sunny enough for the stones to cast firm, dark
shadows. Laura took a bearing, decided upon the direction
she ought to take, and began to pace carefully forward. Sure
enough, at the end of half a mile of downhill walking over the
Downland turf, she came to a little copse, and at the entrance
to it was a monolith the shape of a spire, just one tall stone in a
clearing; and through the clearing (and leading south-east in
the direction which Laura wanted if she were to get to Slepe
Rock) was a narrow path, white and greasily slippery on the
chalk over which it had been trodden.

'Got it!' muttered Laura in triumph. 'Attababy! Here I
come!'

She was so pleased with the results of her reading, deductions
and terrestrial navigation that she began to run down the
path. Downhill it travelled until it was out of the clearing, and
then it climbed up to three hundred and fifty feet above sea-
level and ran along three miles of a narrow ridge until it
crossed a highway which Laura, pausing, recognized as a

secondary road which ran between Cuchester and Welsea Beaches.

The railway then had to be crossed, and Laura hesitated, longing to climb the embankment and see whether her track could again be picked up on the further side of the line.

She decided against this, however, as being unfair to George in case she should be run over by a train or arrested for trespassing on the railway company's property, so she was obliged to walk northwards in search of a footbridge or a station.

Fortunately the road went parallel with the line, and by timing herself she could decide by about how much she had come off her course. By good luck, too, there was a narrow wooden footbridge not more than half a mile along the permanent way, and she soon crossed that and walked south on the other side to pick up her prehistoric trackway.

She had walked just over four miles by this time, including the extra mile up and down beside the railway. By car, she would have had to go into Cuchester, seven miles by any road along which a car could travel, and at that point she would have been no further east and the whole seven miles further north of her objective.

She had reason to congratulate herself. The invisible trackway she was following led past three tumuli and then skirted a long, narrow wood. It then climbed steeply to an ancient fortified camp, entrenched and circular, which Laura would have liked to examine. She crossed it, however, and had the immense satisfaction of finding her track dropping gradually but inevitably past an ancient dyke and then shooting upwards again to its last ridge before it reached another stone circle and then came in sight of the sea.

Laura had walked between eight and nine miles over country as lonely as the grave. She found herself on a headland, looking down at a cross-setting tide which foamed at the foot of the cliffs and thundered below into caves.

She sought a way down, and went to find George and the car. He had parked almost on to the beach. There was not the slightest doubt of his relief when Laura, very warm and with aching legs, suggested that they should drive home.

'And so it went as you thought, miss?' he said, as he reversed the car past the path which led up to the cliff-top.

'Yes,' replied Laura, 'it did. Wait until I tell Mrs. Bradley!'

Mrs. Bradley, regaled with an account of the pilgrimage at dinner that night, was interested but seemed doubtful about the usefulness of the discovery except as a matter of (presumably) archæological interest.

'But you see,' said Laura despairingly, 'what I thought—the way I argued—well, you do see, don't you? There's this circle of standing stones, and there's this place called Slepe Rock, from which somebody once disappeared, and I've proved you can walk from one to the other in, near enough, as straight a line as you could draw on the map with a ruler or measure off as the crow flies—and, well, don't you see what I'm getting at?'

'Frankly, I do not,' said Mrs. Bradley. 'After all, we knew already that Slepe Rock was on your nine-mile circle, didn't we?'

'Ah, yes. But we didn't know you could *walk* the nine miles,' said Laura. 'It seems to me that there must be something different about Slepe Rock from the other places we're interested in, because you certainly couldn't walk from Newcombe Soulbury to the Stones, or from Easey. Look at the map, and you'll see. Don't you think it *does* single out Slepe?'

'It is an interesting theory, child, certainly, and one to which we might well devote some thought.'

'Well, I still say that the number nine has something about it. Take the Nine Stones, for example.'

'Very well, child.'

'Now regard them not as themselves, exactly, but as the centre of another and a greater circle, and what do we get, then?'

'The nine stones as a kind of gigantic boss, child, in the centre of the circle you mention.'

'Right. And what do you suppose then?'

'I suppose,' said Mrs. Bradley solemnly, 'that somewhere or other on the circumference of that imaginary circle with the boss of the Nine Stones as its centre are to be found the homes of all the missing persons.'

'Yes, well, there we are, then!' said Laura. 'Now, what's our next move, do you think? Shall we comb out the circle and try to find out where this fat man lived? It ought to bring results, but it may take a fairly long time. I've worked it out, and it means/a line of two hundred and fifty miles. You'd hardly think it, would you? Too tall an order, would you say?'

'Not at all, child. I think it a most reasonable distance, and I shall enjoy a tour of the County.'

'Well, when can we start?' enquired Laura, after a first suspicious glance at her employer. But Mrs. Bradley seemed serious enough, and merely asked, as a reply to this question:

'May I look at the map once more?'

'Sure. I'll trace out the nine-mile circle on it, shall I? It will give us something to go on. I've slewed the compass round but haven't actually made any marks. I'll make them now.'

The circle, so traced, covered a string of villages, cut across six main roads and several farms, and also enclosed some wild country of hills, woods, moorland and little streams.

'Could be in a village, on a road, or on a farm. Goodness knows how long it will take us!' said Laura, a little despondently, squinting down at the circle she had drawn.

'We have plenty of time before us,' Mrs. Bradley equably replied.

'Plenty of time? We don't know how much time we've got, do we?'

'If your arguments are correct, child, we have very nearly nine years.'

Chapter Eight

★

' "Not for gold or silver; but for flesh and blood." '
Ibid. (*The Lady and the Lion*)

'To-morrow morning, however,' Mrs. Bradley continued, 'we had better rise early, as we arranged to do, and visit the villages of Easey and Newcombe Soulbury. We will ask silly questions and demand unobtainable information. So many earnest persons do this nowadays, many of them sponsored by the government, that I don't suppose we shall seem remarkable. What information shall we seek?'

'Let's fish about with the local history,' suggested Laura. 'No! I'll tell you what! We could be archæologists, trying to find out where to get permission to dig. That will give us a chance to excavate the corpses if those people really have been murdered. What do you say to that for an idea?'

Mrs. Bradley gazed at her secretary in congratulatory amazement.

'I don't know how you think of these things,' she said. Laura looked at her suspiciously, but Mrs. Bradley added, as though she had taken the suggestion seriously, 'But I think that digging will be far more useful a little later on, child.'

'Ah! "Plant her where she'll blossom," ' observed Laura. 'I get it. Right. We become archæologists (and dig up the corpses) later. Meanwhile we are literary tourists with an insatiable thirst for Hardy-ana. That's the best bet in this county.'

'No, no. We will seek the birthplace of William Barnes, child. With any luck we shall be able to lunch in Cuchester and can then complete our round before dinner. And you'd better drive. They may recognize George at those places he visited before.'

'*Time Marches On*,' observed Laura, feeling slightly guilty at the thought that she had taken George to Slepe Rock that afternoon. However, next day she took the wheel and the car drove off towards what she privately termed *The House in Dormer Forest*. This was the place from which the young man Allwright, or, as he had preferred it, Toro, had disappeared in 1939. Mrs. Bradley had decided to go first to Easey on the theory that people might remember the events of 1939 more readily than those of 1930 and 1921.

Thanks to the clear directions supplied by George, Laura found the cottage at Easey and pulled up twenty yards away. It was true that the cottage was concealed in a small wood, but there was nothing either mysterious or sinister about the neat lawn, neat flowerbeds, neat curtains and neat front door. Even the notice-board was neat with its unobstrusive intimation that the property was for sale.

'A great thought strikes me,' said Laura.

'I thought perhaps it would,' Mrs. Bradley remarked.

'Headquarters.'

'I thought you might suggest that, but we need not be in a hurry.'

'Shall I go and enquire, or will you?'

'You go. But don't do anything at present except ask whether we may take a photograph.'

'Mentioning Barnes' birthplace?'

'Not until you have permission to take the photograph, otherwise they will tell you that you have come to the wrong place and close the door on you.'

'What a Machiavelli!' said Laura. 'You ought to have been a lawyer. Well, here goes!'

The door was opened by a middle-aged woman whose respectable black hat, apron worn under her coat and large shopping bag indicated a charwoman about to return to her own home after having 'obliged.'

'Photygraph?' she said doubtfully. 'I don't know. I'll arst, but they'm only holiday folks.'

'Oh, I see,' said Laura. 'Well, perhaps if they'd give permission . . .'

A girl's voice said from one of the inner doorways:

'What is it, Mrs. Bird?'

'Nothing, miss, only trippers,' replied the charwoman.

'Well, they can have some water for their kettle or whatever it is, but we can't give them cups of tea.'

'They want to take a photygraph of the 'ouse, miss.'

'Oh, they can do that, of course. It doesn't sound like trippers to ask!'

'We're not trippers!' said Laura. The girl emerged. 'I mean, not in the sense of paper and bottles and broken glass and catching gorse alight and all that. We thought the cottage rather a beauty, actually, and are doing research and that sort of thing, you know.'

'Well, you can take the photograph, of course,' said the girl. 'All right, Mrs. Bird, you go home. Did you take the dripping you wanted?'

'Thank you, yes, miss.' The charwoman left. The girl watched her until she reached the gate and then turned abruptly to Laura.

'You're not the police, are you?' she asked. 'Because we've had them all over the house already this week.'

'Oh!' said Laura, rather blankly. 'Oh, have you? All we wanted was the photograph and just to ask whether you knew anything of the history of the cottage.'

'No, we don't. We've only been here six weeks. I know the last owner disappeared, but that's nothing to do with us.'

'Oh—I see. I hope I haven't been a nuisance. It was only . . .'

'Oh, that's all right. But my father's a semi-invalid, and the visit of the police upset him.'

Laura was longing to know what the police had given as the reason of their visit, but did not care to ask. She took her leave, and realized that she and Mrs. Bradley were being watched from the windows as they took the photograph from the middle of the garden path.

'Hm!' said Laura, shutting up the camera, waving her hand

towards the girl at the window, and following Mrs. Bradley back to the car. 'Not much to be got out of *her!* I didn't bother to mention Barnes' birthplace. There seemed no point.'

'The cottage was charming,' Mrs. Bradley remarked. 'We must find out whether the police have any information about the inhabitants. I anticipate, however, that the girl will be as innocent as she looks and sounds. Yet . . . police all over the house!' She chuckled grimly. 'Mr. O'Hara's story must have impressed the Chief Constable deeply. I wonder why?'

'It sounds as though the police know something,' said Laura in dissatisfied tones, as though the police had been guilty of sharp practice. 'Will you be able to find out what it is?'

'I doubt it, child. Besides, I imagine that the lines of investigation followed by the police and ourselves ultimately will be widely different. Swallow your disappointment and let us go on to Newcombe Soulbury, where, perchance, we shall meet with good-fortune.'

Laura cheered up at once, and observed, with complete lack of civic morality, that there, at any rate, she proposed to be one jump ahead of the police whatever she had to risk to accomplish this.

The second village lay west by south of Easey, but it could not be reached by car by any very direct route, and Laura, who had to drive twenty-two miles in order to arrive once more on the circumference of her nine-mile circle, had been right in believing that it would not be possible to have walked to Newcombe Soulbury from the Nine Stones. A couple of miles, at last, up a long steep hill brought them to the home of the missing Mr. Battle, whose disappearance dated from 1930.

'I can see the studio,' said Laura. 'It seems as though disappearing from home is a foible confined to painters. Is that so?'

'I have no statistics,' said Mrs. Bradley, getting out of the car and walking towards the cottage, 'but it is a point which ought to be kept in mind during this enquiry.'

'Probably only coincidence that both these chaps were painters,' said Laura. 'The county must be lousy with artists, with all this scenery about.'

The cottage was double-fronted and, built on to it, they discovered, at the back, was a long room, uncurtained, and containing a bar counter. One or two bottles stood on shelves at the back of the bar, the bare floor was of polished boards, and a piano stood in one corner.

They took all this in, and then Mrs. Bradley said loudly (for she saw that they were under observation from an upstair window at the back of the house):

'I don't think this can be the place.

The window was opened, and a head came out.

'Did you want anything?' it demanded.

'We came to see the birthplace,' said Laura. The window was closed, and soon a large, untidy-looking, handsome woman opened the back door and came out to them. She appeared to be about forty years old.

'Can I direct you anywhere?' she demanded in a truculent tone.

'Yes, please. We are looking for the birthplace of William Barnes,' said Mrs. Bradley, briskly.

'Then you'd better look somewhere else,' the woman replied. 'This is a private house.'

'I'm very sorry,' said Laura, hoping for a hint from Mrs. Bradley. 'We thought, perhaps . . .'

'Well, it isn't,' said the woman. 'And the bar is not for customers. It's a freak idea of my husband's, and my husband doesn't like strangers.'

Mrs. Bradley touched Laura's arm, and, under the hostile gaze of the handsome, blousy-looking creature, they moved towards the gate.

'Hasn't helped much,' said Laura, opening the door of the car for her employer. 'What a model for Augustus John, though! I should think she'd be lovely if she took the trouble, wouldn't you?'

'Undoubtedly,' Mrs. Bradley replied. 'And I do not agree that our visit hasn't helped. Do not be in a hurry to start the car. Could you look inside the bonnet or something for a minute?'

It was whilst Laura was carrying out these instructions that the garden gate opened and the woman came out to them.

'Are you going into Newcombe?' she enquired.

'Is that the same as Newcombe Soulbury?' Mrs. Bradley enquired. 'If so . . .'

'Yes, of course it's the same! And . . . and William Barnes was born at a place called Rushay, the other side of Blandford, miles from here. And his statue is in Dorchester churchyard. There's nothing about him round here.'

Mrs. Bradley took out a small address book, and wrote *Rushay*.

'Thank you so much, Mrs. Battle,' she said carelessly, putting the book away. The woman was obviously startled.

'Battle? . . . Oh, you mean the people who *used* to live here! I . . . did you know them at all?'

'I knew of Battle the painter, of course,' Mrs. Bradley replied. 'I assumed, from your manner and appearance, that you were his wife . . . or perhaps (forgive me!) his widow. His disappearance was a great loss to art. The police, I am credibly informed, are looking into it again. But, of course, they will have been here before us.'

'The police?' said the woman. 'Oh, but I could tell them nothing about David! They would have to go to the son, *young* David Battle. Not that he would know any more than I do. I wonder . . .?'

'Yes, Mrs. Battle?'

'But I'm *not* Mrs. Battle!' cried the woman. 'And I tell you I know nothing of David's affairs. And I'm afraid I must ask you to go. My husband will be home at any moment. If you want to see David—the son, I mean, of course—he lives in Cuchester now. I don't know the address, but perhaps you could ask at the Post Office.'

'You were asking whether we were returning by way of the village,' said Mrs. Bradley. 'Yes, we are.'

'Oh, yes, well . . .' She hesitated and then plunged. 'Would you post a letter for me there? You'll see the Post Office. Just the village shop.'

'Most certainly we will post your letter,' Mrs. Bradley replied. 'It must be a great disadvantage to be so far from the village unless you have a car.'

'We have a car. My husband is using it. Thank you so much.'

She went back into the house, and was gone for some time.

'Writing the letter, I should think,' said Laura, abandoning her inspection of the engine and taking the driver's seat once more. The woman came out with the letter and Mrs. Bradley and Laura drove away.

'Well!' said Laura, as the car went slowly downhill towards Newcombe Soulbury village. 'And what do we make of *her*, I wonder?'

'It is too early to be certain,' Mrs. Bradley replied, 'but I should not be surprised if I were right, and that she is the older David Battle's second wife, and that he has not, in the sense that we understand it, "disappeared" at all, but has merely gone underground for his own purposes. And I am truly sorry to disappoint you again, but I have a strong feeling that the police have been there before us, that they have alarmed the Battles, and that the letter we are to post in Newcombe Soulbury contains information relating to our visit. And now we will try Slepe Rock.'

Once they had turned off the main road, their route lay among hills. Great, round-headed slopes lay on either side of the way and rose to meet the car as it headed towards the sea.

Slepe Rock itself was on the seaward side of the village of Slepe, a straggling little place with a poor-looking bungalow or two on its outskirts, some untidy cottages, a house turned into a shop, and a large garage. Laura had seen nothing of the village on her hill-track pilgrimage to Slepe, but had passed through it on the return journey in the car.

Beyond the village was the bay (once, as George had surmised, a smuggler's hole), some limestone caves, a wash of creaming water, like teeth, breaking the surface of the sea, a semi-circle of cliff, a coastguard's hut, and, just where the beach widened to include, between pebbles and backwash, a strip of dirty sand, the refreshment shack of which they were in search.

'Not much future in this,' said Laura decidedly. She regarded Slepe Rock with disfavour. 'I enjoyed my walk over the hills, but, seen from this angle, Slepe Rock is a beastly little place! It's like Lulworth Cove gone hellish. Why should anyone want to live here?—or wasn't it like this when the disappearing Bulstrode lived here?'

It was a question which Mrs. Bradley could not answer.

'The cottage must have been near the sea,' she observed, 'if George's report is correct, and I have no doubt whatever that it is.' She surveyed Slepe with a non-committal eye, and added, 'I think, child, that we ought to put up at the hotel. I wish your David Gavin were here with us. A young inspector of police could extract more information from a barmaid in the space of a quarter of an hour than you or I would be likely to get in a year and a half.'

'O'Hara and Gascoigne,' said Laura, quickly. 'They'd love to help, and they can't be doing anything important, and, after all, they got us into this!'

'An excellent idea,' said Mrs. Bradley, 'but I have doubts about Mr. O'Hara. I don't want him to run into danger on our account.'

'He wouldn't mind danger,' said Laura, 'and, after all, it's because of him that we're going to all this trouble.'

'True,' Mrs. Bradley replied. Gascoigne, however, came alone, explaining that his cousin had gone over to Ireland to a wedding, but would be coming back later and would join them then. He asked what he could do to help the enquiry.

'We want to find out,' said Mrs. Bradley, 'all that we can about the house which used to exist on the site of that shack beside the pull-in for coaches. We want to know why the house was taken down, who lived there, what happened to

him, and we need any other information which happens to
come to light. You shall pursue boatmen and compliment
barmaids. You shall indulge in friendly chat with the hotel
manager and pass the time of day with the men who work at
the pull-in for coaches.'

The god-like Gascoigne promised to do his best, and Laura
announced her intention of keeping a close watch on the hotel
guests.

'You never know,' she said. 'It won't take the villain of the
piece very long to find out that we're on his track, and he
might come here to keep an eye on us.'

'But we don't know for certain that there *is* a villain, do
we?' Gascoigne enquired.

'Well, there must be,' said Laura bluntly, 'or Mrs. Bradley
wouldn't be here wasting her time.'

Chapter Nine

*'And at twelve o'clock the young man met the princess going to
the bath . . .'*

Ibid. (*The Golden Bird*)

So Mrs. Bradley, Laura and Gascoigne booked rooms at
Slepe, and on the day following Gascoigne's admission to
their circle, Laura got up early in the morning and went
down to the beach to bathe. The tide was coming in, and
bathing was comparatively safe. She took off pullover, shirt,
slacks, socks and vest behind rocks, and, in the one-piece sea-
green bathing costume she had put on underneath the rest of
her clothing, she went cautiously seawards, wearing her rope-
soled shoes.

She placed shoes and towel upon a rock which, she deduced,
the sea would not reach until after she had finished her dip,
and waded into the water.

The sea was grey and uninviting. The tide came crosswise,
from the east, into the opening, and the undercurrent was
strong.

Laura, who had been able to swim since she was six, treated
unknown waters with respect. Having swum, keeping level
with the shore, whilst she tested the idiosyncrasies of the
locality, she at last struck out for the caves on the eastern
side of the bay.

The water grew deep and seemed warmer. The undertow
was noticeable, but did not drag sufficiently, she thought, to
be dangerous. In less time than she had allowed she was out
of deep water and was wading towards an opening in the
rocks.

It was a most fascinating cave. So much was soon apparent.

The sand, which, opposite the pull-in, seemed dirty and indeterminate, here was firm and hard. Not much of it was left uncovered, for the tide was coming in fast. Laura would have liked to loiter and explore, but beyond establishing the fact that on the left side as she went in there was a long ledge of slippery rock which would, at a pinch, make a path to the back of the cave, she did not wait or linger for fear of the tide. She promised herself, however, a complete exploration of the cave when conditions were good.

She chose the easy way back. This was to swim with the full run of the incoming tide and let it take her across the bay.

So crosswise did the tide set that her lazy manœuvres took her across to the opposite side and much farther west than the spit of sand from which she had entered the water.

She accepted these conditions, and was brought up opposite a cliff-fall before which some great blocks of limestone had fallen to form great rocks. Even at low tide the water scarcely abandoned them, and they were overgrown with moss-like, slippery weed and small, hard, strongly-adhering shells.

Laura had no intention of making her way barefoot over such stuff to reach her clothes, so, on gaining the rocks, she sat in the water and rested for half a minute, and then set to work to swim round, level with the shore, until she came to her shoes and her towel.

She was within twenty yards of these objectives when a boy on the beach began throwing stones into the sea. He was a lad of about seventeen, and Laura was not aware of him except vaguely until a fairly heavy pebble landed half a yard in front of her. She called out. The boy continued, without, apparently, having noticed her, to hurl considerable numbers of pebbles into the water, most of them fairly heavy.

Finding remonstrance useless, Laura, who was a person of action and short temper, duck-dived, gathered pebbles, and, finding bottom, returned the compliment with all her strength and skill. The third pebble, to her satisfaction, found its billet. The boy yelled, and put his hands to his stomach.

'Now, then!' called Laura. 'Lay off! I'm coming in.'

To her intense fury, the boy, his face like that of a demon, called out and began to pelt her. Hoping that an unlucky missile would not hit her on the head, she still swam in. Then she gathered a handful of pebbles, and soon a brisk battle was in progress. To Laura's satisfaction her aim was considerably better than that of the enemy, whom she now saw as a chunky but undeveloped boy with an unathletic body and rather a large head. When he saw that he could not defeat or frighten her he gave up throwing pebbles and took to flight. Laura, whose blood was up, followed him as quickly as she could on the shifting pebbles, but he had too good a start, and she did not catch him.

She went back and dressed. To her great surprise and annoyance, the boy, accompanied by a tall, grey-haired man, came into the hotel dining-room just as she was finishing her breakfast.

She put down her table-napkin beside her plate, got up, and went over to the table at which the boy was seated.

'Look here,' she said, 'what do you mean by throwing stones at me while I was in the water this morning?'

'I didn't know I should hit you with the stones,' muttered the boy. 'I'm sorry.'

'You didn't hit me with the stones or with anything else,' responded Laura. 'I can only imagine you are not quite right in the head.'

'Which same head,' said Gascoigne, when Laura had returned to her own table and had given an account of the matter, 'it will give me great pleasure to twist off his neck if I catch him annoying you, or anybody else, in that way.' He looked across at the boy and scowled.

The boy gave him a venomous glance, dropped his eyes, muttered something under his breath, and returned to his breakfast. The grey-haired man leaned forward and talked to him earnestly and at some length. Neither of them glanced again towards Mrs. Bradley's table.

'I wonder *why* he did it?' said Mrs. Bradley thoughtfully. 'The boy, I mean.'

'Oh, I don't know. I expect he's just a lout,' said Laura shortly. 'It's a nuisance he's staying in the hotel. Still, I shall be ready for him next time if he tries any more of his tricks.'

After breakfast the grey-haired man came into the lounge where Laura was reading the paper, and apologized for the behaviour of the boy.

'Ivor is rather undisciplined, I am afraid,' he added, smiling. 'He is not my son, of course, but I have spoken severely to him, and I don't think he will behave like that again.'

'He'd better not,' said Laura, very shortly. The man lingered, but Laura returned to her newspaper, and, after a moment, he bowed and walked away.

Laura was fond of swimming, and although the bay was in most ways unattractive and, at some states of the tide, inclined to be dangerous, she went in with Gascoigne in the middle of the morning, while Mrs. Bradley, armed with her shapeless knitting, sat high up on the beach on a flat rock backed by the cliff and watched them.

'Did you ever learn to swim?' enquired Laura, coming up out of the water at the turn of the tide and seating herself at Mrs. Bradley's feet.

'Yes, child. Once I swam the Hellespont, in emulation of Lord Byron and to the surprise of the Turkish authorities.'

'Did you really? I say, tell us about it!' said Gascoigne. 'Did you do it for a bet, or what?'

'I did that I did in envy of great Cæsar,' Mrs. Bradley simply replied; and from this statement she refused to depart, neither would she add one jot or tittle to it.

Laura stared out to sea, and then swung round on Gascoigne.

'Gerry, I'm going to climb the hills and find the hole where my smugglers' cave comes out.'

'Do you possess a smugglers' cave?'

'Of course I do! I found it this morning, before that little beast pelted me with stones. Come on! I'll race you getting dressed.'

She won this contest, and came out from behind rocks to find that Mrs. Bradley had rolled up her knitting in readiness to accompany them.

There was a path from the hotel garden which came out on to the slope of the hill. They followed this path through a little white-painted gate and climbed upwards until they came out at the top of a green-turfed, round-headed Down which broke away to steep cliffs, clean and white, which dropped to the creaming and sullen sea.

'Now, the cave should come out somewhere here,' said Laura beginning to cast around. 'It comes from the edge of the bay, but I don't suppose it goes straight up, do you? I mean, you couldn't get smuggled goods up a sheer perpendicular face.'

'Probably screened by bushes,' said Gascoigne. 'Are there any bushes up here?'

So far as the eye could reach, there were none at all.

'Well, the mouth is almost bound to be hidden in some way, I suppose,' agreed Laura. 'We must just hunt about until we find it.'

But although they hunted until lunch-time, they found nothing which could reward them. Mrs. Bradley did not join in the search. She had brought her knitting and spent the time in studying the sea and the sky from a perch she had found for herself where a dip in the turf gave an uncomfortable but adequate seat.

The afternoon was spent by Gascoigne and Laura in examining the country north of the village. Except that they produced healthy appetites for their dinner they gained nothing but fresh air and the benefits of exercise.

'I'm browned off here,' said Laura, when dinner was over. 'Let's hire a boat and scull about on the bay.'

As it was quite dark by the time she put forward the suggestion, the project was frowned upon by Gascoigne, so Laura went early to bed and dreamt of smugglers' holes labelled Keep Out, and boats that suddenly sprouted arms and legs and ran up the beach towards her.

Next morning she was up early, and, to rid herself of the effect of these nightmares, again went down to bathe. She kept a wary eye on the shore, but there was no sign of the boy who had thrown the stones at her. She had a cold, rough, enjoyable swim, but learnt no more about the cave.

When she got back to the hotel she found the grey-haired

man in the entrance hall turning over the newspapers. He looked up as she came in. At that moment the boy came downstairs. Laura waited. As he passed her she said, in almost friendly tones:

'Hullo, didn't see you down on the beach this morning.'

The boy tried to take no notice, but he received such a determined nudge from the man that he lifted his smouldering eyes, one of which was now black-ringed, Laura noticed, and answered:

'I don't care much about bathing.'

'Ivor was not allowed to learn to swim when he was small,' said the grey-haired man, 'and now he is diffident about trying.'

'Well, it *is* a bit awkward when you're his age,' said Laura frankly. 'Even if you have private lessons in a swimming-bath you're fairly noticeable, and, in these days, when nearly everyone can swim—look here, I'll teach you, if you like,' she suddenly added to the boy.

'No, thanks,' said the boy. 'I don't want to.' He turned and walked into the dining-room. The grey-haired man glanced at Laura, smiled, shrugged, and followed him.

That afternoon Laura went down to the shore with Gascoigne and Mrs. Bradley, and met the boy, who was aimlessly bouncing a ball against a rock. The grey-haired man was nowhere to be seen. The boy greeted them furtively, glanced about him, came up to Laura and said:

'Look out for the Druids.'

'What the devil did he mean by that?' asked Gascoigne, when Laura had gone to get ready to bathe.

'Time will show,' Mrs. Bradley replied. 'I think his guardian ill-treats him.'

When Laura came out from behind her rock, the boy went up to her and said:

'I say, are you going in again?'

'I am,' she replied. 'What about it?'

'Why, only . . . so am I, if you'll take me on,' he said, quickly and awkwardly. 'I'm very good at everything when I want to be. I don't know how it is. I suppose it's just natural.'

'What do you say, Gerry?' asked Laura of Gascoigne, who looked handsomer than ever in a tiny pair of bathing trunks. 'Shall we see how good he is at everything?' Already she was regretting her kindly impulse.

'He can get his things if he likes,' answered Gascoigne, coldly surveying the boy. The boy wilted before this god-like scrutiny, muttered, and walked away. Gascoigne shrugged, and soon he and Laura were in the water. Mrs. Bradley sat down on a flat rock and watched them for ten minutes. After this interval, the grey-haired man came down to the beach and trained a pair of binoculars on a yacht which was tacking across the mouth of the bay. Mrs. Bradley waited until she felt the man was fully absorbed, and then she went back to the hotel. It had not surprised her to discover that the name of the person to whom the woman at Newcombe Soulbury had addressed the letter which Mrs. Bradley had posted was also in the hotel register. It was the interesting and sinister name of Cassius, and Mrs. Bradley had already discovered that this was the name of the grey-haired, courteous, cold-eyed guardian of the oafish and thug-like boy.

'Come here to watch us,' she wrote in a note she left for Laura. 'I knew that there would be repercussions from Newcombe Soulbury. The plot thickens, child.'

She left this note with the chambermaid, with instructions to hand it to no one but Laura herself, ordered the car, and drove to the ancient city of Cuchester.

Chapter Ten

'Heaven have mercy upon us! O if our poor mother knew how we are used!'

Ibid. (*Hansel and Grettel*)

THE woman at Newcombe Soulbury had been correct, Mrs. Bradley was willing to admit, in describing Cuchester as not a very large town, but it was large enough to render unacceptable the notion of going from door to door enquiring for David Battle.

Mrs. Bradley parked her car, therefore, near the cattle market, and walked into the post office to make some enquiries. She obtained nothing there, however, which was of the smallest use to her, except a dozen twopenny-halfpenny stamps, which she put into her handbag before going northwards towards the main road.

She walked until she discovered a shop which had pictures for sale. She went in and asked whether they had any paintings by local artists. She was taken to the first floor of the shop and invited to inspect the canvasses.

It appeared that there were quite a number of local artists. Bold and obscure pictures confronted Mrs. Bradley on every hand. Bright, hard modern greens muscled stubbornly in on both dim and imperial purples; kaleidoscopic variations of sunsets, still, windy, cloudy, clear, were streaked against hills, reflected in water, splashed over levels and indiscreetly displayed behind buildings of historic interest. Water-meadows in the style of the Cromes, and moorland in the style of the Cornish school attempted to distract attention from ladies with flowers in their mouths and horses with ribbons in their forelocks. Here was a touch of Matisse and there a pale shade of Stephen Spurrier. On the left was a still-life displaying a rose and a beer-bottle; to the right a bold attempt at a battle of stags. Cubism was represented by a bull seen on three sides at once, and surrealism by a harp suspended over a pat of butter and a toadstool. In a dark corner hung a canvas which Mrs. Bradley thought at first was a genuine Old Crome.

'I am looking,' said she, 'for a Battle.'

The picture-dealer looked at her with a certain degree of defensiveness, and begged her pardon.

'Battle—a local artist,' Mrs. Bradley explained, waving a yellow claw. 'Among so many examples, you must surely possess a Battle. I came especially to get one.'

The man continued to look dubiously at her.

'We have nothing in stock,' he said, 'but . . . may I ask whether you are acquainted with Mr. Battle?'

'Friends of mine are interested in him,' said Mrs. Bradley vaguely, 'and I should have liked to make them a present of one of his pictures. I wonder whether there is anyone else in Cuchester . . .'

'I don't stock his pictures,' said the dealer suddenly, 'because I don't think they would sell. Not in this place, anyhow. They might sell in London. I don't know. I've only got one of his things—an early work and of no great interest except that, if I were a dishonest man, I could easily pass it off as an Old Crome. I saw you looking at it just now. I took it in payment of a debt.'

'And you don't want to sell it?'

'I couldn't sell it. It isn't a *copy* of an Old Crome, you see. It's a fake. Old Crome never painted that subject, so far as we know. I believe Battle painted it for a bet, but he tried to pass it off as genuine. His later work is, shall I say, French?'

'You shall say French by all means,' Mrs. Bradley cordially replied. '*Chacun à son gout*, no doubt. And as I happen to recognize that the subject of the picture under discussion is part of the Isle of Wight——'

'San fairy Ann,' said the dealer, entering into the spirit of the discussion, and suddenly grinning. 'But Battle is certainly a bit too hot for Cuchester.'

'That being the case,' said Mrs. Bradley, 'if you will oblige me by writing down Mr. Battle's address . . .' she produced

notebook and pencil in a flash . . . 'I shall attempt to assuage
the natural disappointment of my friends with . . .' She
looked around her. 'Ah, yes! With . . .' She picked out a very
large canvas priced modestly (considering the amount of paint
on it) at twenty-two pounds ten ' . . . with this!' The picture-
dealer, looking at her for a moment with a degree of incredulity
which, but for the practice she had had in the art of converting
unbelievers, she would have found disconcerting, said, on a
high note of pleasure:

'But I congratulate you! You have selected a masterpiece.
That, madam, is the only Toro in my establishment.'

Mrs. Bradley was more interested in this information than
the art dealer could possibly know, but she did not betray her
feelings. It might well be the only Toro, if he hoped to sell
pictures, she thought.

The painting was wrapped up for her and taken to the
ground floor of the shop. Armed with the address for which
she had sought, she went in search of David Battle. A single
enquiry was enough to set her upon the right road, and she
found him on the second floor of an old and dilapidated house.
He was a tall, myopic, rather handsome young man. Three
minutes' conversation and the sight of two dilapidated but
genuine seventeenth-century picture-frames each containing a
boldly-splashed and obviously freshly-painted picture, led
Mrs. Bradley to decide to tell him frankly why she had come.
She felt that only by taking him into her confidence could she
obtain from him any assistance.

He listened carefully, and without attempting to speak,
until she had reached the end of her story. Then he said,
blinking through his spectacles:

'I can't do anything to help you, you know, and if I could I
wouldn't. I hated my father. I have no intention of trying to
find out why he disappeared, or what happened to him after
he left me. I believe he might have been murdered. I've
thought so for the past ten years, and, if he *was* murdered,
rather than attempt to track down the murderer and get him
punished, I'd like to shake him by the hand. He is the best
friend, except my mother, I ever had.'

'I see,' said Mrs. Bradley, slowly nodding her head. 'Your mother died, I imagine, before your father disappeared?'

'Yes, she did. While she was alive she protected me. She held the purse-strings, you see. After she died my life was hell. I was half-starved and ill-treated. Then, when I was twelve, my father went out one night and never came back. I waited up all night, but he did not come.

'For a week I lived in dread of his reappearance. After that I lived go-as-you-please for a couple of months. Then I got into trouble for poaching. I had to keep myself alive, and I had no money except a pound or two which I found in one of the drawers of the dressing-table in my father's bedroom. The magistrates made some enquiries, but nothing came of them. Some of the villagers thought that my father had deserted me, and was living with a woman in London.

'My uncle heard of all this before I could be sent to an Approved School as being in need of care and protection, and he made a good many enquiries, but nothing came of them, so he took me to live with him, and, later on, sent me to school. He was good to me; so was my aunt—my mother's sister—but they wanted me to go into business and, of course, I wanted to paint.

'I painted. That's all there was to it. And if you suppose I am going to move an inch to find out what happened to my father, you are, I'm afraid, mistaken. I'm sorry, but there it is. I've simply no need of my father, dead or alive.'

'I am not, primarily, concerned with your needs,' Mrs. Bradley pointed out, 'and I sympathize with your feelings; but will you tell me just one thing before I go?'

'I expect so.' The young man smiled. His face, when he was not brooding upon his wrongs, was pleasant enough. 'What is it?'

'Are you aware of any connection between your father and the people who now live in what used to be your house at Newcombe Soulbury?'

'I don't know the people at Newcombe Soulbury at all. I've never seen them. My uncle sold the cottage and invested the money for me when I came of age, for it seemed unlikely by that time that my father would ever come back. It was my mother's property, in any case, not his.'

'Then you don't know so much as the name of the people who bought it?'

'I've got their name somewhere, yes. Wait a minute. I think I can remember. . . . A peculiar name. Reminded me of melons . . . What was it, now? Ah, Cantelope. That's it. John Alexander Cantelope. But I don't know the man himself from Adam.'

'And now,' said Mrs. Bradley, 'do you know anybody called Allwright, who painted his pictures under the name of Toro?'

'I knew *of* him, of course. I never met him. A very fine painter. Would have made a name for himself if he had lived. Went to London, so I've heard, and was killed in the blitz in 1940.'

'No, I don't think that was it,' said Mrs. Bradley. 'It seems more likely that he disappeared some time in 1939.'

'Really? I never heard of that! I knew that his relations wanted news of him, but that, I happen to know, was in 1940. I remember it because I'd just been seconded for a camouflage job, and was at home on a few days' leave, and an uncle and aunt of his called to see me.'

'Why did they come to *you?* You say you didn't know Mr. Allwright personally?'

'I don't know, exactly, how it was, but I think they had found my name among his papers.'

'Had you ever corresponded with him, then?'

'No, I had not. My father may have done so. His name was the same as mine, you see, David Battle.'

Mrs. Bradley thought it unwise to press him further; therefore, armed with the information which she had contrived to obtain, she went back to the picture-dealer's shop, claimed her canvas, and returned to Slepe Rock.

Whilst she was dressing for dinner she turned over in her mind some yeasty thoughts to which the Cuchester pilgrimage had given rise. There was also the fascinating connection between the cottage at Newcombe Soulbury and the appearance at Slepe Rock of the sinister and urbane Mr. Cassius now that she had identified him as the guardian—or, more probably, the father—of the boy who had thrown stones at Laura.

Laura, meanwhile, had come back from bathing, had received Mrs. Bradley's note, and had crossed the road from the hotel to the refreshment shack. It was much like all other such temporary structures, and was inside the open yard of the pull-in. It was patronized chiefly by drivers of lorries and coaches. Opposite to it was a garage.

Laura went back to the beach and conversed with the oldest boatman. A friendly atmosphere having been maintained for some quarter of an hour, she mentioned the shack and the pull-in.

'Been here the last ten years. Built just before the war,' she was told. 'Been a bungalow or something afore that, and before that again a cottage. The bungalow people was drownded out in the bay. Sailed their own dinghy. Reckless. 'Andled 'er well enough, too. But there's a nasty lift on the bay when the wind blows contrary to the tide. Pity. They was a nice young couple. 'Ad the cottage left 'em in somebody's will, and pulled it down and 'ad the bungalow built. Never lived there 'ardly six months. Then these motor-lorry folks took over, and pulled down the bungalow and put up the garridge and that shack. 'Course, it be better for Slepe in a way, but in my opinion it brings the wrong people to the place.'

'And both of those who lived in the bungalow were drowned?'

'Ay, like I told ee.'

'Were—were the bodies recovered?'

'No, they wasn't, although they was looked for. But the boat was found. Gybed they 'ad, us reckoned, beyond the point out there, and overturned. No, there was never no sign of the neither of 'em. They went out, but they never come back.'

'Were you surprised the bodies weren't found?'

'Not a lot. The tides be very funny round 'ere when the wind's across 'em. That's what us said at the time.'

'But the bodies would come ashore *somewhere* along the coast, surely?'

'That I couldn't very well say.'

'What sort of a man was that one who left them the cottage?'

'I don't recollect much of he. Bit of a poet, they *do* say.'

'What was his name?'

'Blowed if I know. 'Twere all of thirty year ago.'

'Twenty-seven since he died,' thought Laura; but she did not say this aloud.

'I *did* 'ear as it was the poet chap as left the cottage to them as was drownded and built the bungalow,' the old man went on. 'The young 'ooman was a niece of his or sommat. I don't recollect how it went, but I believe it was family property. Howsomever, it must ha' been sold to these garage folks, seemingly by the lawyers. Of course, it brings trade to the village. No doubt as to that, but we done very nice, all the same, wi'out all the likes of them trippers.'

The conversation continued along these lines until Laura went back to the hotel. Brooding upon the conversation, it seemed to Laura that the first use to which the information it had produced could be put was to find out the name of the lawyers who had sold the bungalow and discover from them whether the dead poet or the drowned couple had been named Bulstrode. She discovered the name of the lawyers by asking at the hotel.

'The lawyers were Thorn, Thorn and Butterthorn, of Burehampton,' she told Mrs. Bradley next day. 'I got it from the landlord here this morning. We talked about lawyers in general, and it came out almost at once. The trouble is,' she added, 'that the police will have explored that particular avenue long ago, and it can't lead anywhere, or they would have found out more than they did. Is it worth our while to follow up those deaths by drowning?'

'Oh, yes, child, of course it's worth while. Anything which adds to our knowledge will be valuable, because we shall soon be following a different line from that so far taken by the police.'

Following, Laura gathered, this different line, she returned to Cuchester on the next afternoon and went again to see David Battle.

'Did a man named Bulstrode have anything to do with your father?' she demanded.

'Bulstrode?' said David, who seemed very much on the defensive and whose smile was not once in evidence. 'I don't think I've heard the name before. Why? What about him?'

'He disappeared,' said Mrs. Bradley, waving a yellow claw. 'Nine years before your father. A poet, I understand. I thought you might know something about his work.'

'Not a thing. Sorry. I say, I wish you'd sit for me some time.'

'Not if you are going to give me an odd number of eyes and noses. I sat for a Cubist once, in my younger days, and the result was not at all gratifying.'

'You wouldn't have to buy it if you didn't like it, you know, although, if you're rich, I wish you would.'

'Are you as badly·off as that?'

'I'm pretty well down to bedrock. But I didn't mean that. At least, well, yes, I suppose I did. But I think you *would* like it, you know.' His manner changed. In a persuasive voice he added, 'You've got lovely bones. It wouldn't be difficult to flatter you.'

'You had better paint my secretary,' said Mrs. Bradley decisively. 'She has time to spare, and I haven't. Besides, her young man would like to have a flattering portrait of her, no doubt. Oh, you needn't look distressed. Laura is well worth painting. I'll send her round. Mind you're polite. She is quite capable of felling you to the ground if she finds you irritating. I thought, by the way, that your mother left you some money?'

'She did, but that brute got through most of it. There was only the house when he went, blast his ugly soul!'

Mrs. Bradley looked searchingly at him.

'Did you, by any chance, *murder* your father?' she asked. To her great interest, Battle looked amused.

'When I was a little tiny boy?' he asked mockingly. 'What do you take me for?'

'More of a villain than you look!' said Mrs. Bradley decisively. 'And more of a liar than you think I do,' she added in her sardonic, secret thoughts. She did not like the young man.

Chapter Eleven

★

*'Who they are that have come to live there I cannot tell, but I am
sure it looks more dark and gloomy than ever, and some queer-
looking beings are to be seen lurking about it every night, as I am
told.'*

Ibid. (*The Elfin-Grove*)

LAURA went for her first sitting accompanied by her
employer. She went unwillingly and under orders, but
regained her good temper when she discovered that
Battle was prepared to chat to her whilst he made his
preliminary sketch.

'The thing that stands out a mile,' she remarked to Mrs.
Bradley when they had returned to Slepe Rock, 'is that this
Battle loathed his father with the deep and intense sort of
loathing which would very likely lead to murder. And you
know what he said when you asked him whether he *had*
murdered him!'

'Yes. He said he had often thought of it, but that he was no
more than a child when his father left him and disappeared.
We must admit that he *would* have been rather young, at the
time of his father's disappearance, to make an effective
murderer, don't you think?'

'Oh, I don't know. I've read of kids murdering people.
Morbid kids, and those sort of half-baked ones that nowadays
you'd get a psychiatrist to look over.'

'Even supposing that he did kill his father, do you think
that, at the age of eleven or twelve, he could have contrived to
hide the body so that the police could never find it?'

'Oh, I hadn't thought of that. Well, anyway . . .'

'And if he *had* murdered him and hoodwinked everybody so

successfully, would he still hate him quite so fiercely? Would
not his attitude be different from what it is? And wouldn't he
have some plausible story to account for his father's disappearance? He merely states that he hated him and doesn't want
him back.'

'All right, all right. I withdraw. But he seems quite a
murderer to me, but then, of course, I dislike him.'

Mrs. Bradley forbore to contest these unreasonable and
unscientific views, chiefly because she agreed with them. She
was interested to learn that Laura held them, however, and
enquired:

'What else do you think of him, I wonder?'

'I don't think anything. By the way, he wanted to charge
me so much an hour for the sittings, but I wasn't going to
agree. I might have to go a dozen times. I believe in piece-
work from painters.'

'I heard the conversation, and am also aware that you lent
him two pounds,' said Mrs. Bradley, with a slight but
appreciative cackle.

'Oh, that's all right, because, if he doesn't sub up, I shall
simply knock it off his bill,' said Laura hastily.

'You are prudence and foresight personified. But let us,
before we go further, make an inventory of what we know.
First, we have two painters and a poet. Three painters, if we
count this young Battle. There ought to be something significant
about that, as you would say.'

'All creative artists?'

'Very well. We have four creative artists, three of whom
disappeared without trace. Secondly, we have the odd and
possibly significant fact that these disappearances seem to be
on a cycle of nine years.'

'Thirdly,' said Laura, 'the disappearances seem to take
place nine miles from the place where O'Hara's fat man was
last seen. Fourthly, there seems to be no sort of motive for the
disappearances so far as we know at present. Fifthly—is there
a fifthly?'

'There is. You should keep your eyes open and apply your
knowledge, child. Fifthly, there are two seventeenth-century

carved picture frames in David Battle's rooms, and there is a wonderful pseudo-Old Crome on the walls of the Cuchester picture dealer.'

'Painted by David Battle. What about it? And, of course, we shall discover that David's father disappeared in September because, although I never realized it until now, September is the ninth month of the year! So that would settle it.'

'And the month is still September, said Mrs. Bradley. 'I wonder . . .'

Laura waited a minute, but Mrs. Bradley left the sentence unfinished. Laura decided to prompt her.

'You wonder what? she said. Mrs. Bradley shook her head.

'A passing thought, that's all, child, and quite a foolish one, no doubt.'

'Don't be aggravating,' said Laura. 'You're not the only person who dislikes harvest festivals, but *I* don't mind mentioning *my* dislikes.'

At this startling piece of thought-reading Mrs. Bradley cackled loudly. Her secretary grinned.

'You know, what we ought to do, as I see it at present, is to go to the stone circle every night and hide ourselves, and wait and watch in case the Druids dance. And do you know what I think about that?—I've been thinking it over, and I perceive a secret society behind all this, you know.'

'A *what?*' said Mrs. Bradley sharply.

'Oh,' said Laura, waving a shapely palm, 'I've been doing a good deal of solid considering since Mike O'Hara and Gerry Gascoigne came to us with that story, and, as I see it, there's a kidnapping gang at work. The gang is nine strong, operates at nine-yearly intervals, holds some sort of horrid festival in the ninth month of each ninth year, and captures people who live on a nine-mile radius from their centre of operations, which is the nine-stone circle to which O'Hara helped them take that fat man. How else can you work it all out?'

Mrs. Bradley was lost in amazement, and gazed rather anxiously at her secretary.

'Are you feeling quite well, child?' she enquired. Laura

strode to the hotel window and looked out on to the sea.

'It's going to blow,' she said. She watched the rollers come combing across the bay, and then turned to face her employer. 'You may laugh,' she went on, 'but there's something behind all this—I know there is!—and we've got to work very much quicker. And if those Druids dance I'm jolly well going to see them do it, and then we shall know where we are!'

'I do beg of you,' said Mrs. Bradley, looking, this time, genuinely alarmed, 'not to get into mischief. As I have already pointed out, if your deductions and surmises are correct, we have nearly another nine years in which to solve the problem of these disappearances, and if you are *not* correct, then idiotic antics among the Druids will not assist the enquiry and may be dangerous. When do you go for your next sitting?'

'To-morrow,' said Laura gloomily. 'I thought you heard me arrange it over the 'phone. Oh, Lord, how I hate being painted!'

'I know, child, and you have my utmost sympathy. And I did hear you arrange it. I was, however, desirous of changing the subject. You alarm me very much when you get ideas into your head. Now, whilst you are occupying the attention of David Battle, I am going to London. I may be away for a day or two, and I do not want anybody to know that I have left you here alone. In fact, I do not intend that you shall be alone. You will take Mr. Gascoigne to Cuchester with you to-morrow, and you will not go anywhere without him. We have made enemies, I suspect, over this business, and it would be most embarrassing for me to have to explain to your mother that you had met with an accident.'

'Nothing would surprise her less than to hear I'd broken my neck,' said Laura cheerfully. 'All right. I'll watch my step. But I'm not prepared to promise not to go out and about, and not to poke my nose here and there if it seems to be needed. You can't ask that sort of thing. I'm turned twenty-one, and . . .'

'I ask you to exercise reasonable discretion and to take reasonable precautions,' said Mrs. Bradley. 'Not that I think you understand the meaning of the words, but to quiet my conscience, that's all.'

'If you're so bally anxious and old-hen, why on earth don't you take me with you? Oh, I know! I've got to keep Battle in play. Never fear. I'll watch him like a hawk. How long do you want me to keep a line on him?'

'Until four o'clock to-morrow afternoon, child.'

'Easy!'

Escorted by Gascoigne, she went again to Battle's studio on the following day. They took Mrs. Bradley's car, for its owner's mysterious errand could best be accomplished, it appeared, by taking the train.

'But where will you get the train?' Laura had demanded. 'It's miles to a station from here.'

'I shall manage,' Mrs. Bradley had replied.

'She told *me* not to get into mischief,' said Laura gloomily, when she and Gascoigne had garaged the car at the Bournemouth end of the town and were going towards David Battle's studio, 'but she's far more likely to get landed in the soup than I am! I don't like this business of going off cagily by herself. It must be something dangerous, or I'm sure she'd have taken me with her. It's all poppycock pushing me off like this for this beastly portrait.'

'Never mind. Play up, and for heaven's sake look pleasant,' said Gascoigne. 'You don't want that horrible expression bequeathed to posterity. Think what your grandchildren would say. And, another thing. Mike is coming down this evening. Says he's got news and must see me. What do you say to that? Look here, if we can get hold of another female, let's go to Welsea for dinner. I'm becoming rather tired of Slepe Rock. What do you say?'

Laura accepted the invitation immediately, and they mounted to Battle's studio. The artist was already in front of the portrait.

'Come on, come on!' he said irritably, 'I'm in form to-day. How long can you give me, Miss Menzies?'

'Oh, an hour,' said Laura, picking up a piece of newspaper and dusting the model throne before she sat down. 'This is Mr. Gascoigne.'

The two men nodded to one another. Then Gascoigne said, 'Haven't I seen you before?'

'No, I don't think so,' said Battle, messing with oil paint which he squeezed from fat and filthy-looking tubes. 'I have never seen *you*, anyway. I'd remember if I had. I always remember faces.'

Laura thought that this was not an idle boast. A painter most likely would always remember faces. No more was said, and Battle was soon at work, concentrating with a frown, and never stepping away to look at his work. Gascoigne had brought a book, and, after glancing a little doubtfully at the only chair in the studio, he surreptitiously placed the jacket of the book on the seat of the chair before he sat down to read.

An hour passed, and Battle continued to paint. Laura, catching Gascoigne's eye, shrugged helplessly. Mrs. Bradley's witching hour was past. It was five o'clock by Laura's wrist-watch.

'I say, aren't we nearly through for to-day? I can come again to-morrow, if you like,' she said at last.

'Keep still,' said Battle, squeezing out more paint and daubing it rapidly and in chunks and lumps on to his canvas. 'I've got it! And you can't have the portrait until after I've shown it. It's good.'

'But, look . . .' said Laura. The artist took no notice. He put down his brushes, and, going at the picture with great energy, proceeded to work at the oil colour with his fingers, a dirty piece of thick linen, and what looked like an empty paint-tube.

'There,' he said at last, stepping back. 'You can go home when you like now.'

Laura got down stiffly.

'Thank heaven for that,' she observed. She walked over and looked at the painting. 'Hm! Not bad.'

'It's good,' said Battle, shortly. 'And I'm tired.'

Gascoigne looked at his watch.

'Let's all go and have some tea,' he suggested. 'Plenty of places in the town.'

'Not for me,' said Battle. 'I'll clean this muck off my hands and then I'm going out to get drunk. I'll never do better work than I've done this afternoon, and I'm going to celebrate. So long.'

'I suppose,' said Gascoigne, detaining him, 'you don't know a fellow named Firman?'

'Firman? I've some cousins named Firman, I believe. I've never met them. My father's sister's kids. Gosh awful, at that. Why do you want to know? I hate the thought of them.'

'It isn't you I've met before, then; it's your cousin, that's all,' said Gascoigne. He enlarged on the resemblance between Battle and Firman to Laura on the way back to Slepe Rock. 'And the queer thing is, of course,' he added, 'that Firman was one of the hounds that day when Mike helped to carry that fat fellow to the car. It seems to me that we might do worse than get Firman to answer a few questions. It wouldn't do any harm. And I'll put Mike on to this chap Battle. He may get more out of him than I can.'

'I should hardly think so,' said Laura. 'If your fatal charm doesn't do the trick I shouldn't think Mike would get anywhere. Still, anything you say. And although I've more or less promised Mrs. Croc. that I won't step high, wide and handsome while she's out of the way, I don't see why we shouldn't explore an avenue or two now she's gone. You go ahead and get Mike down here, and let's see what we can ferret out amongst us. I should like to surprise the Old Lizard. She's been putting on dog a bit lately.'

O'Hara arrived by motor cycle at ten o'clock that night, too late for dinner. He was in high spirits and announced that he was ready and willing to take part in carrying out any plans that might be proposed by the others.

'And what I wanted to tell you is this,' he added. 'You know that queer house—the big one with the four dead trees in its grounds? I've discovered, from looking up old records, that it used to be called Nine Acres. The recurrence of the number noted by Miss Menzies and sent along by you, Gerry, seems a bit of a pointer, and so I propose that, instead of keeping out of that house as ordered by the notice on the gate, we jolly well go in. I've been thinking over the details of that day we had our run and I think I've stumbled on a clue.'

'Say on!' said Laura, with enthusiasm. Gascoigne looked interested but said nothing. O'Hara continued quietly:

'It's this: you know I thought I spotted you, Gerry, from the path round Grimston Banks? Well, the fellow I saw was Firman. We're pretty certain of that. He was making for a gap in the hills, and he wasn't so very far ahead of me. I ought to have caught him, but I didn't, because of my gammy ankle. After that, I was misdirected by that fellow in the car. Now, if Firman had turned into that house, that would account for my having seen no more of him. It's a long shot, I know, but the house is on the way to that farm, and we've had a hunch, all along, that there's something fishy about Firman.'

'It's odd you should revive that,' said Gascoigne. 'A fellow down here, whose father disappeared and has never been traced, is cousin to Firman. It's a coincidence, certainly, but there it is. I still don't see, though, what the house has to do with it, or quite why Firman should turn in there.'

'It's only this,' said O'Hara. 'If Firman had done what he said he did, and gone to his uncle's, I shouldn't have spotted him at all. You remember we worked that out from the map. Also, if *you* did what you said you did—and I'm absolutely certain you did, allow me to say!—I couldn't have seen you either. Therefore we inferred that it was Firman I saw. Now, Firman has a gammy leg, and I know I had a gammy ankle, but, even so, I ought to have caught him. Instead of that, I never saw him again. Ergo, he went to ground and for that there's still no explanation, nor is there any explanation of why he said he went to his uncle's.'

'Well,' said Gascoigne, looking at Laura. 'We mustn't be hampered. There's a club event billed for Saturday which I had not intended to dignify with my presence, but in a good cause . . . What do you say?'

'We've no guarantee that Firman will turn up for the run,' protested O'Hara.

'He'll turn up all right, if only to disarm suspicion,' said
Gascoigne shrewdly. 'Therefore——'

'In the changing-room when the runners have all set forth,'
said O'Hara, nodding.

'Oh, well, that takes care of that,' said Laura carelessly.
'Now, about this house. When do you think we should go
there? Before or after Saturday?'

'I think to-morrow would be best,' said Gascoigne at once.
'I don't think to-night would be feasible . . . not for a first
visit, anyway. After all, we may be barking up quite the
wrong tree, although . . .' he glanced at his cousin's thin, dark
face, deep eyes and proudly-carried head . . . 'Mike's hunches
are almost monotonously sound.'

Laura looked upon the gifted youth with favour.

'Attaboy!' she observed. But she had sighed with relief when
she heard that the two young men did not intend to visit the
house that night.

Laura was bold as a lion, but was as superstitious as a war-
lock. She was full of dark fancies drowned in primordial deeps.
She also believed, with healthy, female instinct, that dangerous
and delicate missions were less unpleasant in the daylight than
in the dark. With respect to the house itself, she was torn
between a frantic desire to visit it and an equally strong
determination not to go anywhere near its boundaries. She
was, in fact, like a child who both dreads and longs for a
ghost-story just at bedtime. The thrill would be worth it, the
aftermath definitely not. In other words, although Laura was
both practical and hard-headed, and although she was brisk,
jimp and daring in all that she undertook, she was also the prey
of an inherited belief in the legends, spectres and bogies of a
Highland ancestry. It was one of the many reasons for her
adherence to Mrs. Bradley, who was legend, spectre and
bogie all in one, for she felt, without realizing it, that the
greater demon kept lesser demons at bay.

However, before the three parted that night, they were
pledged to visit the house very early on the following morning.

'Well, now,' said Gascoigne, climbing into the car, 'boot, saddle, to horse and away!' The morning was fresh and fine as the car drove off for the house with the four dead trees.

'But I can't see what we're going to do when we get there,' said Laura, when they had left Cuchester and were crawling along a very narrow lane on the east side of the level-crossing. 'It's been keeping me awake all night.'

'We're going to test Mike's password,' said Gascoigne mysteriously.

'Has he got a password? Oh, yes, of course! I think I know it. Mrs. Bradley said something.'

'I bet she did,' said O'Hara. 'It must have stuck out a mile to anyone with any intelligence.'

'Ah, well!' said Gascoigne. As they approached the turning which led to the house, they had to pull over to the right almost into the ditch in order to pass a large lorry loaded with great blocks of ice such as are delivered to fishmongers in the summer. The lorry had broken down, and the two men in charge of it were seated at the roadside smoking cigarettes. The bonnet was raised, and there were tools lying on the edge of the grass verge.

'Lazy devils,' grunted Gascoigne, as the car crawled round the lorry.

'Ice?' remarked O'Hara. 'I wonder where they're going? They're coming away from Cuchester, and there's nowhere much down this way until you get to . . .'

'*Ice!*' exclaimed Laura dramatically. 'I bet I know where it's going and what it's for! Tell you what! When we get to the house we'll hide and watch it go in.'

'But we don't know . . . how do you? . . . oh, I see what you mean!' said Gascoigne. He looked amused. 'I should hardly think so, you know.'

'Well, we could hide the car in that little wood we're coming to, and snake along to the house, and keep watch for a bit. If the ice is delivered there, it might very well mean what I think it means.'

'Tell you what,' said O'Hara, who took Laura's suggestion

more seriously than his cousin appeared to be taking it, 'let's stroll back in a minute, and ask them where they're bound for. That can be done without arousing any suspicion. Anyway, they won't know, ten to one, what the ice is to be used for. That is, of course, supposing it *is* delivered to the house we're thinking of. Though, for my own part . . . Oh, well, it won't hurt to find out.'

'It's a very good idea,' said Laura. 'You two go back and ask, and I'll keep the engine running, ready to make a dash for it if necessary.'

Gascoigne seemed doubtful, but O'Hara's strange experience on the evening of the hare and hounds had predisposed him in favour of wild schemes, for nothing, he felt, could be as wild as his unforeseen adventure.

'Come on,' he said briefly; and the two young men got out of the car and strolled back towards the ice-cart.

They returned in about a quarter of an hour.

'Go on,' said Gascoigne to Laura.

'Well?' she said, after she had let in the clutch.

'The name of the house is Cottam's,' said Gascoigne. 'And these fellows are down on their luck. They've come from Poole Harbour, lost their way after Brandencote, and have been all night on the road. They've just about had enough of it. Ought to have been back by now. Nothing but trouble all the way. Never been to the house before, and will take care they never go again. (I'm glad you weren't there to hear their language!) Anyway, they've given us a reason for calling. The ice is wanted urgently, so I've promised to say they are coming with it and I'm to swear it isn't their fault that they've been so long upon the road.'

'What do they think the ice will be used for?' asked Laura. Gascoigne laughed.

'They didn't say what they thought it would be used for, but they said they could tell the people what to do with it when they got it, which is not, perhaps, quite the same thing. Of course,' he added, 'as we don't know that the house with the four dead trees is now called Cottam's, it's quite possible that our destination is not the same as theirs. It was no good describing the house to them, because they only know it by name.'

'But we *do* know it's called Cottam's! Mrs. Bradley and I know. Are the people called Cottam, or only the house?' said Laura quickly.

'The people are called Gonn-Brown.'

'Gonn-Brown? But that's a film company! I've seen their offices in Wardour Street. Mrs. Bradley vetted the psychiatry in one of their films.'

'Really?' said Gascoigne. 'Remind me of that a bit later. Like the heavenly Yvonne Arnaud,* I've got an idea!'

'Well, here's the house,' said O'Hara. 'Drive past it, Miss Menzies, and we'll park the car where it can't be seen from the windows.'

Laura took the extremely narrow turning very slowly, and the car bumped over a culvert and then over a humped bridge a little farther along.

'About here,' said O'Hara.

Laura pulled up, and the three got out. She locked the car, and then they strolled back along the way by which they had come until they reached the gates. These were propped wide open, and the notice board with its terse instruction to keep out was now covered by a piece of paper affixed to the board by four drawing pins.

The paper read TRADESMEN ONLY.

'This is us,' said Gascoigne. 'Look here, you'd better not come up to the door, Mike, in case you're recognized. And you, Miss Menzies . . .'

'I'm coming,' said Laura flatly. 'A man and a woman are far less remarkable than one or other on their own. Just give the message about the ice-cart, and then we'll see how they react.'

Gascoigne did not argue. They walked up to the ecclesiastical door, and Laura stood looking at it whilst Gascoigne pulled at an ancient bell. They could hear this clanging, and then came the sound of footsteps along a stone-flagged passage. A woman opened the door. She was younger than middle-aged (but not

* In *Tons of Money*.

at all youthful), full-fleshed, handsome and blowsy. Laura, with the swiftness of a panther, slipped to the outside of the porch.

'Good morning,' said Gascoigne to the woman. 'We promised to bring a message. The ice you are expecting is on its way, but the lorry has broken down. They'll be here as soon as they can.'

'The ice?' said the woman. 'I don't know anything about it. I'll enquire.'

She went to the back of the house, leaving the front door open. Gascoigne watched her all the way along the stone-flagged passage until a door closed behind her. Laura made tracks for the gate. The woman returned. She looked Gascoigne over as though she were memorizing his face, and then said:

'Sorry you've had your trouble. No ice expected here.'

'I beg your pardon,' said Gascoigne.

'I'm sorry you've been troubled,' she repeated, and closed the door very gently in his face, giving him, as she did so, a lustful and conciliatory smile. It was evident she had had no eyes for Laura.

'Thank goodness for your comely face,' said the latter, when Gascoigne joined her. 'You could have knocked me endwise! That was the woman from Newcombe Soulbury, that was! Ah, well, let's wait and watch the lorry drive in. There's something delightfully fishy about all this—or don't you think so?'

She walked beside Gascoigne slowly back to the car. O'Hara was not to be seen. They climbed in, and had scarcely done so when a car came from the opposite direction, slowed down, and stopped. A boy got out from beside the driver, and went forward to open the lodge gates.

'Well!' said Laura. 'What do you make of *that*? That's the kid from the hotel! The one who threw rocks at me the other morning!'

The boy pushed the gates back as wide as they would go, and the car drove in past the lodge.

Of O'Hara there was still no sign. Gascoigne lit a cigarette

for Laura and another for himself, and had scarcely put away
his lighter when O'Hara dropped over the high brick wall
which shut the house off from the road, came down in the
ditch, picked himself up and hurried towards the car.

'The boy seems in a hurry!' said Laura, starting the engine
as O'Hara opened the door and scrambled inside.

'That woman you spoke to . . . I was hiding in the bushes . . .
she's the one at the farm . . . the one who told me she was
alone in the house. And those people who drove up just
now . . .'

'Are the man and the boy from our hotel at Slepe Rock.
Yes, we know,' said Laura.

'And there goes the ice-cart,' said Gascoigne, as the lorry
drove in at the gates. 'All liars, aren't they?'

'I don't know about liars, but they may be murderers,' said
O'Hara. 'I heard that man who came with the kid—I heard
him speak. That's the fellow called Con, I'm almost certain.'

Chapter Twelve

★

' "Ha!" thought she as she looked at it through the window.
"Cannot I prevent the sun rising?" '
Ibid. *(The Fisherman and His Wife)*

Now what?' said Laura, full of pleasurable excitement as the car drove on towards the farm. 'What do you think we ought to do?' she added, elucidating this query.

'Return, one of us, and suborn that old' man with the barrow,' said Gascoigne readily. 'We shall find out what he knows of the people from Slepe Rock, and perhaps he can tell us what the ice is to be used for, although I should rather think he can't. Pull up round the next bend, anyway, and I'll go back, and see what I can find out.'

'Both of us will go back,' said O'Hara firmly.

'But you may be recognized, and that would hardly do.'

'It can't be helped. You stay here,' added O'Hara to Laura, 'and be ready to help us make a dash for it if anybody chooses to be annoyed. Good-bye. We will see you later.'

'You'll see me sooner,' retorted Laura. 'What do you think I am? If there's going to be any fun I'm all for being in the thick of it. None of this women and children business with me! I'm a lot older than either of you, and, furthermore, I'm Mrs. Croc's accredited representative. Besides . . .'

'All right, then,' said O'Hara, hastily. 'If you feel like that about it, I think you'd better come. What do you say, Gerry? Shall we take her with us?'

The handsome Gascoigne assumed a reproachful expression, but did not voice his sentiments, and the car was reversed as far as the nearest gate. Here Laura turned it, and the three were soon near the house with the four dead trees.

'This is about as far as we should go, I think, before we get out and walk,' suggested Laura.

'And now,' said Gascoigne, when they were almost opposite the gate, 'you two had better stand by, I think, whilst I contact our aged friend. He won't talk to three of us at once.'

This seemed a reasonable suggestion, and therefore O'Hara and Laura remained under cover of some bushes whilst Gascoigne walked up to the gate. By good luck the aged gardener was not more than ten yards away. He was standing on the brickwork of a tiny culvert which carried the weedy drive across a brook, and was gazing into the water and scratching his mossy-looking thigh.

'That there old water-rat,' he said, without turning his head, 'do be rousing his whiskers at all of us. Catch a holt of him I don't somehow seem to, seemingly.'

'Tough luck,' said Gascoigne, joining the ancient man, putting his hands in his trouser pockets and peering sympathetically into the ditch.

'Live under that arch, he do, and laugh his way through against all of us,' the old man continued. 'And my fowls fattening, and him with his eye on 'em like he had on the chicks last August twelvemonth, was a Sunday night, as I remember.'

'I suppose that was before the new owners took over?' said Gascoigne. 'I mean, they haven't always been here, have they?'

'New owners?' The old man spat. 'Tenants, um be, not owners. Film people. Money and no sense. Ice by the cartload for their drinks. If beer wants ice, must be funny beer, says I. And if sperrits wants ice, give me water. Neither Englishmen nor Yankees, them don't be.' Upon saying this, he turned his head and gave Gascoigne a long look.

'I suppose they have lots of visitors,' remarked the young man, kicking a stone from the culvert into the ditch.

'Not so many. Secret proceshesses, they says. Trade rivals, they says. Keep out, they says. Well, there y'are. Mr. Concaverty, round at the lodge, he has his orders, and, being in their service already, before they comes here, no doubt he carries 'em out. But this old water-rat, drat him, ain't nobody's business but mine. Mr. Concaverty, he don't keep fowls. He don't know this old water-rat like I do.'

He picked up a bit of stick, and, stepping from the culvert
on to the bank of the ditch, poked industriously and with
considerable vigour underneath the arch. Gascoigne waited a
moment or two. Then he said gently, but with a persistence
which Laura would have approved:

'What about some beer that's *not* iced?'

By way of answer, the old man took off his cap and held it
up. Gascoigne dropped half a crown into it. The old man
scooped up the coin, bit it, nodded indulgently, said that that
was a bit of all right, and ambled off.

'Concaverty!' said Laura, as soon as Gascoigne had told the
others the gist of the conversation. 'We must get to him before
the old man gets round there. And, this time, it had better be
me! We don't want them comparing notes, and thinking
you've been snooping, although, of course, you have.'

'Do you think . . .?' began O'Hara. But Laura insisted that
her idea was the right one, and Gascoigne was inclined to
agree.

'We must get what we can,' he said gloomily.

All three young people were conscious of a feeling of slight
flatness. If the inmates of the house with the four dead trees
were film people, all idiosyncrasies on their part immediately
lost any tendency to seem dramatic, improbable, lethal or, in
fact, at all exciting, and it was a deflated although outwardly
debonair Laura who marched up to the lodge and enquired
for Mr. Concaverty.

An older woman opened the door, and one whom Laura
again did not fail to recognize. It was the caretaker from
O'Hara's mysterious farm. Laura, who was not altogether
unprepared for this, since some connection between that farm
and the house with the four dead trees by this time could be
taken for granted, smiled naturally and asked for a bucket of
water. She needed it, she said, for the car.

The woman supplied it without a word. Laura thanked her,
took the bucket of water to where she had left her friends, set
it down and told them the news.

'I don't see how to ask again for Concaverty,' she added. It
proved unnecessary to do so, however, for, when she returned

the empty pail and made a remark upon the weather, the woman asked curiously:

'What did you want with Mr. Concaverty?'

'Actually, to know whether my friends—a man and his son—a boy of about sixteen—have left the house yet. We know they came, but don't know how long they intended to stay.'

'Oh, *them!*' said the woman. She looked at Laura curiously. 'Ain't you the young lady I put on the way to Little Dorsett? Would these here be *friends* of yours, then?'

'Well, we are staying at the same hotel in Slepe, and hoped to meet them for tea,' explained Laura, seizing upon the first excuse that came into her head.

'You'll not see them at tea to-day," said the woman decidedly. 'They're to stay a night or two to see the Druids dance. It's the great night around these parts, and, films or no films, everybody, so they tells me, goes up at midnight to see it.'

'The Druids? How queer,' said Laura, racking her brain for some means of prolonging the conversation, but finding none that she thought it would be wise to employ.

'Oh, there's things queerer than that,' said the woman, 'and I would advise you to keep clear of them.' She lowered her voice to a confidential huskiness, and added, 'And this Mr. Concaverty, too. You're a real young lady, you are, and not for the likes of him, though he pays my wages.'

She shut the door on these words, and Laura walked back to the others.

'I've put my foot in it,' she said gloomily. 'I've made her suspicious, I think.' She recounted the conversation. O'Hara whistled. Gascoigne said:

'We'll see the Druids dance, too. That must be on the ninth of September. But, I think, not you, Laura dear. This sounds to me like men's work.'

'Sez you!' retorted Laura with her usual force and inelegance. 'And let's drive on. I want to think, and I think better in a vehicle that's moving.'

The first result of her thinking was a letter to Mrs. Bradley which she sent to the house in Kensington, knowing that it would be forwarded at once if Mrs. Bradley were not at home.

'Essential to see Druids dance,' wrote Laura with telegraphic brevity. 'Don't write back to say not. Mind made up. Should appreciate blessing on enterprise, and will promise to duck if guns brought into play. Hope you are well. Come back soon. Deep doings at Slepe Rock re.man and stone-slinging kid. Regards. Laura.'

Mrs. Bradley received this missive whilst she was at breakfast on the following morning.

'Dear, dear!' she observed to her maid Célestine who was removing the plate which had held Mrs. Bradley's egg on toast. 'What do you think Miss Menzies is up to now?'

'That passes comprehension,' said Célestine, whose attitude to Laura was one of the amused admiration of a human being for a young and lively elephant. 'That one, she has of the most surprising stomach.'

'And we, as we get older, have no stomach at all, surprising or otherwise,' said Mrs. Bradley. 'Ah, well! Tell Henri I shall be in to lunch and that there will be two gentlemen as well . . . my son Ferdinand, in fact, and the Assistant Commissioner of police. Will the butcher have offal, do you think?'

'It will be surprising if not,' replied Célestine with vigour. 'Again, Henri has a chicken. It is from America, that land of the loan. It is frozen, like all the assets. I speak of the chicken, you understand.'

Mrs. Bradley cackled. Lunch consisted of very good giblet soup, some poached turbot, chicken *en casserole* and devilled pigs' liver on toast.

'It is for the gentlemen, this lunch,' said Célestine, sniffing slightly. 'Ladies are less appetizing.'

Mrs. Bradley cordially agreed. She herself looked very far from appetizing in a sage-green costume and a bright red blouse, an heirloom brooch of vast proportions whose only virtue was that it did at least conceal some of the blouse, stout shoes with crêpe rubber soles, knitted stockings and a rakish diamond clip on the side of her shining black hair.

'What devilment now, Beatrice?' enquired the Assistant Commissioner, finishing off Mrs. Bradley's satisfying lunch with a glass of her equally satisfying brandy. 'And where did you get this?' He held up his glass. 'Not bad!'

'Imported under licence from the government,' Mrs. Bradley replied with a smirk.

'Oh, rot! Where did you get it?'

'Henri has friends.'

'I bet he has! Yes, I'll have one more. And some more coffee? Thank you very much. Now, then, what's all this about a cat with nine lives in Dorset?'

Mrs. Bradley told him at some length, whilst her saturnine son Ferdinand listened without offering a word.

'But you can't prove anything?' the Assistant Commissioner suggested.

'Not at present. But the chief point is that I don't want this young O'Hara murdered.'

Ferdinand grunted (a sound which his mother correctly interpreted), and the Assistant Commissioner added:

'All right. We'll keep an eye on him for you. Don't let your Miss Menzies get into trouble. Lots of peculiar happenings since the war.'

'This may well have begun before the war,' Mrs. Bradley pointed out.

'Interesting,' said the Assistant Commissioner, stealing Jove's thunder without a second thought. 'Ah, well! More brandy? Thank you, I think perhaps I will. Ferdinand owes us something over this last case of his, so I'll take it out on you. The woman always pays. How true that is!'

'Well, I suppose I had better go back,' said Mrs. Bradley. 'I don't know what mischief Laura will get into if I am not there to prevent her.'

'The thing is,' said Laura earnestly to her escort, 'that we have to take up our positions early enough. It's no good to get there after *they* do. The thing is, how are we to dodge this Con person at the hotel?'

'The best plan by far,' said O'Hara, 'is to lay him out before we start. I will undertake to do that.'

Laura and his cousin Gascoigne gazed at him in surprised admiration. He continued, calmly:

'It should be easy enough. A sock full of sand, which sand I can collect from the beach, a strategic point, a minute of co-operation from you, Gerry, to help move him into an inconspicuous position, and from you, Miss Laura, to divert the attention of that unprepossessing infant . . .'

'Sisyphus?' said Laura, who had contrived to learn that this was the boy's second name, and who was fascinated by this baptismal error.

'Right. Let us work out the details. I think perhaps that passage which leads to the lounge. Then we could plant him outside those French doors at the side . . .'

'Good idea!' said Laura, always the apostle of violence.

The business in hand having been despatched successfully and the victim having been put out to grass by Gascoigne and O'Hara, the three uninvited witnesses set out by car for the circle of standing stones.

'How did you manage the kid?' asked Gascoigne; for to Laura had been delegated this share in the responsibility of the attack.

'I didn't. He's been sick all the evening.'

'How come?'

'I don't know, but it's genuine all right. The head waiter told me. They had to have the doctor. A bit of luck for us, but tough on the poor little thug.'

'Yes, quite. Not that I love the little beast. I expect he's got food poisoning. I thought myself that the rabbit stew at lunch was just a bit off, didn't you?'

'I didn't have it,' said Laura. 'I had cold.'

'Wise woman. However, two double whiskies kept the bunny in place so far as I was concerned. Kids are less fortunate in their access to these obvious remedies.'

'He's not such a bad kid,' said Laura, with female untruthfulness.

The car held the main road for about seven miles and then swung left and south again across the open country. The hills began to gather in, and the gloom deepened. It was nine by Laura's wristwatch as they by-passed Cuchester, and nearly half-past by the time they approached, up the straight and sand-surfaced avenue, the house with the four dead trees.

Over the little bridge and past the lodge went the car, and then the narrow road dropped downwards past the golf-course until it took the lane to the farm.

'Where do we park?' enquired Laura, slowing as they reached the little wood.

'Among the trees. Can't very well drive into the farmyard,' O'Hara responded. 'Edge gradually over to your right. Your headlights will show you the opening.'

Doubtfully Laura obeyed, fearful of crashing into tree-trunks, but O'Hara's topographical sense proved to be flawless, for a kind of mossy passage opened among the trees and she was able to take the car bumpily but with safety off the road.

She put off all the lights except the rear light, felt in the pocket of her tweed coat to make certain that she had her torch, and the three walked out of the wood. Laura, with a curious but half-scared glance towards the dark mass of the farmhouse, followed the others up the muddy, cobbled road which ran through the cartshed, and all three were soon on the miry ascent which led towards the circle of standing stones.

'Now for it,' muttered Laura, wondering what her much-admired *döppelganger* Jo March would have made of the situation. 'Wonder whether the Druids really dance?'

'You can be sure they dance,' said Gascoigne.

The going was heavy with mud, and treacherous with large, uneven stones. Twice Laura slipped and three times she tripped up, but each time her escort, closing in on either side, saved her and kept her on her feet. Considering that Laura was both tall and well-made and weighed more than eleven stone, their sense of chivalry, she felt, was over-developed.

'Don't bother, really,' she said, as they saved her for the fifth time from measuring her length on the muddy field they were mounting.

'No, don't,' advised a singularly rich voice from a bush on the left of the speaker.

'Good Lord!' esclaimed Laura. 'Ghost of Mrs. Croc!'

'Not yet,' said the reptilian, joining them like the shadow of Lady into Fox. 'And I wouldn't make so much noise if I were you. The vultures are gathering above on the top of the rise. I've just been up there to see.'

'The Druids?' muttered Laura. 'Sakes alive!'

'Their congregation, maybe, child. Now, watch, but do not make your presence known. We are in sight of mysteries, and our appearance may not be welcomed.'

'But suppose they offer a human sacrifice or something?' demanded Laura. 'Or suppose one of the corpses is on view? Don't we do anything then?'

'My advice . . . indeed, my urgent request . . . is that you take no part in the proceedings whatsoever. We are uninvited guests, remember.'

'Oh, all right, if you say so.'

'I do say so. And now I am going to leave you for a while. I shall look forward to your report later,' said Mrs. Bradley, living up to her reptilian appearance by sliding rapidly away among the bushes.

'Well, I'm dashed!' said Laura, with the frank surprise which her employer's doings had still the power to arouse in her. 'What's the old crocodile up to now, do you suppose?'

'We mustn't queer her pitch, anyway,' said O'Hara, who had conceived a warm admiration for the elderly lady. 'So no squeals, my dear Laura, when the sacrificial knife descends!'

'Ass!' said Laura amiably. 'Dry up, now, and let's get along.' She looked at the luminous hands .of her watch. 'Although I don't suppose,' she added in parenthesis, 'that they'll start before midnight, and it's only a quarter past ten.

How much further, do you think, to the Stones? I'm no judge of distance in the dark.'

'Half an hour, just about, at the rate we shall go,' said Gascoigne. 'Look out! I hear somebody coming!'

The three crawled into the hedge, and a man on horseback, with two others holding on to his stirrups, went slowly but noisily past them. Laura screwed up her eyes, but there was not the remotest chance of recognizing any passers-by, for, in spite of a clear sky, the night was dark, and dawn some hours away.

'Come on!' said Laura when the horseman was a blur against the top of the hill. Her cavaliers, nothing loth, went forward with her, and, gaining the summit, all crouched beside the broad posts of a farm gate and saw, ahead of them, a deep gold glow in the sky.

'Not exactly carrying on their doings in secret,' muttered Gascoigne, bearing sideways away from the dimmed head-lights of a car which was grinding its way on its lowest gear from the farmyard and up the airy road.

It passed between the gateposts beside which the watchers lay crouched, and swayed unevenly southwards across the grass. The three uninvited guests, now keeping close beside a tall, sparse hawthorn hedge, and one of them, at least, thinking uneasily of cow-pats, followed in the wake of the car, and were rewarded at last by the sight of a ring of figures bearing golden torches from which occasional showers of sparks descended and splashed like rain. These torches lighted the ring of standing stones, for a neophyte bearing a torch stood beside each of the nine monoliths. A dark and considerable concourse of people formed a thick belt of darkness outside the circle of the Druids, and a murmur, rising and falling, of polite conversation could be heard.

'Good Lord! It's a set of mummers, or folk-lore what-nots, or something!' said Laura in deep disgust. 'There's nothing here for us, and nothing to keep quiet about, either. Oh, well, let's join the throng!'

'Not so fast,' said Gascoigne. 'Keep out of it as long as we can. This is a wheel, by its shape and semblance. Look at those people going forward to form the spokes! There are sometimes wheels within wheels, and we'd better, perhaps, not forget it!'

So the three went to ground and then gradually crept nearer to the Druids. The ceremony proper, they gathered, had not begun, for a man beside the tallest of the stones was in earnest consultation with three others, and there was still a murmur of conversation among the crowd, although the ranks of those forming the spokes (or, as Laura thought, the rays of the sun), were now completed and still.

'I should think they'd begin community singing soon,' muttered O'Hara into Laura's left ear. She hushed him. They were all three lying now in the shallow ditch which bordered the stone circle, and, as the crowd was thin on this side, they were able to see what went on, although their view was impeded comparatively often by the movements of the (presumably) invited guests nearer the stones.

Suddenly there sounded the blast of a horn. It came from far away, in the direction of the round barrows which O'Hara and Gascoigne had noticed on their first visit to the neighbourhood by daylight.

'The horns of Elfland,' said Laura, slightly rearing herself. With a brotherly pressure on her skull, Gascoigne forced her head down again. The note of the horn was repeated from the opposite side of the hill. There was silence from the crowd. The torches burnt smokily, and shrouded some of their holders from view. The air became acrid, and the silence of the onlookers was broken by spasmodic coughing. The horns called and answered again, and then, from various points on the hillside, coloured bands of light began to play across the circle of the stones. The coloured bands wavered and shifted at first, then they were laid upon the ground to form segments of a circle. A horrible greyish colour lay to the west, and to the south-south-west a brilliant green changed to blue-green, and met a deadly white light at full south. To the east the ground was purple, and from north-east towards north-north-east it shifted in bands of light with an effect of dark blots on a white ground very dazzling to the eyes of the watchers. To the extreme north, and round to the north-west, there was a deep and awe-inspiring darkness made intense by the brightness of the lights. The effect was crude but somewhat frightening. The faces of the people looked ghastly.

'Talk of a Witches' Sabbath!' muttered Laura.

'I wouldn't be surprised,' said O'Hara suddenly, 'if they're trying to raise the devil! I have read of these colours in that orientation before. It is the Celtic circle of good and bad luck they have there. I wonder, now, what they are after?'

'Do you think they'll go on all night?' demanded Laura, aware that she was excited, and therefore trying to give her voice flatness and a casual tone. 'If so, I don't see much sense in staying. Nothing much will happen in front of all these people. We're wasting time! It's like the Helston Flurry on a Bank Holiday!'

As she said this, the lights went out, and a man holding a torch stepped into the centre of the circle of standing stones whilst the people forming the spokes or rays submerged themselves in the crowd. Another man joined the first. They held their torches high, and a third man stood between them with a sheet of paper in his hand from which he commenced to read.

Laura and the two young men crept closer. Nobody seemed to notice them. The reader coughed once or twice when the reek of the torches caught his throat, but he went on gallantly with the peroration, which sounded remarkably like one of the Hebrew biblical genealogies.

When he had done, the two torch-bearers flung their torches on the ground. All the other torchbearers followed suit, and then they and the spectators joined in the task of stamping them out with their feet.

Laura and her escort withdrew, for fear of being trampled on, and watched from a respectful distance but without enthusiasm.

'I suppose that's the dance?' said Laura. 'If so, I don't call it particularly impressive, do you?'

'It's some crack-brained society carrying out what they imagine to have been an ancient rite,' said Gascoigne. 'Blessing the crops, or something, I suppose. At any rate, it's very nearly over.'

He was right. Already many of the onlookers had ceased their leaping and stamping, and were walking in quiet groups away from the stones. The three young people remained in hiding until all the people had gone. They noticed that none of them returned by the track which led down to the farm, but they could see the tail-lights of several cars on the way which led towards the main road. The farm gates, they imagined, had all been removed for the occasion, and would be put back in the early morning.

'Well, that seems to be that,' said Laura, standing up and brushing vegetation from her skirt and stockings. 'What it was all about I don't seem to know or care. I wonder what the film people made of it? Should you think there was much to film in that? Oh, well, let's beat it, shall we? I could do with a spot of sleep.'

But O'Hara put a hand on her elbow.

'Never mind about sleep,' he said quietly. 'Listen, will you? Can you hear anything, or is it my imagination? No; I'm sure it isn't! Let's get into the hedge! I rather fancy that this is where the fun begins! Keep close!'

Chapter Thirteen

★

'... but the moon was cold and chilly, and said, "I smell flesh and blood this way!"'

Ibid. (*The Seven Ravens*)

LAURA listened intently, but the sound was not repeated. The three lay crouched where they were for perhaps a quarter of an hour, but nothing stirred. Laura murmured, 'I know now.'

'Know what?' asked O'Hara, his long body sprawled beside her on the turf.

'Those lights and colours. Don't you remember the Ferguson one-act play, *Campbell of Kilmhor?* It comes: *The blue and the green and the grey fires* . . . That's what they were making. I wonder why?'

'*For the destruction of your soul,*' said O'Hara softly. 'I *said* they were trying to raise the devil. Will you be quiet now! I think I hear them coming.'

'This is it!' muttered Laura, feeling, she confessed to Mrs. Bradley later, a chilly sensation down her spine. 'Who comes, though?—and why?'

'Lie close,' murmured Gascoigne. 'They're coming this way, I think. I only hope they haven't been tipped off that there are strangers in the House!'

Laura listened. Very soon, through the thick darkness, could be heard the approach of several persons, one of whom almost immediately revealed, by the light of a lantern from which he had slipped the cover, that he was wearing riding breeches and boots, and was, in all probability, therefore, the horseman whom the three had seen go past when they were on their way to the circle of standing stones.

When this man had reached the middle of the stone circle he set down his lantern upon the ground and thus provided

enough light for Laura and her companions to see the number
of persons who were with him. There were eight of them, the
man himself making nine, and Laura, tapping heavily with
her forefinger upon Gascoigne's shoulder, indicated that this
magic number was again of some importance and interest.
Just as she had concluded this unnecessary observation, the
party she was watching began slowly to disperse until one of
the standing stones hid each man and the lantern alone could
be seen, glowing bright as a topaz in the middle of the ring of
stones.

Led by Gascoigne, the watchers began to crawl towards the
stones. Minutes passed. There was the silence of death. Then
began a slight sound too loud to be called breathing, too quiet
to be called grunting. Laura heard it first, and, for a reason she
could not afterwards explain, but which was due to some
instinct acquired by females as opposed (in all senses) to males,
she leapt up, shouting, 'They're on us! We should have kept
to the hedge!'

It was true. There ensued a curse and a shout, followed by a
tense moment of dramatic fervour as her cavaliers went into
battle. Laura, prompt always for action, went bounding to
help them, and then heard two shots as she wound her long,
strong arms about a stranger who loomed up in the light of
the lantern. Then came a cry from her left in a voice she did not
know; that, apparently, of one of the postulants of the Druids.

'Look out! Someone else! Look out, boys!' Her opponent
wrenched himself free, but Laura had a coat button and a lock
of his hair. Gascoigne grounded his man and fell on him, and
muffled cries could be heard as he bumped the man's head on
the turf. The man, however, showed sudden agility. He rolled
over, kicked backwards at Gascoigne's face, leapt up and raced
off. Gascoigne, pursuing him, ran into a bush he had not seen
in the dark, and tripped and fell.

There was the sound of a rich cackle. A formidable beam of
light was switched on. Mrs. Bradley, her revolver still in her
hand, swept her torch across the ground in widening arcs. By
this means O'Hara was discovered sitting masterfully on one
of the foemen.

'I think he's dead,' he said. 'I tackled him low, and I think he hit his head.'

Mrs. Bradley knelt down and examined the fallen man. She gave Laura the gun to hold. The man opened his eyes.

'Well, well!' said Mrs. Bradley, as he sat up and felt the back of his head, and winced. 'And what game is this that has to be played by midnight among the relics of pre-history?'

The man, who was young and badly needed a shave, looked sheepish and scrambled to his feet.

'It's just a ceremony,' he said. 'I'm afraid it's ruined for this year. Was it you that fired the gun?'

'It was,' replied Mrs. Bradley. 'Pick up your lantern and go home. And don't drink spirits until a doctor has examined your head. You might regret it. But, first, who are you?'

'I'm with the film people,' he responded sullenly. 'We weren't doing any harm. You'd no right to attack us like that. We only came up for a lark because . . . because . . .'

'Because the Druids might dance? Don't lie,' said Mrs. Bradley peremptorily. 'Be off with you. And you children, too,' she added. 'Every one of you ought to be in bed! This is all very foolish and frightening. Which is your way, young man?'

'Oh, the village,' said the young man crossly. 'I'm in lodgings there.' He limped away from them. Mrs. Bradley kept her torch trained on him. He picked up the lantern and, using it to light him on his way, went slowly, half-dragging one leg, in the direction of the path which eventually gave access to the main road near the village of Upper Deepening.

'And now,' said Mrs. Bradley, as the wavering lantern disappeared from view, 'to your car as quickly as you can.'

Guided by her torch (Laura still holding the revolver), they returned to the wood in which they had left the car. They could see its rear light among the trees, so they made their way to it, climbed in, and made room for Mrs. Bradley.

'No, no,' she said. 'I have George to drive me back. Laura, I suggest that you come with me, too, then these young men can sleep in their car. I also suggest that neither of you two returns to Slepe Rock until the morning,' she added, addressing Gascoigne and O'Hara. 'There have been strange happen-

ings to-night, from what I hear at the hotel! Sandbags, indeed!
Drive back towards the outskirts of Cuchester, and park the
car in the lane that leads to the ancient fort. You, Mr. O'Hara,
will know the lane I mean.'

'Yes, ma'am,' said O'Hara, in a gravely obedient tone. 'And
you'll pick us up there in the morning?'

'At ten o'clock,' said Mrs. Bradley briskly. 'Now good night,
heaven preserve you, and don't run into any more mischief.'
She stood away whilst Gascoigne, who was driving, backed the
car on to the road, but as soon as its tail-light had topped the
rise, she seized Laura's sleeve and said urgently, 'And, now,
child, back to the stone circle, for we cannot remain in this
unenviable condition of doubt.'

To Laura's astonishment, excitement and secret, slight
dismay, they were soon dodging under the cartshed. Then
they set their faces towards the north-east and approached
what Laura, with some lack of originality but with a nice sense
of what it would feel like to be permanently agoraphobic, had
begun to think of as the, wide open spaces beyond the farm
and on top of the hill.

'Don't speak, if you can help it,' said Mrs. Bradley, suddenly, 'after we pass the next gate.'

'I was wondering what had happened to the horse,' said
Laura mildly, taking advantage of the permission implicit in
her instructions to speak at least once before they reached the
gate. 'One of those men was on horseback.'

'The horse? Oh, I led it away. It is in one of the stables at
this farm,' said Mrs. Bradley carelessly. 'It came from here, I
expect.'

'What do you think the men with the lantern were up to?'
Laura then asked.

'Oh, an interment—or a disinterment,' Mrs. Bradley
replied. 'I thought it would be a very good idea to find out
which. The Chief Constable and his men should be in position
by now. I only hope they haven't frightened our birds away.'

The cheering news that the police had been brought into
the adventure reassured Laura. To Mrs. Bradley's amusement,
she stepped out briskly.

They passed the gate which Mrs. Bradley had mentioned, and were soon walking upon turf, for Mrs. Bradley had left the track, and was bearing over to the west towards the barrows.

As they approached the circle of standing stones, Laura gasped, for in the middle of the circle stood another group of figures, one of whom was holding a lantern.

'Keep close to the hedge,' murmured Mrs. Bradley, in her ear, 'but don't fall over the Chief Constable, who should be in hiding near here.'

But it seemed that the drama of the earlier part of the night had expended itself, for when at last a sharp sound like a sibilant hiss informed them of the presence of the police, Mrs. Bradley and Laura lay under the hedge and grew gradually cold and stiff whilst the party whom they could still see on the higher ground did nothing more subversive than to produce more lanterns and light them and then hold a midnight picnic. The popping of corks, the sound of women's voices, some laughter and conversation could be heard, and, after about an hour, the Chief Constable muttered into Mrs. Bradley's ear that he was damned cold, felt a damned fool, and was damned well going home.

'Those film people, that's all that is!' he said in a blasphemous mutter.

'Well, at least go up and have a look at them,' said Mrs. Bradley, at this. 'You'll be sorry, later on, perhaps, if you don't.'

'I've no earthly right to go and look at them!' he retorted, this time in his ordinary voice, for conversation among the picnickers was so general and so noisy that no other voice was likely to be heard. 'Come on, Inspector. Bring your people. Do you recognize any of those voices?'

'Ah, I do, sir,' the Inspector replied. 'One of them's Mr. Battle, the artist, I reckon, him that lost his father in the circumstances you asked us to look into. We questioned him last Monday, and I know the voice. At least, I reckon I do.'

'Good for you, Inspector,' said Mrs. Bradley. 'But the tones seemed to me deeper than those of Mr. Battle.'

'I say,' said Laura suddenly. 'I thought I recognized another of those voices.'

'Yes, so did I,' Mrs. Bradley agreed. 'In fact, there was no thought about it, child. It was the voice of our acquaintance from Slepe Rock, the aptly-named Mr. Cassius.'

'Funny, if it was,' said Laura, 'because Gerry and Mike laid him out with a sandbag before we left there this evening. I suppose they didn't like to hit him hard. His real name's Concaverty and he owns the house with the four dead trees. We found all that out since you went to London. Not bad for amateurs, eh?'

The police, moving with Boy Scout swiftness and silence along by the hedge, soon led the party to the gate. The last Laura saw of the picnickers was an unnaturally tall figure darting from side to side of the stone circle like a witch-doctor smelling out the damned. She watched for a moment, but decided that he was probably only handing round food.

'Oh, well, that's that,' she said, unable to keep from her voice the note of anti-climax as she joined the others.

'Oh, no, it isn't! Not by a very long way,' said Mrs. Bradley. 'For one thing, there is some indication that David Battle is in league with the film people who've rented the house, and that might mean the turn of his fortunes! Who knows? He says he is poor. Perhaps he has been engaged as a designer.'

Laura received this suggestion in silence. They reached the farm and found the police cars parked beneath the cartshed.

'Ah!' said Mrs. Bradley benevolently. 'So the curfew could scarcely be expected to ring to-night!'

'Oh, that farmhouse is empty,' said the Chief Constable. 'Can we give you a lift?'

'No, I have George,' she replied. 'He awaits us this side of the golf links.' She walked off into the night, taking Laura with her. It seemed a long way to the golf links. George lifted his head from the wheel, upon which he had been dozing, and, without instructions, drove into Welsea Beaches just as the dawn appeared.

'Do you really think that first lot meant to bury something?' Laura enquired.

'Frankly, no, child, but the Druids might dance on more than one night in September.'

Chapter Fourteen

★

'. . . and how the devil sat upon the top of the house and cried out, "Throw the villain up here!"'
                    Ibid. (*The Travelling Musicians*)

'AND now,' said Mrs. Bradley, when her henchmen had slept and breakfasted, 'I am going to the nine standing stones with a party of archæologists. Do you know anything of archæology?' she added, turning towards the young men.

'Well, I did some digging once,' observed O'Hara, 'when I was a kid of twelve. That was with my uncle and some friends in the south of France.'

'Splendid. You shall certainly come and help. We shall be filmed at the same time. It will be most interesting.'

'Filmed?'

'Yes, child. All our party, with the exception of ourselves, my nephew and a friend of mine, an expert upon the Early Bronze Age, will be film extras hired for the occasion at union rates plus their tea. At least, I hope so!'

She gave such a horrible leer that the two young men did not know whether her remarks were to be taken seriously or not. Then she added:

'To-morrow, then, we meet at the circle of standing stones. If you could bring a spade or two, and perhaps a pickaxe, a measuring-tape, a theodolite and a packet of sandwiches it would be as well, but no matter if you cannot get them.'

'Have you hired the film extras?' asked Laura.

'Not yet. It will be a very good excuse, however, for calling at the house of the four dead trees, will it not?'

'You know we've already been there?' said Laura, a trifle

uneasily. 'That's how we knew about Concaverty. Oh, and about that woman you called Mrs. Battle. I didn't tell you about that.'

Mrs. Bradley heard the news with great interest and much satisfaction, and, to Laura's relief, passed no judgment upon her secretary's activities.

'I'll go and hire the film extras, if you like,' Laura added. 'That is, if you think I can.'

'I have implicit faith in your abilities,' said Mrs. Bradley solemnly. 'When would you like to go? This afternoon? By the way, I wonder whether our Mr. Concaverty-Cassius is still at the Slepe Rock Hotel?'

The afternoon was cloudy and dull, and promised rain, and, although the rain held off, the atmosphere was depressing, and the blue-grey hills looked very far away. The sky remained threatening.

Laura set out from the hotel at Welsea at half-past two, with George to drive the car, and approached the house with trepidation. She was not at all sure what effect the previous visits had had, and she was uncertain, too, whether the woman whom Mrs. Bradley called Mrs. Battle had seen her with Gascoigne and O'Hara. If so, her present mission might be dangerous.

She went boldly up to the door, however, and rang the bell. It was answered by a scowling man whom she affected to take for Concaverty. She even addressed him by this name, and received, in response, no denial of the patronymic but merely a growling enquiry as to her business.

'I want to hire some film extras,' she replied. 'I thought you might be able to tell me where to find some.'

'You talk as though they were primroses or birds' nests,' he responded, giving her a bleak smile which had the effect of making his face look like a piece of carved wood.

'I know,' Laura meekly agreed. 'But I've been told to get hold of a dozen or two for some *March of Time* sort of stuff by a distinguished amateur, and some people at the hotel told me they thought you had an outfit here that you might be willing to hire out.'

This clumsy expression of her requirements drew, rather to her surprise and trepidation, a morose invitation to go in, and Laura, a feeble and most unwilling Daniel, entered the lions' den in the wake of the wooden-faced unknown. She was glad to see that he left the door wide open.

The interior of the house was not alarming. It was furnished modestly and in good taste, so far as Laura could see, but she saw little, for she was conducted to a small room containing a large desk and a picture by A. J. Munnings and there was invited to sit down. She was left alone for ten minutes, and then a young man in horn-rimmed spectacles came in, seated himself at the desk and unscrewed a short, thick fountain pen.

'Name?' he asked, with no preliminaries.

'Menzies,' Laura responded.

'Business?'

'To hire about a dozen or two dozen film extras for private and non-commercial work.'

'Destination?'

'Oh, I should want to film them here and there about this county, you know.'

'That is location, not destination.'

'Oh? Well, in that case, they wouldn't have destination, but only location.'

'I see. Well, I am not at all sure that we could do that, Miss Menzies. The usual rates, of course, if it turns out that we can spare our extras? I mean, there's a Union to consider. And then, of course, when would you require them?'

'I don't know exactly. By the end of the week, I should think.'

The young man rang the bell and the man whom Laura had addressed as Concaverty answered it.

'Show Miss Menzies out, Sorensen,' said the young man briefly. To show that the interview was definitely at an end, he picked up a pen and began to write.

Laura left the house forthwith. She felt more than bewildered. Not thus, she thought, was crime conducted, unless the young man had been instructed to get rid of her with all speed. She wondered what they all knew about her and what the terrifying Sorensen suspected.

'You ought to have those four trees cut down,' she said, when they reached the front door.

'What four trees, madam?' the man enquired, giving her again his teakwood smile. 'Oh, you mean the *dead* trees!'

'That's what I said,' said Laura.

'Yes, madam, but, you see, we *need* them at the moment. There may be shooting to-morrow or the next day.'

'Shooting? Oh, you mean shooting the film!'

'What other kind of shooting could I mean, madam?'

Laura did not answer this question. She walked towards the gate feeling like a person caught in a dream which he knows is a dream and from which he cannot awake.

'Crazy,' she muttered to herself, as she came to the little culvert over the ditch.

'I don't think I've done the slightest good,' she confided to Mrs. Bradley when she returned, 'but I have been inside that house, and it doesn't seem particularly sinister.'

'You have done bravely, child,' her employer cordially responded. 'You have established, I think, that Mr. Concaverty, under his pseudonym of Cassius, is still at the hotel at Slepe Rock, and that is exactly what we wanted to know. Did they promise you any helpers?'

'I don't really know,' said Laura, looking and feeling perplexed. 'Do you think they'll send us an answer?'

'I expect so, if you left an address.'

'I didn't! And they didn't ask for one.'

'Excellent, child. And now for your smugglers' cave. We hired a sea-going cruiser from Welsea Beaches, and from there we shall go to the cave and explore its interior. I have very great hopes of that cave.'

'I *say!*' said Laura, enthralled. 'You didn't tell me! How decent! It'll clear our cobwebs away! Who's going to handle the navigation, I wonder? I can't, because I don't know the coast.'

'We are taking a boatman from Welsea.'

'Won't he wonder what on earth we're up to exploring a cave? I mean, it's kids' stuff, really, and if he sees *you* . . .!'

'Geology knows no law,' said Mrs. Bradley complacently.

'We shall take our little hammers and a specimen or two, and then we shall chip rocks and collect bits and pieces, and place them with tender discernment in little bags discreetly but obviously labelled. It won't be scientific, but it will pass. At least, I hope so.' She cackled with great enjoyment.

Laura giggled. She spent the evening helping to prepare for the 'great camouflage' as she herself termed it, and early on the following morning, she, Gascoigne, O'Hara and Mrs. Bradley set forth in a motor cruiser, a chunky, sturdy, sea-worthy affair in charge of an old man and a boy of fifteen, with the geological apparatus well displayed.

They stood out to sea to avoid the shore-setting currents around the headlands, and arrived off Slepe Rock at lunch-time. They had lunch on board, and then the motor-cruiser ran in, slacked off when it came almost opposite the cave, and took advantage of the tide to back cautiously under the cliffs.

The dinghy was soon lowered from the cabin top where it had been slung, and its little outboard motor, with full pivot reverse for driving sideways or astern (a very necessary feature for the kind of work which the dinghy might need to perform in the cave) having been started up, away went Mrs. Bradley, Laura and O'Hara, whilst Gascoigne remained on board with the man and boy.

Laura, who was skilled in such matters, edged the dinghy into the cave, keeping just enough way on her to avoid her stern being swept round on to the rocks.

The cave was dark and cool, and smelt of seaweed. The water into which they nosed with such circumspection and finesse ran deep, as might have been expected, and was wonderfully smooth once the yard or two of surf at the mouth of the opening had been crossed, but it had been a tricky little passage, on the whole, and Laura felt that she merited the congratulations offered by her crew and passenger.

'Well, anyway, we're in,' she said modestly. 'I should think we'd better have lights.'

Mrs. Bradley and O'Hara, who were already well forward, switched on powerful electric torches which lit up the glisten-ing walls and indicated the dark distances of the cave. Laura cautiously started the engine again, for the cave was too narrow for oars.

'Good heavens! This cave must run inland for several hundred yards!' exclaimed O'Hara. This estimate proved to be an exaggeration, but the tunnel was fully one hundred and fifty yards long, and in a few minutes the young man, who had given Mrs. Bradley both torches and was using the boathook as a lead-line, announced shoal water.

Laura cut out her engine, which, in any case, was barely functioning, took the second boathook, and helped to fend the dinghy from the side. The cave had widened into an almost circular end, but on the port side of the boat was the natural shelf which Laura had noticed on her first visit. Moreover, as they reached shoal water, they came upon a pinnacle of slimy rock which stood up like a pointing finger.

Laura caught at it with the boathook, but the metal hook slipped off the weedy surface and the dinghy, answering the pull, began to heel. She drifted stern in and bows out, but, being well fended, she did no more harm to herself than to bump her port quarter gently against the side. At this, she tried to head herself towards the opposite wall, but Laura, leaning out boldly, caught at the slimy finger of rock, and held on long enough to arrest the drift of the boat and bring her head-on again. O'Hara came to the rescue with the deft dropping of a mooring rope over the pinnacle. Then he stepped ashore and made fast.

'Take care how you come!' he said, offering Mrs. Bradley a hand. 'It's beastly slippery up here.' He was on the rocky shelf, which now formed an unsafe but possible path.

The elderly lady, disdaining assistance, landed without mishap and shone an inquisitive torch all over the walls before she led the way onwards. The cave, now an upward-sloping passage, still ran on into the hill.

It seemed a long way to walk, and the rock had changed to a damp and crumbling landslide of chalk, trampled and marked by footprints, before the smell of the seaweed was out of the venturers' nostrils, and a strong reek of petrol took its place.

'Stop!' said Mrs. Bradley, speaking quietly. She had returned one of the torches to O'Hara, and Laura had a small one of her own. 'Put out the lights. I think I know where we are! I took a compass bearing at the mouth of the cave, another as soon as we had tied up the dinghy, and a third one minute ago.'

Suddenly from over their heads came a noisy and terrifying rumble. O'Hara and Laura instinctively ducked their heads, but Mrs. Bradley, more knowledgeably, remained bolt upright and smiled into the petrol-scented darkness. She explained that she had no doubt whatever, from her compass bearings and from what rough estimate she had been able to make of the distance the three of them had travelled since the dinghy had entered the cave, that they were now below the concrete floor of the pull-in for coaches, and that the noise was that of a motor coach driver or a lorry driver racing his engine.

'We can go back now,' she added.

Laura, entranced by what she termed 'the boys'-book atmosphere of the proceedings', was in favour of repairing forthwith to the pull-in and finding the trap-door or other aperture which opened on to the cave.

'What we need,' said O'Hara, 'is a car that wants repairing. They've a pit for repairs at that place. I've seen it. I should think it is bound to be the opening we want. If the cave is used in the way Mrs. Bradley thinks, they wouldn't risk having a suspicious-looking opening into it. Nobody would think of looking at an inspection pit in a biggish garage, which the pull-in certainly has. If we could only manage to get hold of a damaged car, we could gather round the inspection-pit while they dealt with it.'

'We will see what can be done. George will know about things like that,' said Mrs. Bradley.

'One thing,' said Laura, as they reached the tied-up dinghy, 'it looks fishy about those people in that yacht.' Mrs. Bradley did not question this statement.

'I shall again appeal to the Chief Constable,' she said. 'He is so angry with me already that one more red herring—if it should turn out to be that—can scarcely annoy him more.'

This refreshing point of view appealed to her hearers, and it was with gusto that they climbed into the dinghy and reversed her out of the cave.

'Well, you found plenty in the hole to interest you,' said the boatman encouragingly when they rejoined the cruiser, and the dinghy, after some trouble, had been hoisted aboard. For answer, Mrs. Bradley peered with an expression of vulpine rapture into one of the little linen bags she had taken with her, and produced for the boatman's inspection one or two specimens which she had had the forethought to borrow from her archæological friend before she had returned from her visit to London.

'Ah,' said the fifteen-year-old mate, coming up and peering politely over Gascoigne's left elbow, 'if you found them there in that 'ole, it's where somebody must have dropped 'em.' To the horror of three of his hearers, the stupefaction of the fourth and the cackling delight of the fifth, he continued, pointing, 'That there be a bone of *bos longifrons*; that be part of the blade of a Stone-Age sickle; and that un be a bit of the turnover top of a Neolithic collared urn. I don't hardly reckon none of they would be found in a hole like that un, but maybe they would.' *

'Well, here they are, anyway,' Mrs. Bradley briskly replied, for she neither could nor would give the erudite child the lie.

The motor cruiser took up her anchor and moved off on her return journey to Welsea Beaches. The short passage was as uneventful as her crew and passengers could desire, and the latter were back at the hotel in time for dinner. They did not return to Slepe Rock. Mrs. Bradley feared for O'Hara's safety there, although she did not give that as her reason for remaining in Welsea.

'But when can we take the damaged car to the pull-in?' asked Laura. 'That is, how soon can we get a damaged car? George won't let us mess up our own.'

'Soon; I can promise that,' said Gascoigne, looking at Mrs.

* This boy afterwards became Assistant Keeper in the Department of Archæology in the University Museum at Padmancaster, and wrote a standard work on Bronze Age Survivals in Britain.

Bradley. 'You've simply got to say when. If we can't find some legitimate means of getting into that pull-in and using their garage without exciting suspicion, I shall be surprised and will eat my hat.'

'Yes, but I don't think you wear a hat.' observed Laura. 'By the way, what about our film extras? I don't think it's much good depending on those people, somehow, at the house with the four dead trees. But perhaps you don't want any now?' she added, eyeing Mrs. Bradley narrowly.

'Oh, yes, I do want them, and we shall get them,' Mrs. Bradley responded. 'My nephew Denis knows someone who is in film circles in some managerial capacity, and this man rang up the Gonn-Brown company and the extras will be sent to us on loan at the usual rates.'

'Good,' said Laura. 'I shall sleep soundly to-night. Hope I don't dream of our cave!'

'And I that I do not dream of that terrifying child on board the cruiser!' said Mrs. Bradley.

Chapter Fifteen

★

' . . . where they say the great Emperor Frederick Barbarossa still holds his court among the caverns.'

Ibid. (*Peter the Goatherd*)

MRS. BRADLEY, as always, was as good as her word. By nine o'clock in the morning she and her host of extras were in full swing. The stone circle presented a lively spectacle and was, as the now refreshed Laura expressed it, positively crawling with ant-like archæologists, almost all of whom had been hired for the occasion, although not by Laura.

The work was in charge of Mrs. Bradley herself and a tall young man in disreputable shorts who turned out to be one of her many nephews. The expert upon whom Mrs. Bradley had been counting was suffering, it transpired, from lumbago, and could not come. He had, however, been responsible for providing the reason for hiring the helpers, for the excuse for all the activity (if anybody asked any questions) was that a 'dig' was to be filmed for educational purposes.

'And if we can't outshine *Charley's Aunt*,' announced Laura darkly, 'in competing for the educational hogwash, I shall be gloriously surprised. By the way, how come Denis? I thought he only played the violin!'

'I remembered Denis just in time. He helped to excavate some hut circles in Wiltshire last year. He will make it look as though we know what we're doing, and will also prevent us from doing any damage,' said Mrs Bradley, waving an explanatory claw. 'The great thing,' she added, gazing benevolently round upon her ant-heap, 'is to have *enough* people busy. It disarms suspicion. And the Chief Constable, as I told you yesterday, is not pleased with me. I have kept him out of his bed and caused him to creep in the lee of hedges and get the knees of his trousers dirty. It will be as well to demonstrate our own continuing zeal.'

She concluded this peroration with a startling yelp of laughter, and then called up her nephew and presented him to the other young men.

'Denis *does* play the violin,' she added, waving a skinny claw again as though to excuse this idiosyncrasy on the part of her nephew. 'You will have much in common.' She walked off, hooting mirthfully.

'Aunt Adela is very full of beans to-day,' said Denis. 'She feels she's up to mischief, and that, in my experience, always makes old ladies very cheerful.'

O'Hara and Gascoigne, who had taken to him at sight, would perhaps have liked to know what his experience had been, but they did not ask that, but only what was the plan of campaign on the site of the digging.

'We have to fool about as long as possible without *doing* any actual *digging*,' Denis replied. 'So if you two wouldn't mind taking this measuring tape and this fairly large protractor, and assing about over there for a bit without doing anything in particular, but just looking busy and intelligent, it would be handy. We lunch at twelve and shall spin the picnic out until two-thirty. Then we resume the fooling until four. By that time we hope to have attracted a fair amount of attention, and to have demonstrated our fat-headed innocence. Then we can push off home. At least, so Aunt Adela says.'

Gascoigne and O'Hara accepted the implements presented to them, retired to the north-west segment of the circle, and began a series of elaborate measurements. O'Hara produced a notebook and a fountain pen, Gascoigne a few unpaid bills and a pencil, and the two young men wrote down records and calculations of distances, angles, direction and length of shadows, and such other data as occurred to their yeasty intelligences or were suggested by the circumstances of the survey.

They also named, for their private satisfaction, all the nine stones, beginning with the names of the eight great planets, but as it was a matter for argument how then to name the ninth stone, they compromised by deciding to call all the stones after the most eccentric dons at their University. This exercise in ingenuity took some time, as it seemed necessary to relate each stone in some way to the person after whom it was to be called, and the time passed pleasantly enough.

At last there was a halt for the picnic lunch. A firm of caterers from Welsea Beaches, suborned or intimidated by Mrs. Bradley, appeared at ten minutes to twelve with lorry-loads of excellent food and a sufficient number of crates of bottled beer, and drove cautiously through the open gateway on to the site of the dig.

The archaeologists knocked off work at once, and, with completely comprehensible enthusiasm, unloaded and fell on the provisions. Laura sat between two of the film extras, a young man in velvet trousers and a young woman with hair so thoroughly bleached that it had turned white. Laura was an expansive, friendly person, and was soon conversing with the extras and listening with great interest to what they had to say about the cinema.

They were on location, she learned, to shoot half a dozen sequences involving a background of open hill-country, some pasture and a Tamworth boar.

'Although what a Tamworth boar looks like, unless our producer,' said the velvet-trousered one frankly, 'beats me, what I mean to say.'

Laura agreed, although she knew perfectly well what a Tamworth boar looked like. She had not, so far, met their producer, however, and so reserved judgment on the aptness or otherwise of the velvet-trousered comment.

'I suppose you've got digs down here?' she said. 'I mean, if you're staying some time. How do they put you up?'

'If you call it that,' said the silver-haired one. 'Digs, I mean. We've been given the attics in that house by the golf links. I suppose it's all right if you're not choosey, but being seventh lead, as you might almost say, I did think I ought to get something better. But it's no use talking. Anyway, it's dry and fairly clean, and the food's not bad, and they give you a drink occasionally. Free, I mean.'

'Iced?' enquired Laura, upon what she hoped was a casual note; for she felt sudden excitement at the news that these people were actually housed in Cottam's, of the four dead trees, a mansion which, she was still certain, contained a corpse.

'Iced? Oh, I suppose so, if you like them that way. Personally, a gin is all I care for, and you don't want that iced, do you?'

Laura said that she supposed not, and, the conversation showing signs of languishing, she was moved suddenly to enquire:

'What sort of man is Concaverty?'

The silver hair and the velvet trousers exchanged glances which indicated indecision and a certain degree of embarassment.

'Oh, well,' said the velvet trousers, 'he's an old so-and-so, actually. Too big for his boots. In fact, too big altogether. But, look here, don't say I said so. I don't want to get the wrong side of him. He rents us the house, you know. The Gonn-Brown pay him five hundred a week, and, even then, he doesn't much want us, we've been told.'

'If he's here, I wish you'd point him out,' said Laura. 'I believe I've heard of him. Better still, I wish you'd point your producer out to a friend of mine who's in the O.U.D.S. and wants a small part in a film.'

'Him? Oh, he wouldn't be here, don't you believe it! Probably still in bed. Oh, no! I'm wrong! Here he comes. The fellow with the battleship jaw.'

'Oh!' said Laura, realizing at once that this was a man she had never seen before. 'Oh! I suppose you're sure?'

'One's usually sure of the boss!' the lint-haired seventh lead replied.

'Hullo, who's that talking to young Bradley?' asked Gascoigne, joining his cousin. 'Looks a bit of a bruiser, doesn't he? What do you make of him? Your face has gone all expressive!'

'Why, that's the fellow!' said O'Hara. 'I recognized his voice at once. I wonder what his name is? I'll go over and claim acquaintance. I'd like to find out what he's got to say about the body we carried down those stairs.'

'Do you mean the producer?' asked Laura, coming up to them.

'Good Lord, no! I mean that fellow talking to Bradley. Mrs. Bradley's watching them, do you see? She smells a rat, and no wonder.'

He strolled over to where Denis was in conversation with a thickly-built, tallish man who looked like a professional boxer.

'Hullo,' said O'Hara casually. 'How goes it?'

'It looks all right to me,' the man replied, 'but I don't know much about . . . Good Lord!'

'Yes, exactly,' said O'Hara, eyeing him. 'How did our friend get on?'

'Eh? . . . Oh! Poor old Chummy! Yes, that was a very bad business! But what possessed you to get out of the car like that? Still, he managed the journey all right, and we got him to hospital. Hæmorrhage, too! The most extraordinary thing. I've never heard of it accompanying typhoid fever, have you?'

'I don't know much about illness,' said O'Hara slowly, 'but I knew he was pretty bad. I had an idea he was dead when I left the car.'

'Of course not! There wasn't any question of that! He was pretty bad, certainly, but he's progressing well enough now. We didn't think much of the local hospitals, so in the end we ran him up to London, and that's where he is! Well, so long! Be seeing you!' He turned and strolled away.

'I wish I'd got that kind of cast-iron nerve,' said O'Hara, when, at the end of the afternoon, the film extras and all other strangers had gone, and he, together with Gascoigne, Laura, Mrs. Bradley and the useful and decorative Denis, were getting into the two cars to return to Welsea Beaches. 'He didn't attempt to put me off. Just said that the sick man was progressing well and was now in London. Looked me in the eye as bold as brass, and asked me why on earth I'd got out of the car that night. Did you ever meet such an example of complete, copper-bottomed cheek?'

'If we could only find that body, and get it identified!' said Laura. 'If only we could find out *anything!* I hate being kept in the dark.'

'To-night,' said her employer mysteriously, generously omitting all reference to the discovery of the smugglers' cave and the important and entrancing theory that it ended under the pull-in at Slepe Rock, 'we go on a mysterious quest. You wait and see. I think we have started our hare.'

'That's good,' said O'Hara. 'What do you want us to do?'

'I don't want *your* company, child. I have something most important for you and Mr. Gascoigne to do. You must all get what rest you can in the next few hours. Matters, if I mistake not, approach their zenith.'

She refused to add to this Elizabethan platitude, but cackled harshly in reply to further questions.

Although she was dogged by the supposition that Mrs. Bradley was indulging in an Indian midsummer madness, or had caught a touch of the sun, Laura agreed to spend the whole time between tea and dinner at rest on her bed at the hotel. She even fell asleep for a time, and did not wake until seven. She dashed in and out of a bath in record time, and hoped that the main dish would still be 'on' when she got to table, for at Welsea Beaches, as at most seaside places of the decade, it was necessary to be early unless one was prepared to eat some extraordinary mixture concocted from the remains of food left from the previous day, or something based on sausage-meat or macaroni.

Mrs. Bradley, however, had reminded the waiter to see that Laura received the portion due to her. She advised her young secretary not to hurry over her dinner as there was not the slightest need to do so. Hiccups, she pointed out, would be out of place at that evening's special gathering at the standing stones, as silence was to be the chief consideration and even the most involuntary sounds taboo. To Laura's questions she returned no answer except a hoot of laughter.

They set off as soon as dinner was over. The night sky, overcast as it was with cloud, had already brought darkness sufficient, Mrs. Bradley decided, for their purpose, and from the large and fashionable hotel at Welsea their departure would cause no comment, and probably would go unnoticed.

Laura, wide awake and conscious of excitement, noticed that the car, instead of making direct for the objective, went from Welsea Beaches for some miles along the London Road before it turned off at Coshill for Dimdyke, Allis and Hafford. This string of hill hamlets took in a wide oval beyond Cuchester and finished by the south-west border of the county. At last the passengers found themselves on the way (up a long narrow lane of potholes and the old tracks made by the caterpillar wheels of tanks) to the village of Upper Deepening. From there the car dropped gently, and, to an imaginative person, inevitably, to the stile from which they would reach the Dancing Druids.

'What do we do now?—walk?' enquired Laura, as the car drew up, and she and her employer got out.

'There is nothing else to do,' Mrs. Bradley replied. 'But please be guided by me. Do not speak unless I speak first, and leave our course of action entirely in my hands, no matter what may be forthcoming.'

'Right. Do we leave George here again in charge of the car?'

'We do.'

'Where are Gerry and Mike? We haven't seen them since . . .'

'They are in position, I hope, by this time.'

'By the Druids?'

'Nowhere near the Druids, child. On the shore of the bay at Slepe Rock, if they have carried out instructions. And from now on, no talking, unless I speak first.'

'Complete silence,' agreed Laura. 'Right.'

She and Mrs. Bradley then climbed the stile and walked towards the circle of standing stones. Mrs. Bradley went first, and Laura kept close behind her but left sufficient space between them for Mrs. Bradley to pull up short, if she wished to do so, without having Laura butting into her. They made no sound as they walked, and Laura, in spite of (or, possibly, because of) tightened nerves, began to enjoy the expedition with that kind of tingling excitement mixed with fear which is felt by young children with a sense of adventure when they embark upon the unknown or the previously untried.

The ground rose gradually from the road, for the steeper side of the hill was that which dropped to the farm on the opposite slope. The night, in the classic phrase, was chilly but not dark, and Laura was glad of her tweed coat. The hedge rustled beside them as they walked and gave its customary impression, in the darkness, of being full of eyes.

Laura began to wonder what Mrs. Bradley intended. Nothing so far had been said of the object of the excursion, but Laura connected it vaguely with the 'archaeological eyewash' as she herself expressed it, of the afternoon. She gave up further speculation, and began to wonder, instead, exactly how Mrs. Bradley would react if, on this hair-lifting excursion, something, coming out of the hedge, stabbed Laura soundlessly to death in the dark, and Mrs. Bradley found herself, at length, alone with the Dancing Druids. She embroidered this theme until she felt sufficiently terrified to abandon it.

At this point it occurred to Laura that the Druids themselves formed a sinister rendezvous, and that she and her employer were, after all, a very young and a very old woman to be undertaking a night tryst with them, especially in view of the lonely and exposed position in which the Druids stood. She dared not conclude this thought, but the one which followed it was not more comforting. Who knew, she wondered, what ghastly sights and sounds the stones had been witnesses of in long-past times and under the ancient sky? Why, anyway, were they called the Druids, and, again, why should they dance? She saw them, enveloped, like witches, in cloaks of mist. She saw them writhe out of the ground, and, with slow contortions, shuffle towards their victims, avid for blood.

These terrifying images disappeared as Mrs. Bradley turned off from the path through a gap in the hedge, and muttered to Laura to keep low. Dark thoughts forgotten and the fever of wild adventure again in her blood, Laura crouched down. Mrs. Bradley paused for no more than three minutes, and then moved on again. Laura followed with bold and tightened heart, and she and her employer began to creep across the turf towards the stones.

It was a long and uncomfortable trek, but at last the stone circle was reached, and Mrs. Bradley, extending a skinny claw, drew Laura to a halt, and then, without speaking, thrust her gently behind one of the stones.

'Keep under cover unless I tell you anything different, child,' she muttered. 'Our business to-night is to watch. I hope nothing else will be necessary.'

Chapter Sixteen

★

'Night came fast upon them, and they found that they must, however unwillingly, sleep in the wood.'

Ibid. (*The Nose*)

LAURA, behind her stone, touched its roughly-scored surface. She felt it rasp beneath her fingers. It felt warm. Superstition came flooding back into her mind. The stones, she thought, after all, were alive. They lived some strange, remote life of their own, up there on the barren hill. They were kept alive by human blood . . . by the innocent blood of murdered men!

She was thinking these wild but archæologically reasonable thoughts, when Mrs. Bradley leaned over from her own stone and murmured:

'Prepare to repel boarders! In other words—by the pricking of my thumbs, something wicked this way comes! Stand firm, child! We have visitors!'

There followed an unpleasantly eerie pause, whilst Laura held her breath and the whole hill seemed to listen. Suddenly, from the opposite side of the circle, someone spoke.

'This'll be the one he meant. Curse those idiots and their damned dancing about!'

'Thank 'eaven they didn't start digging!' said another voice. 'That would have torn it proper! Now what about the leanin' tower of Pisa? Is this the one?'

Opposite Laura, on the north-east side of the circle, was, by daylight, a particularly noticeable stone, for it leaned over away from the rest of the circle as though at some time it might have been uprooted and had been put back carelessly.

'Yes. Here, where have you got to?'

'Feelin' it. Yes, this is it. Easiest to take out of the ground. That's what he thought, and I daresay he was right. Easiest to describe, too, if it had to be us as didn't bury it.'

'Can two of us tackle it, do you think?'

'Sure. Put the rope round it and carry the slack over the top of the next stone, the higher one.'

'Right. Carry on, then. Can you find the one you want?'

'I guess so. I'll have to have a light for the job, though. I'm not a cat as can see in the dark, and we don't want to mess the thing up.'

'Not more light than we can help, then. Sing out when you're ready, and Ben will bring up the horses to do the pulling. Your job, once you've rigged up your tackle, will be to stand by, and see that the rope doesn't slip.'

'Oh, that's the notion, is it? And what about *you*? I suppose you're the gentleman, as usual!'

'Get *on*, man, for God's sake! We haven't all night to mess about. Get that rope round, and look slippy.'

'O.K. Say when. Here she goes!'

There was a fairly long pause and some sounds indicative of effort.

'Got it over the second stone yet?'

'Nope.' A torch was switched on, but Laura could see little of the men. She knew, from the voices, that one was the man from Slepe Rock. The rougher voice she did not know.

'All set. Bring up the horses,' said this unknown man at last. 'I'll be glad to be through with this job!'

There was another pause. After a while Laura could hear the trampling of the great beasts as they were brought up the hill from the farm. A man carrying a lantern was with them, and, from his muffled oaths and muted cajolery, he seemed to experience some difficulty in getting them up to the stones.

After great efforts on the part of all three men, the horses were backed and manœuvred into position, the end of the rope was secured to a pole which dangled from their harness, and which Laura could see in the lantern-light, and the work began of heaving up the stone.

The great horses snorted and blew, the men cursed and

grunted, and the work proceeded (grimly and spasmodically, it seemed, from the comments which Laura could hear) until at long last, with an enormous sound of tearing, up came the long, tilted stone.

'Hold!' cried the man from Slepe Rock. 'Wait while we get in the crowbar!'

There was a pause of a second or two, and then the other voice observed, in a high, impatient tone:

'All right? Get busy and don't mess about! I'm not breakin' my back to suit you, as you haven't even humped yourself yet! All right now? . . . I can't hold on much longer. Something's got to go, and it might be me!'

'All right so far, but you'll have to hang on for a little bit longer,' said the first voice. 'Come here, Harry, and put your weight on this crowbar. We *must* relieve Bud. He can't hang on much longer.'

'Can't be done! The horses won't stand it,' said the carter.

The man from Slepe Rock became angry.

'Never mind the horses! You, Bud, hang on a bit longer. We're doing all we can. Oh, for God's sake, man! Use your guts!'

'That's all very well,' said the other; and Laura could hear him panting. Suddenly there was a shout which was almost a scream.

'Oh, heavens!' said Laura, aloud. Her imagination supplied the rest of the picture, but, before she had finished constructing it, the rope had parted over the top of the stone which was used to take the strain of the lifting, and the tilted stone which the men were raising had bumped down on to the turf.

Mrs. Bradley moved far more quickly than the girl. She was out of her hiding-place and on her knees beside the ghastly wreck pinned by the stone before Laura had collected her wits. The horses, relieved too suddenly of their burden, were stampeding over the hill. They uttered sounds of excitement and fear as they thundered off. The man from Slepe Rock and the carter both went after them, apparently regarding the rounding-up of the animals as of greater importance than the fate of their unlucky companion.

Mrs. Bradley switched on her torch and surveyed the scene
of the accident. She knelt beside the fallen stone which had
pinned the man underneath it, told Laura to keep off, and
soon rose.

'Quite dead, thank goodness,' she said. 'There's nothing
here that I can do.' She switched off her torch, put her hand
into the capacious pocket of her skirt and drew out a flask.
'Here,' she said, going over to Laura. 'Where are you? Un-
screw this carefully. It's brandy. I expect you can do with it.'

'I'm quite all right,' said Laura, in the husky tone of shock.
But she took the dram and was glad of it. 'I suppose we get out
of here quick?' She screwed on the cap of the flask.

'Not until we've looked into the hole,' said Mrs. Bradley,
taking the flask and testing its screw cap before she returned it
to her pocket. 'I was pretty sure this morning which stone it
was, but they've proved it beyond a doubt, as I knew they
would if our archaeological bluff came off, and it has! Come
along, before those men get back, if you will, and help me look.
I think that two witnesses will be more satisfactory than one.'

Laura, with shaking legs, at once followed her over the
turf. Mrs. Bradley kept the light from her torch on the
ground, although there were no sounds to indicate that
the men were returning.

'Don't look at *him* unless you want to,' she said decidedly,
as they approached the fallen stone and the dead man.

'I'd better look,' said Laura. 'I saw air-raid casualties.
This won't be anything more dreadful. I shall only imagine
it's all the worse if I don't see it.'

It was not, in fact, a particularly dreadful sight. The great
stone had fallen across the man's body and he had crashed
face-downward on the turf.

'Broken back, among other things,' said Mrs. Bradley, dis-
missing the incident and concentrating the beam from her
torch on to the hole torn in the turf by the lifting out of the
stone. It was the thought of what was buried in the hole, far
more than the sight of the dead man, which Laura dreaded.

'Don't touch anything,' Mrs. Bradley added. 'Just let's look. Take your time, and look carefully and closely, for we may need to be able to swear to what we have seen.'

There was nothing fearful in the hole. All that Laura could see was the loosened soil, and, a long distance down, something dark and metallic protruding.

'What is it?' she whispered, surprised, for the contents of the hole seemed strangely innocent.

'A funerary urn, perhaps,' said Mrs. Bradley, 'or, possibly, buried treasure.' She knelt beside the hole and shone her torch more directly on to the object which it contained.

'I don't think the two of us could get it up withiout assistance,' she said, 'yet I confess that I should like to have a closer look at it.'

Laura, thrusting from her mind the story of the *Treasure of Abbot Thomas* which had chosen this obvious but inconvenient time to obstrude itself upon her memory, rolled up her sleeve and thrust a strong arm into the cavity.

There was a handle on the end of the container, and upon this she took a good grip and began to heave and struggle.

'Don't trouble,' said Mrs. Bradley. 'I doubt whether it would be wise, after all to move it.'

'Thank goodness,' said Laura subsiding.

'And now,' said Mrs. Bradley, snapping off her torch, 'let us listen intently. It would never do for those villains to find us here, yet I do not intend to move until I know what they are going to do next.'

Laura became the prey to wishful thinking.

'I wish Gerry and Mike were here,' she observed. 'We could hold our own, then, whoever turned up. They'd soon settle anybody's hash. I wouldn't even mind a policeman, or Denis, or George. Or even the Chief Constable,' she added.

'I could whistle for George,' said Mrs. Bradley. 'An excellent idea, child.'

She produced a small whistle and blew it twice. Then she and Laura listened.

'I'm awfully glad we're wanted!' said Denis' voice from the hedge. He came quickly towards them. 'Where are you?' Mrs.

Bradley switched on her torch to guide him. George was with him.

'How do you come to be here, Denis?' enquired his aunt.

'George heard noises, ran the car back to the hotel and routed me out,' explained Denis, 'and here we are. What do you want us to do?'

'I trust I did not take a liberty, madam,' said the second figure, coming forward. 'Desiring to witness the course of events, I must confess that I climbed the stile and followed you part of the way, and then hid in the hedge. I remained there until it was certain that one of the malefactors had been injured. I heard the horses stampede, and, having a long switch in my hand, I did what I could to drive them further. The men pursued them as heartily as one could have wished. I then went for Master Denis . . . I should say *Mr.* Denis, madam . . . thinking we might both be of service.'

'Good for you, George,' said Mrs. Bradley. 'You've given us extra time. But we are in no danger at present. We have had an interesting evening. We have provided ourselves with buried treasure, and a man has been killed.'

'Killed?' said Denis. 'You don't mean . . .?'

'Murdered? No. The Druids danced, I think, and trampled him underfoot. Come over here, and you shall know as much as we do.'

All three went with her, for Laura disliked the idea of being alone. Mrs. Bradley shone her torch on the body, and then showed her followers the metal receptacle which the fall of the stone had disclosed.

'I think we might raise that up, Madam,' George observed, 'if those men have left any rope. What do you think, sir?' he added, turning to Denis.

'With a rope I could help,' said Laura.

A portion of the rope which the stone had chafed through was found, and, whilst Mrs. Bradley kept guard, the others, by mighty exertions, drew a long, wide metal container from the hole, and, quite exhausted, lay on the grass beside it.

'Now what,' said the wiry Denis, recovering first.

'Laura and George could take it away in the car, if we could possibly get it to the car,' said Mrs. Bradley. 'I myself would prefer to stay. I want to know what will happen here when those men return.'

'I don't see why we shouldn't get it into the car, if I give George a hand,' suggested Denis, 'and then he and Laura can go back to Welsea with it.'

'I could bring the car a lot closer, I think, sir,' said George, 'but I would respectfully suggest that we carry the receptacle to the shelter of the hedge at once, in case those fellows return and find us with it.'

'A good idea, George,' said Mrs. Bradley. 'Up with it at once, if you can.'

Although the metal container was bulky and very heavy, the two men, with Laura to take one of the handles occasionally, contrived to get it over to the hedge.

'And now you can take your time about getting the car a little nearer, and getting the box in,' Mrs. Bradley observed. 'And then Denis may rejoin me if he thinks fit to do so.'

'Look, I know you employ me and so forth, but couldn't I stay? It was me you brought, not Denis,' objected Laura. 'And he and George will be far more use to lug that thing about than George and I will,' she cunningly added.

'True, child,' said Mrs. Bradley. 'Off you go, Denis, with George and our treasured although ill-gotten gains, and you will not need to return. I have my revolver.'

'Oh, but . . .' Denis began. His aunt gave him a slight, authoritative push.

'Laura will be quite safe with me,' she promised. 'Otherwise I should not keep her. Besides, there is man's work to do at Slepe Rock to-night. Go there as soon as you have left this cylinder in some place of safety. You might find out whether Gerald and Michael need help. It is likely they do.'

'Oh!' said Laura. 'Well, I'm . . .'

'Not yet, child,' said Mrs. Bradley, thinking of Robert de Baudricourt and Saint Joan. So George went off, and very soon the almost unmistakable sounds of a car being started up came faintly upon the air.

'Now, sir,' said George, returning, 'I've brought her as near as I can. We must tote it the rest.'

Laura assisted them again, and returned, rather breathless, to report the trove safely on board.

'Thank goodness!' she added. 'I should think it weighs even more than Mike O'Hara's fat man.'

'The weight of the iron box more,' said Mrs. Bradley; but Laura, who was massaging weary muscles, apparently did not hear her.

Mrs. Bradley waited, and then she looked at her watch. She and Laura prepared for a long and tiresome vigil, and this mood proved to be of service, for a long and tiresome watch indeed it was, once they had returned to the Stones.

It became rather chilly towards morning, and Mrs. Bradley and her secretary, both by this time cold and stiff, took turns in coming out from cover, and walked about flapping their arms. At about half-past four, Mrs. Bradley saw, against the grey-black light of the sky, a horseman ride over the hill. She watched him for more than a minute as he headed towards the Stones, and then, with a word to Laura, she scuttled into cover like a rabbit making for its burrow.

Chapter Seventeen

★

' *"That is strange,"* said the other; *"let us follow the cart and see where it goes."* '

Ibid. (*Tom Thumb*)

LAURA had seen the man, too.

'Oh, lor!' she said. 'Here we come!'

The horseman gained the summit and reined in his mount. He seemed to be trying to make out the lie of the land in the greyish deception of the half-light, and took some time to satisfy himself. He then turned his horse and thundered off.

'I suppose he will bring his friends to finish the task,' said Mrs. Bradley grimly. 'I wonder how soon we may expect them?'

She took out her revolver, and she and Laura stood behind their respective stones and waited for what might be coming. They had not long to wait. There was the sound of hoofs over the hill, and the horseman reappeared, the darkish shadow of a centaur against the grey of the sky. He turned in his saddle to look behind him. After a short pause, three men came after him on foot, lumbering up the slope at a half-trot. He spurred forward, followed by these companions, and rode straight towards the stone beneath which the dead man was pinned. Here he dismounted, and waited for the others to come up. It was the biggish man whom O'Hara had recognized as the one whom he had assisted on the Saturday evening of the hare and hounds.

'Quiet enough,' he remarked. 'Now we've got to get him away, and we haven't much time. Get busy. Free him first, and then for the box. All set? Now get a move on. Con's expecting us.'

He received no answer, so he remounted, and remained on

watch. Paying no attention to him, the other three knelt
beside the hole from which the stone had come, and one of
them reached down into it. He found nothing, so, changing
his position to that of lying flat on his face, he thrust his arm
further into the hole. The others watched him. He got up,
shrugged, and the three of them glanced towards the horseman, whose back was towards them, and then went over to
where the dead man lay with his face in the turf, and looked
attentively at the respective positions of the man and the
fallen stone.

Meanwhile Mrs. Bradley and her secretary, behind their
respective stones, were playing a grim game of hide and seek
with the horseman, moving stealthily round the stones as he
kept his watch so as to remain out of sight whichever way he
manœuvred his horse. As the last place from which he was
expecting scrutiny was from behind the stones, their task was
fairly simple.

He soon seemed satisfied that there was nothing to be
feared, and rode quietly back to where the men were working.
The one who had groped in the hole had unwound a grappling
chain which ended in a hook, and this he passed round the
end of the stone and secured it. When he had tested it, he
passed the end of the chain to one of the others. This man
carried it to the horseman, who turned his mount so that the
chain could be fastened at the back of his saddle.

'All set?' he called, when this was done. He obtained a
growling assent from his obviously unwilling helpers, and
turned in the saddle to say angrily:

'Well, you take your cut, don't you? And you've got to do
what's to be done!'

'Us didn't reckon on deaders,' said one of the men very
sullenly.

'Oh, go to hell, and do as you're told, or we're all in the
cart,' said the horsemen. 'Once let anybody find poor Bud
like this, and they've got us all in the bag.'

At this, the men, one at the mouth of the hole and astride
the stone, the others between him and the horseman, took the
chain in hands on to which they had pulled stout gauntlets,

and, at a word from the first man, took the strain and began to haul and tug with the greatest determination with the object of lifting the stone from the body of their dead companion.

The man at the hole was the biggest and presumably the strongest. He gave the orders, panting them out as though the strain of the lifting was almost too much for his strength. The others, too, strained and sweated, and the rider, urging his horse, was swearing softly and continuously as, for half an hour by Mrs. Bradley's watch, they toiled (though with frequent pauses for rest and to wipe off the sweat which was running into their eyes), to move the great stone off the body. Their efforts were vain.

Mrs. Bradley and Laura watched with the greatest interest. At last the two men stood back, then flung themselves on the ground and declared that the job could not be done. The big man, who at first had been as unwilling as they, now cursed, cajoled and bullied them, but they refused to go back to the work. He spoke to the horseman, who glanced at the eastern sky, and then unhooked the grapple from his foam-flecked horse and rode off. He was absent for about a quarter of an hour, during which time the others, although they were resting, betrayed all the known and obvious signs of anxiety, for the sun was rising and their time, it was clear, was running out. At last the horseman came back, flogging his horse up the hill and over the turf to the stones, as though he, too, was most desperately pressed for time.

In his left hand he held a short axe, or, rather, a billhook. Mrs. Bradley watched interestedly, but Laura covered her face, for both had guessed the use to which the implement was to be put. The rider handed the billhook to the biggest man, and the others got to their feet and stood away. The biggest man looked at the billhook and then at the corpse, whilst the rider dismounted and pulled a large sack from his saddle.

'Now then,' he said, 'have a smack at it.'

'Not me,' said the big man, dropping the billhook on the grass. 'Do your own bloody butchering.'

The horseman lost no more time. There was a horrid

interval, during which Laura, behind her stone, was sick twice, and then the horseman kicked the head and hands of the dead man into the sack, wiped his boots very carefully on the turf, twisted the neck of the sack, and approached the horse with his burden.

The animal, however, squealed and backed, and the horseman could not control it. It would not suffer the sack to be brought nearer than about three yards, and the horseman was dragged at the end of the rein as the animal pranced and whinnied. It was not until two of the others came to his assistance that the horse was brought sufficiently to a standstill to enable him to get upon its back. As he did this, another sound could be heard, and over the brow of the hill came an ancient and lumbering farm-wagon half-filled with dirty straw which looked as though it had made a bedding for calves and stank accordingly. It stopped at the open gateway, and then creaked onward again, but remained on the rough but well-defined path which led along the side of the field.

The carter jumped down as soon as it stopped next time, and clumped across the turf towards the hole. As he came up, the men beside it indicated the corpse—or what remained of it—and the carter swore with horror, and for some time argued whether or not he should take the sack on the wagon.

'It's worse nor a murder,' said he. 'I tell ee, it's worse nor a murder.'

'Oh, don't talk such muck,' said the horseman. He tossed the reeking billhook on to the straw in the wagon. 'Listen, now, cully,' he went on. 'That'll take some explaining if I don't pick it up out of there. You've heard of fingerprints, haven't you? Well, it's more than your neck's worth . . .' he made a suggestive gesture indicative of the tightening of a noose . . . 'to touch that billhook and leave your fingerprints on it. His are on it . . .' he jerked his head towards the big man, who with the other two, was making off towards the farm . . . 'and mine are superimposed on his. Follow? So if yours get on top of mine, you know what the police'll think, don't you? Now don't be a fool. I don't touch that billhook again until we get to the farm with that sack and I can get it into a safer place, and you know where that is, don't you?'

The carter was not so easily bullied or convinced. He turned stubborn.

'You promised me it 'ud be poor Bud's body, and willing enough I am to take that along to the farm. But this is different. Bodies do be resurrection matter, but 'eads and 'ands be offal and most on-Christian.'

'Oh, don't be a fool!' shouted the horseman, almost dancing with impatience and fury. 'Do you want your cut or don't you? I'll report you to Mr. Concaverty, that's what I'll do, and when the next pay-off comes you'll be left with nothing except a prison sentence. How would you like to do a three-year stretch, eh?'

'Not by myself I shouldn't be, nohow,' said the carter morosely. 'Still, suit yourself. But I ain't going to touch the sack, mind that. Dollars is dollars, and if they turns into a quid or two now and then, that ain't no odds to no one, supposing a man keeps his mouth shut . . .'

'Oh, go to hell! Off with you! Off with you! It'll be full daylight in half an hour, and we'll have people all over the place,' yelled the horseman furiously. 'Here, take the beastly thing, and shut your trap!'

'It's again my conscience and it's a-dimmin' of my holy lights,' said the carter. The horseman, consigning his holy lights, in a crisp phrase which Mrs. Bradley appreciated without wishing ever to employ, to what he suggested would be their ultimate destination, slung the sack into the cart on top of the billhook, heaped the filthy straw over both, and, having caught his horse which seemed to have forgotten the sack and was grazing quietly at a short distance from the cart-track, he mounted and galloped away.

The carter, with fearful mutterings and some darkly suspicious glances towards the stones, drove slowly off down the hill towards the farm.

When both horseman and wagon had disappeared, the witnesses quietly emerged.

'If anybody comes, pretend to be gathering mushrooms—or,

at any rate, looking for some,' said Mrs. Bradley producing two large paper bags from her pocket and handing one over to her secretary.

But no one appeared, and by the time they had reached the open gateway they could see the wagon almost at the bottom of the hill.

'Keep under cover,' said Mrs. Bradley, putting the paper bags away again, 'and you had better begin cutting a stick from the hedge if the carter chances to look round. We're a couple of holiday-makers out for an early-morning stroll.'

'I could do with an early-morning breakfast,' said Laura with feeling. 'When do we resume our archæological pursuits? I rather liked fooling about on these ancient hills.'

'We could, of course, "discover" the corpse, child. Somebody will do so, sooner or later, you know.'

'Oh, no! Not us!' said Laura, horrified. 'What on earth made me mention breakfast? I don't think I'll ever want anything to eat any more.'

'We had better report to the Chief Constable as soon as we know what they propose to do with the wagon,' said Mrs. Bradley. 'After that, I think we will let the police discover the body. It will be less embarrassing for them and for us that way.'

'No more archæology, then?'

'The police will provide all the digging that is necessary—at any rate for some time,' Mrs. Bradley replied. 'I anticipate their taking up all the nine stones to see whether anything else is buried beneath them. The police are nothing if not thorough.'

'What do you think is in the box?'

'I *did* think it was a body, but now I am not so sure. It is possible (as so many people seem to be involved) that it is the proceeds of robbery. But no doubt before long we shall know.'

'I'm dying to get it open,' said Laura. 'At least, I think I am. It couldn't be money, could it?'

The wagon bumped on down the deeply-rutted cart-track. Once or twice the carter looked back, as though aware that there were people behind him, but they were a long way off, and all that the man could see, Mrs. Bradley hoped and believed, were two early-morning walkers intent on the view, or deep in conversation, or, in the case of the young one, on switching at the nettles in the hedge.

The wagon made heavy weather of the turn at the bottom of the hill, but was into the farmyard at last, and there was left, an innocent-looking adjunct, in the cartshed, whilst the carter went off to his breakfast, or perhaps to polish up his holy lights, whatever these ostensible manifestations of dark superstition (for as such Mrs. Bradley interpreted them) might be.

She and Laura, who had hung back until it was certain that the carter had gone, now turned in their tracks, climbed part of the hill once more, kept low behind a hedge which ran at right-angles to the cart-track, and then sat down to keep an eye on the farmyard, which was now directly below them, and to decide what their next move should be.

'One of us,' said Mrs. Bradley, 'had better remain whilst the other goes back to breakfast, and then we can perhaps change places. The vigil will not last long, because whichever of us goes first can inform the police of what has occurred, and no doubt they will very soon be on the spot.'

'But what do you make of it all?' enquired Laura. 'I said it was a secret society, but it's a gang of crooks, I should imagine. Have you heard of any robberies in the neighbourhood?'

'No, child. Neither shall we do so. At least, if we do, they will not, I may venture to predict, be the work of those men.'

'Do you think Mike's fat man was murdered?'

'I have very little doubt of it, child.'

'You don't think that's him in the iron box?'

'I have very high hopes of it, I confess.'

'You really think that's not treasure?'

'I really think that the iron box contains the corpse of the painter Toro.'

'Toro? Oh, but . . .'

'If the rest of my deductions are correct, I do not see who else it can be but Toro, child. When we have concluded our present business, which is to see that the head and hands in the wagon come into the possession of the police so that the dead man can be identified, we will persuade my picture-dealer in Cuchester to describe Mr. Allwright for us.'

'But why shouldn't it be Mr. Battle? Why do you say so definitely that it's Toro?'

'I don't say it definitely, child. It may not be a body at all. But if it *is* a body, then I say it is Toro. It could not possibly be Battle, because Battle, to the best of my belief, is not only alive, but is in constant touch with his son David.'

'Then all that story of David's is a lie?'

'Most of it, I think, is untrue. Its own internal evidence is against it.'

'And he doesn't really hate his father at all?'

'I think he hates his father as deeply as he says he does.'

'Then . . . But *why* do you think his father is still alive?'

'Because I think we have seen him this morning.'

'This morning?' Laura was almost shouting in her excitement.

'Of course, the horse may have thrown him and broken his neck for him by now,' said Mrs. Bradley.

Chapter Eighteen

★

' . . . so at last he let them come in, and they bespoke a handsome supper, and spent the evening very jollily.'
                                                    Ibid. (*Chanticleer and Partlet*)

THERE was a saloon bar at the side entrance to the hotel at Slepe Rock, and thither Gascoigne and O'Hara went to drink beer and pass the time away until the hour should come to carry out the instructions they had received from Mrs. Bradley. They discovered that it was the barmaid's night off, and that the proprietor, a genial man (now in his waistcoat), was doing her work for the evening.

'Quiet here to-night,' said O'Hara.

'Yes,' the host replied. 'People are going home from their holidays now. We shall be very quiet indeed until about the end of May. Then visitors start trickling in, and by July, of course, we're full. Then they fall away in the first two weeks of September, and by the end of the month we're practically clear. Funny thing happened this evening . . .'

'No permanent guests?' enquired Gascoigne.

'Permanents? No. Don't encourage 'em. My experience of permanents—not here, but when I was in Welsea—is that they get a wrong sort of vested interest in the place. They get to thinking they can always take the same seat in the lounge, and the same place by the fire or near the windows or in the garden, or wherever it might be. Why, some of them even look upon the hotel servants as their personal lackeys and chambermaids, and make all sorts of demands on them which no servant to-day will put up with. And not much in the way of tips or presents, either. No, when I took this place I said to Mrs. Cooke—that's my wife—I said to her plainly: *No*

permanents. So we don't encourage them. I suppose Mr. Cassius
and his ward are the nearest, but I don't mind men. It's the
ladies . . . God bless 'em! . . . that make all the trouble in
hotels. And talking of Mr. Cassius, that reminds me. Funny
thing happened here this evening . . .'

'Mr. Cassius?' said Gascoigne. 'Has he gone?'

'Well, more or less. Said he might be back for a fortnight,
later on, without the boy. The boy will be at school, no doubt,
next week or the week after. Then Mr. Cassius will be down
again, I daresay. But it will only be his usual short visit. We
generally see him for the last fortnight in September, and
then no more until May. But I was going to tell you . . .'

'He's a regular visitor, then?'

'Regular enough, the last ten years.'

'Don't you mean *nine* years?' asked Gascoigne. The landlord, who had accepted a half-pint of beer and was about to
light his pipe, paused with the match already aflame. He
shook it out as the flame reached his fingers, and scratched his
head with the matchstick.

'Funny you should ask that,' he remarked. 'Now let me
see . . .'

'Like to bet on it?' asked O'Hara of Gascoigne, quickly
taking up his cousin's lead.

'A pound,' said Gascoigne.

'Done. Come on, Mr. Cooke. The bet's made.'

'Let me just serve these three gentlemen, and I'll get my
book,' said the host.

The three gentlemen wore padded overcoats, hats pulled
well down, beautiful shoes, and indulged in almost no conversation. Their hands were in their overcoat pockets, but
whether for warmth, or because they carried guns or knuckle-
dusters, it would have been difficult to say.

'Doubles,' said the first of them, slapping a pound note
upon the counter. 'Serve yourself one.'

'Thank you, gentlemen.' The host, abandoning his custom
of serving nothing but single whiskies, poured the drinks and
placed them in front of his customers. He then raised his half-
pint of beer. 'I have a drink on, thank you all the same.' He

turned and placed the pound note in the small black japanned cashbox on the shelf behind the bar, took change from the till, placed it neatly on the counter, and resumed his conversation with O'Hara and Gascoigne. The three men drained off their whisky and went out.

'Spivs,' said Gascoigne. 'How come, Mr. Cooke, in this part of the world?'

'That's just what I was wondering,' replied the host. 'I haven't seen gentry of that kidney since I was in Brighton last. We certainly don't see their like around here, and glad of it I am. I'll get my book now, gentlemen, and you can settle your bet.'

Regardless of a prominently-displayed notice above the inner door of the bar which forbade any form of gambling on the premises, he departed.

'Good for you, Gerry,' said O'Hara. 'That was very neat.'

'You weren't bad yourself at catching on and following my lead,' said Gascoigne. 'I say, he's trying to tell us about this fellow Cassius getting knocked out, you know. I suppose we must give him his head. We can't keep on fobbing him off. Oh, here he comes!'

The hotel register, to the great interest of two of the hotel guests, showed that the oddly-named Mr. Cassius and his ward Ivor—Sisyphus to Laura Menzies and Mr. Cassius-Concaverty's son to Mrs. Bradley—had been regular visitors to the hotel at Slepe Rock during the past nine years, war or no war. Their permanent address, it seemed, was London.

'Alias Cottam's, alias Nine Acres,' observed Gascoigne to O'Hara later.

An influx of thirsty customers prevented the two young men from hearing the story the host had been anxious to tell them. They were not at all sorry about this, although both, from valuable experience gained at school, were able to keep their countenances when their sins were mentioned in their hearing.

Having finished their drinks, they strolled down to the shore at Slepe Rock. Several of the guests at the hotel had done the same thing, so they lighted meditative pipes and discussed the business of the evening.

'How are we going to get out to-night without being seen?' enquired O'Hara, as they stepped on to the spit of dirty sand. 'It seems to me absolutely necessary that we should manage without being spotted, but I don't see how it's to be done.'

'I've been thinking about that,' said Gascoigne. 'I think the best way will be to seem to go to bed at our usual time, and then come straight down the servants' staircase. Of course, we may run into one of the maids, but we must risk that. If we *do* meet one of them, I shall act as though I'm tight, and you'll have to pretend to get me back into our part of the house. After which, we'll try again, and hope for better luck.'

'What about the fire-escape?' asked O'Hara.

'I had thought of that, but I think we'd be spotted rather easily. Once we're out at the servants' door, we've nothing to do but shin over the wall at that place where the trees hang over. They should give us plenty of cover, and I loosened a brick this evening.'

'And once we get down to the shore?'

'I don't know. Mrs. Bradley herself didn't know. It's a hunch she's got that they're going to take action to-night before the police get on to them. We're to watch and wait, and not to attack anybody or join in any fights unless it's to save our own skins. That's all she could say. Our main job is to keep an eye on that cave. That's where the fun may begin. It's their last base on land, and is used, she thinks, to smuggle something out of the country.'

'Stolen goods or faked money, I suppose,' said O'Hara. 'Well, there's nothing doing at present, so let's get back and make ourselves obvious, shall we?'

'Oh, I say, no! There's no need to be conspicuous! And, talking of that, we still haven't settled with Firman.'

'Finding him is going to be the trouble. And don't repeat his name. We don't know who knows it round here. And, to change the subject completely, it's your turn to stand me a drink.'

They went back to the hotel, passing, on their way, the shack and the pull-in, interesting now not only because they

were built on the site of the cottage from which the man
named Bulstrode had disappeared, but because they
were certainly screens to the uppermost entrance to
the cave.

The night was not yet so dark as to obscure all objects from
view, and O'Hara, without realizing that he had done so,
noticed that the pull-in was occupied by a large lorry. This
was unusual. It had so far been empty at night. The hotel had
its own lock-up garages for the convenience of its guests, and
the lorries and motor coaches which used the pull-in during
the day were almost always gone by six o'clock.

The two young men went inside the hotel and to the lounge.
They remained there until eleven, spoke to several of the
guests, and then went up towards their room. At the top of the
first flight of stairs was a long corridor. They traversed it, and,
opening a baize-covered door, found themselves on the
servants' staircase.

They were lucky. It was long after the time when maid-
servants were likely to be about. In fact, they could hear girls'
laughter and snatches of talk from the floor above. The young
men descended to the back door, which was not yet bolted and
locked, crept out, slipped noiselessly across the garden, and
were soon up and over the wall.

There was an alley at the side of the hotel. They emerged
from it into the only street of Slepe Rock, and, keeping in the
shadow of the wall, they gained the beach, and, with the
utmost carefulness, made for a group of rocks, high and dry
beyond the tide-mark, from which they could watch the sea,
and the headland into which the cave penetrated.

'Now for dirty work at the crossroads,' said O'Hara with
quiet enjoyment. 'Sister Ann, Sister Ann, oh, do you see
anyone coming?'

'Dry up, you ass! You'll attract attention. We don't want
the local watch committee down on us or something,' said his
cousin, with crude common sense.

'Shouldn't think there's even a village policeman,' replied
O'Hara. 'Still, perhaps, if you say so. Wonder how the old
lady and Laura are getting on?'

'Dry up!' said his cousin, who seemed nervous. The beach was entirely deserted, and the snarling of the sea sounded ominous and might blanket, he thought, the approach of undesirable persons. It had occurred to him more than once that O'Hara's recognition of Cassius as the Con of the first adventure might have placed his cousin's life in some danger. He had put this to Mrs. Bradley. Her serious acceptance of the theory had done nothing to modify his anxiety, but he agreed with the elderly lady that, as nothing would impress O'Hara less than the fact that he might be in danger, Gascoigne should continue to shoulder the responsibility of acting in partnership with him, and guard him as far as that was possible.

'For we'll never get him to give up the fun at *this* stage,' he observed.

Chapter Nineteen

★

'Then the soldier went out and told the people to take up the
square stone in the market-place and dig for water underneath.'
Ibid. (*The Crows and the Soldier*)

In spite of Gascoigne's uneasiness on his cousin's behalf, the
long period of waiting made him drowsy, for it was well
after midnight when the sound of boots on the shingle
attracted O'Hara's attention.

He touched his cousin, and Gascoigne, who had been more
than half asleep, roused himself and they listened. The footsteps approached them and then stopped, and a torch began
to flicker like a will o' the wisp over the shingle.

Then round the point beyond the eastern end of the bay
came the masthead light of a vessel. A lamp from the ship
winked twice, went out, winked twice and again went out,
this time for good, and the masthead light disappeared.

Gascoigne and O'Hara watched and still waited. The torch
repeated what was undoubtedly a signal, and then was
switched off. No word was spoken, the boots returned by the
way they had come, and all was quiet again.

Nothing more happened for about three-quarters of an
hour. Then there came the sound of voices muted by distance,
and, shortly after that, the sound of oars. A boat was pulled
up on to the shingle where the road came almost to the sea,
and men began to tramp up the beach.

It was impossible to see them in the darkness. Apparently
they knew their way well, for, black though the night was,
none of them carried a torch.

The watchers—or, rather, the audience, for there was
nothing to see—heard them leave the shingle and step up on

to the road, and then there was nothing else to hear but the drag of the tide on the beach.

'Wonder if anyone is left in charge of the boat?' O'Hara muttered.

'It wouldn't be more than one man,' replied his cousin, alive to the implications of this question.

'Scrag him?'

'I think so. No light indicates no good. And why that signalling?'

'You'd think the coastguards would spot it.'

'I should hardly think they would see. It was very discreet. We'd hardly have seen it ourselves if we hadn't happened to be just where we are. Come on,'

'He'll hear us as soon as we move, but never mind.'

'That's if anyone's there. There may not be. Keep by the cliff, and mind how you go. It's a booby-trap walk in the dark.'

By keeping close to the cliff they found that the shingle was not quite so liable to slide away under their feet. They advanced by inches, testing each step before they took it. No sound came from the boat, and they began to think that it was indeed unoccupied; but as they drew nearer to where the cliff dropped to the road, a voice from the water said softly:

'Thought you was never flippin' well comin'. Get a move on! I can't ruddy well stop here all night.'

'Sh!' said Gascoigne, with the loud hiss of a jet of escaping steam. He and O'Hara stepped on to the road and strode towards the edge of the water. 'Where are you?' O'Hara demanded, as the gunwale of the boat made a dark mass suddenly before him.

' 'Ere!' said the man in the boat; but he was throttled into silence by O'Hara before he could say any more.

'Quiet, you!' murmured Gascoigne into his ear. He pricked the man's chin with the point of his pocket-knife. 'One bleat, and you'll get this in your neck. Now, then, who are you, and what's the game?'

'Oo're *you?*' grumbled the man. 'What's *your* game?'

'Oh, don't be a fool! The boss sent us,' said Gascoigne, upon inspiration. 'Somebody's mucking it up, and he wants to know why.'

'Then he'd better ask Mr. Cassius,' said the man. 'Mr. Cassius' orders is as good as *his*, any day, I reckon. We got to get some young feller as is dossin' down at the 'otel. He give us the number of his room.'

'Well, you get out of it,' said Gascoigne, 'and go and fetch the B's back. Those orders are countermanded.'

He and O'Hara seized the man and bundled him over the side; then they shoved off, scrambled aboard, put the oars in the rowlocks, and, pleased with the form which the adventure appeared to have taken, rowed out to sea.

The tide was still onshore, but would turn in less than an hour. They had nothing to guide them, but they had a clear idea of the shape of the bay, and, after a brief discussion, they decided to go to the cave. Somewhere off the headland lay the ship which had signalled the boat, but how big she was, and how many men she had on board, and what they were to do if and when they gained the cave, they had not the faintest idea. Gascoigne was happy. Mrs. Bradley had foreseen that his cousin might be attacked at the hotel, and, by sending him down to the beach, she had put that particular experiment out of court.

'Up the old lady!' thought Gascoigne.

'Let's lie off a bit, and see what happens when those fellows get back and find the boat gone,' said O'Hara. 'It can't be long before that fellow contacts them and lets them know what has happened.'

They lay offshore for forty minutes or so, but no sound came from the beach, and at last they were forced to conclude that the men had not intended to return to the boat, or else that the loss of the boat had brought about an alteration in plan.

'But they'll have to signal the ship again, I should think,' remarked O'Hara; and almost upon these words they saw a signal go up from the beach at the point, as nearly as they could guess it, from which their boat had put off.

'Three flashes,' said Gascoigne, dipping his oars (for the tide by this time had turned, and was drifting them farther out to sea and towards the ship) and giving the short shallow strokes which the circumstances seemed to demand. 'Now, where will they get the answer?'

But no answer came, and the young men deduced from this that the ship was now hidden behind the headland, and must be off a lonely stretch of the coast on the east of the bay.

'It won't be healthy, once the day breaks,' said Gascoigne, his anxieties suddenly returning. 'What do you think we ought to do?'

'Capture the ship, like that idiot Jim Hawkins,' said O'Hara. 'This is a smuggling gang. There doesn't seem much doubt about that. The thing is to find out what they are smuggling, if we can. And, further to that, a great light dawns on me.'

'It will dawn on both of us in about another couple of hours,' observed Gascoigne. 'Nevertheless, say on. And pull on your left oar a little. We're drifting too far and too fast.'

'I rather think,' said O'Hara, 'that Mrs. Bradley is trying to clear this smuggling gang out of the way. They have nothing to do with the murder of my stout party down on the farm, and they're cluttering up the enquiry. What do you say to that?'

Gascoigne thought it over, and then proceeded to discredit it, and the two young men might have gone on until the morning alternately dipping their oars and discussing this no longer intelligent and barely tenable theory, but that there came a sudden break in their tranquillity. This took the form of their seeing distress signals fired from some point beyond the headland.

'A Verey light pistol?' suggested O'Hara. 'Anyway, someone in trouble.'

'Rockets, I think,' said his cousin, as the night was again pierced. 'It might be from that same ship. If so, I wonder what's happened? There's not much of a sea running, and she was a long way out. She must have tried a quick run in, and fouled the rocks.'

'Out of control, perhaps. Come on, we'd better get to the cave and see whether they've started running the stuff, or whether this alters their plans.'

They bent to their oars. It was not much further to the cave, and as they came opposite its entrance they could see a light within its depths. The ship which was signalling for help lay farther over to the west, and was carrying all her navigation lights. She was nowhere near any rocks, and might have been a couple of miles offshore. As they came in sight of her—for her flares lit up her hull sufficiently to allow her to be seen for an instant—she released several more flares in quick succession.

'I say,' said O'Hara, as they rested on their oars, 'I've had another hunch. I think those signals may be fakes, and they're going to run the smuggled stuff when they've drawn off the lifeboat, and attracted the attention of the coastguards away from the headland. The lifeboat will be bound to put out, and all attention will be centred on the wreck. There'll be two ships out there, I'd bet a pound, this one with lights and the other lying closer to the shore and further west—in fact, between this one and the cave. It's not a bad scheme, and I'd like to foil it.'

'Then in we go,' said Gascoigne. 'This is amazing good fun! Ship your oars. We must quant her in.'

'There's only one boathook,' said O'Hara, 'so I'll use an oar as a quant-pole. Good thing we've been in before. Oh, no, I forgot. You haven't, so I'll give the orders. Go easy, now. We're almost on to the rocks.'

The mad project of entering the cave in pitch darkness was safely accomplished. Once in, the cousins found themselves in a blackness so unrelieved—for the light at the further end had disappeared—that it was almost a necessity to glance back, as Gascoigne did once or twice, to the almost luminous sea at the mouth of the cave.

'I'll use my torch in spurts,' said O'Hara. 'That should help us a bit. We must trust to luck nobody sees it. There's nobody here at present. We're in luck.'

He switched on his torch and disclosed that they were far enough into the cave for the rocky path to be discerned above the water-line on the port side of their boat. Quanting the boat against the outrunning tide was heavy work, and they were glad to be able to tie up. This they did, to the rock pinnacle for which, for some time, O'Hara groped in vain.

'Sure proof the cave's what we think it is,' murmured Gascoigne. 'I wish I'd come in with you before. I'd no idea it had been such grand fun. How is she for depth, by the way?'

'Very nearly aground. We couldn't get in any further.'

'Good enough.' Gascoigne switched off the torch which he had placed on the ground to light the moorings, and put it back into his pocket. 'Let's listen a minute.'

But they could still hear nothing but the sound of the sea at the cave-mouth, and they thought it safe to use their torches again as they walked with great caution into the deep interior of the cave.

At last they found that they had penetrated beyond the tide-mark, and, as they began to ascend, there came to their nostrils the smell of petrol from the garage.

'Off torches!' whispered O'Hara. 'We're almost underneath them. Better take cover whilst we listen.'

He had already become aware of a suitable hiding-place. This had been unexpectedly provided. Since he, Mrs. Bradley and Laura had been inside the cave, three very tall packing-cases had been placed there. A man six feet high could easily take cover behind the smallest without being seen, even if he stood up on tiptoe.

'Now I wonder what's in them?' muttered Gascoigne. 'And I wonder how soon they'll be shifted? Any minute now, I suppose—or are they smugglers depending on our boat?'

'Shut up!' whispered his cousin, whose sharper ears had caught a sound unconnected with the booming of the sea. 'I think somebody's coming down from the garage above. Stand ready!'

Whilst O'Hara and Gascoigne were proving their blood and mettle, Mrs. Bradley's discreet but equally bold and mettle-some nephew, accompanied by George, Mrs. Bradley's chauffeur, had come to Slepe Rock, but had failed to contact the Irishmen, who, by this time, were out in the borrowed rowing-boat.

Denis had left the car—to George's mute regret—in a lane about a mile from the beach, and the two had come on foot to Slepe Rock. The hotel was in darkness, the inhabitants of the cottages asleep, and the road rough, stony and not at all easy to follow.

'I can't see how we get hold of these fellows,' said Denis. 'Anyhow, everything seems quiet. What do you suppose my aunt had in her mind?'

'I don't think anything definite, sir,' replied George. 'If, on the beach, we don't contact the gentlemen, I should suppose it is up to us to formulate a plan of campaign.'

'Yes, but who are the enemy, dash it? You can't campaign without an enemy. Who are the party of the other part?'

'It passes me to say, sir, but I have my suspicions of that pull-in for coaches a little further up, near the hotel. I take it that madam has told you of our geological expedition?'

'The cave? Oh, yes. All right, then, George. Look here! Let's go and break into the place, and see what we can discover. What do you say?'

'Very good, sir,' replied the sober man. 'If I may say so, it would be an anti-traumatic act, and, as such, it would please me greatly.'

'The war has altered our outlook, don't you think, George?' Denis enquired, amused and delighted by the man's acceptance of the scheme.

'Not so much altered it as enhanced it, sir, perhaps.'

'You mean we're all thugs at heart? It's very likely, and seems an inspiring thought. Anyway, here we go. Have you any suggestions to offer before we muscle up?'

'Yes, sir. I think perhaps the indirect method would be the most successful. I will go back to where we left the car, and there, with your permission, I can effect some trifling mishap to the engine. Nothing to hurt, sir, of course. Then we can put on a bold face, knock up the people at the little shack and ask for a garage hand to help us. Even if help is refused, we may

get a look at the place. It is better than a direct storming of
the beach-head, sir, I think.'

'Right, George. You go and nobble the car, then, and I'll
have a look round on the beach for those two lads of Irishmen.
I wonder where they've got to by this time? Might be anywhere. I've no idea what their plans were, if any.'

'From an elementary knowledge of the Irish temperament,
sir, I should be inclined to suppose that by this time they are
in the thick of whatever is going on. Irishmen are not so much
born to trouble, sir, as born to look for it, irrespective of
whether the sparks fly upward or not.'

George went back to the car and Denis onward to the
beach. Denis was both elated and satisfied; elated with a sense
of adventure all too seldom experienced since the war, and
satisfied with the hiding-place which he and George had
found for the iron box which had been pulled up out of the
circle of standing stones.

The beach, at first glance, seemed deserted. Then he was
aware of a groaning noise not very far to his right. He stepped
on to the dirty shingle and began to explore. It might be one
of the Irishmen in trouble, or it might be one of their victims,
he reflected. In view of the groans, he was inclined to the latter
view, and so went warily, not knowing whether he might be
ambushed as he approached.

'Where are you?' he called. 'Are you hurt?'

'Boss, there was all five of 'em. Five on to one,' groaned the
voice. 'And me not doing nothing but me plain duty, as anyone
but suckers might know.'

'Are you *hurt*?' demanded Denis.

'Boss, they've pretty near done for me, I reckon. I couldn't
'elp it if the boat was took while I was laid out bleedin' on the
beach!'

'Nonsense, man!' said Denis vigorously. 'Get up, and don't
be a fool!'

It did not surprise him to hear a scrabbling sound on the
shingle, followed by the noise of heavy boots beneath whose
impact the shingle began to shudder away.

'Where are you, boss?' asked the voice.

'Here!' said Denis, flinging himself suddenly sideways, and not too soon, for a draught past his ear was followed by a tinkle of metal falling on to the stones.

'You rat!' he said, leaping forward. The man was taken unawares. Denis was fairly light, but was young and tough. The impact with the shingle as he went to ground with his man sent pins and needles up his arm, but he had made his kill. He got up and the man stayed down.

'You beauty!' said Denis. He picked the man's head up and bounced it on the shingle for luck, and then stared out to sea to where a ship was making signals of distress.

'Hullo,' he thought, 'someone in trouble. I suppose the coastguards will spot the flares, but just in case they don't...'

He turned, wading over the shingle. It would be necessary to contact George, but the first consideration must be to give the alarm. He raced along the road to the hotel. There was no night-porter, but one of the servants, in his dressing-gown, answered the bell.

Denis cut short his announcement that it was too late to take in travellers, and informed him of the wreck. The man left him standing at the door, and hurried back into the house to arouse the landlord. He was obviously more excited than upset.

It seemed to Denis that he had done what he could for the ship, and that his duty was now to George and the car, and to Mrs. Bradley's errand. It occurred to him, too, that, if he were quick enough, he might be in time to prevent George from disabling the engine, for it would be easy enough to arouse the whole village, the men at the pull-in included, with the news of a wreck in the bay. From Denis reading he had deduced that such tidings brought every soul in the village on to the beach, if only to salvage the cargo. He was anxious to avoid putting the car out of action unnecessarily, for it was not good tactics, he felt, for George and himself to handicap their chances of escape by nobbling their own transport. He was light on his feet and in good shape. He ran up the road at twelve miles an hour, and caught George before the latter had reached the car.

He gave him the news. George, glad enough to leave the car intact, for she was his pride and joy, returned with him to the pull-in. There was no doubt of the excitement in the small village at the news of the wreck, but when Denis hammered at the door of the shack a light went on, and a fully-dressed man with a smear of white across the sleeve of his dark blue suit, opened up with an oath, and demanded to know what in hell had gone wrong now. Denis was greatly disappointed to find the place still occupied, but he spoke up cheerfully.

'All right! All right! There's a ship on the rocks in the bay. Can you go and help?—or tell me whom to send?'

'Get out, you——!' said the man, as he slammed the door. George pulled at Denis' arm.

'Come on, sir,' he said. 'That fellow has come from the cave. Did you spot the limestone on his sleeve? They're running the stuff to-night, whatever it is. I should think we could leave 'em to the coastguards. They'll never get by if boats are all going off to a ship in distress. They're absolutely sure to be spotted, and smuggling was one thing that madam suspected from here.'

'I *do* want to see that inspection-pit in the garage of the pull-in,' said Denis, with deceptive mildness. 'Come on, George. Let's go. Even the wreck may be a put-up job. I wouldn't put much past the brains of men that my aunt thinks it's worth while to try and outwit, don't you know,'

Shaking his head in a middle-aged manner which indicated that he thought the plan ill-advised, George followed him across the yard to where stood the double doors of the garage belonging to the pull-in.

'Now,' said Denis, producing a small electric torch, 'I wonder how much one can see?' He shone the torch into the crack between the double doors, and tried to squint through the opening.

'Dash!' he began; but he stopped at the sound of a whistle.

'Look out, sir!' said George. Both shot away from the doors and took cover at the side of the garage. At the same instant a broad shaft of light came across the yard from the shack. A man stood silhouetted against the light as the door was flung open, and the whistle apparently was still at his lips, for he blew it before the man who had opened to Denis' knock reached out and pulled him inside again. The door of the shack slammed shut, and the yard was in darkness once more.

'Now's our chance, sir, I think!' muttered George. 'They'll be out here again in a minute.' He drew a large file from his pocket, inserted one end between the doors of the garage and gave a sinewy jerk. The doors came open towards him. He and Denis went in, and Denis pulled the doors to.

'Odd they weren't padlocked,' he said.

'Lends colour to what we think, sir,' George responded. 'They get to the cave this way, and back to the shack. The mistress imagined—here's the inspection pit, you see, sir—that the little cottage which stood here used to have a cellar, and that the cellar was connected with the cave.'

'Then the cottage itself originally formed part of an inn, I daresay,' said Denis. 'A cottage would hardly have a cellar. It's not as though it's built on a hill. Come on, George, let's go down.' He looked into the empty pit. 'It's obvious it's still a cellar. Look, you can see the steps.'

'I would suggest, sir,' said George, 'that you don't venture into that rat-trap minus the means of self-defence. Here, sir, catch hold of this spanner. I've got my big file for myself. I think . . .'

'Hands up!' said a voice from the doorway.

'Jump, sir!' said George, suiting his own actions to this advice, and disappearing with some suddenness from view.

Chapter Twenty

★

'Alas, dear sir . . . yonder lies the granite rock where all the costly diamonds grow.'

Ibid. (*The Salad*)

THE strange sounds heard by O'Hara were those of Denis and George descending into the cave. The jump into the inspection pit had been a strategic measure calculated to confuse the enemy, but it could not do more than throw him mentally off-balance for a moment or two.

This moment on which George had counted was lengthened by several seconds whilst the man fired six shots after them into the pit, but the opening into the cave was under the right-hand side of the hole and they had ducked in before the second shot was fired.

Regardless of what might be ahead of them, they switched on torches and were soon on a flight of stone steps which led down to a long ramp and ended in front of the packing-cases in the cave.

The Irishmen, from their hiding-place, were astounded to hear Denis' voice, as he called back to George:

'I can't see a thing, and heaven knows what we do next. Hide somewhere, I suppose, and put up a fight if we're followed. I'm not so sure I think much of our chances, you know.'

'Oh, I don't know,' said O'Hara, shining his torch. 'Here are two good men to come to the aid of the party.'

There was mutual recognition and rejoicing, and adventurous accounts were exchanged among the three young men whilst the middle-aged one, working in silence, removed first the twine and then a board from the packing-case behind which he sheltered to find out what was inside.

'Can't think why nobody followed us down,' said Denis.

'If the chap fired six shots he's had to reload, I expect, and that may have meant returning to the shack. If that's where he went, I expect he's taking counsel with the fellow whose boat we've borrowed, and whom you laid out,' said Gascoigne. 'I should think that bloke's had a sticky evening, throttled by Mike, beaten up by his pals and then knocked out by you. By the way, what's happened to George?'

'Sir,' said George, 'I have succeeded in prising open one of these packing-cases with my file. I think that, whilst we are still undisturbed, we should look to see what is inside. I feel that madam would be interested.'

Before he had concluded these observations the young men were shining their torches into the packing-case.

'Good Lord!' said Denis. 'The thing's full of pictures, I think! Framed pictures, too, by the feel of them. Here, let's have one out.'

'Pictures?' said O'Hara, doubtfully regarding the object drawn forth by Denis.

'Yes, of course. Done up in sacking and packed between shavings. You can feel the edges of the frames. It must be pictures. No one would smuggle mirrors out of the country. Besides, this isn't heavy enough for glass. They're oils, I suppose. I wonder what's the idea?'

Scarcely had he spoken when there was the sound of persons descending from the garage, and at the same time there were shouts (from the mouth of the cave) which came booming in the ears of the listeners.

The young men and George crouched low and prepared for battle. George had his file, a tasty weapon in skilled hands; O'Hara depended upon his fists; Gascoigne was limbering up, in a surreptitious way behind his packing-case, a limb of Attic shapeliness whose merit, as he saw it, was its ability to deliver, when called upon to do so, a French kick in the face; the wiry Denis was still possessed of George's spanner, and had taken off his jacket and rolled up his sleeves.

There was a considerable amount of confusion at the mouth of the cave. The boat left by Gascoigne and O'Hara was in the way of the motor boat which was bringing the enemy in, and an argument was in progress which came, with sound and fury, but without recognizable words, hollowly to the young men and George.

Suddenly down the ramp at the landward end, from the garage, appeared two men, the second one carrying a lantern. O'Hara leapt out and smashed his fist into the first face. Denis went for the lantern and knocked it out of the second man's hand by tapping him hard on the elbow with the spanner. George, with a neat flick, smacked his file across the side of the fellow's neck, and then Denis pulled out a whistle and blew three police blasts on it.

The effect on the men at the mouth of the cave was instantaneous. There was a bellowing sound suggestive of panic-stricken orders. The next moment the engine of the motor boat was started up again and the enemy put back to sea.

'You've spoilt the fight!' grumbled Gascoigne, picking up the twine which had been tied round one of the packing-cases, and kneeling by the prisoners to secure them.

'Can't help that,' said Denis, who was practical. 'Our job is to get these packing-cases away before any more of those chaps turn up. The thing is, what to do with these two fellows.'

'I've frisked them, sir,' said George, who was helping Denis. 'You'd better take their guns.' He handed these over.

Behind an ubiquitous hedge Laura and Mrs. Bradley were deciding which of them should go to the police and which should remain to watch the cartshed.

Morning was broadening before they came to any conclusion, but Laura had her own way, in the end, and remained in hiding whilst her employer walked back towards the stones on her way to the village of Upper Deepening from which the buses went to Cuchester and to Welsea Beaches.

Mrs. Bradley took the Welsea bus with the intention of

contacting the nearest police station. Laura, left alone, prowled restlessly up and down the hedge, keeping low so as not to be seen above it, and prayed that adventure might follow.

It did, in dramatic fashion, for at just after eight o'clock by Laura's wristwatch a small lorry drove into the farmyard from out of the wood and pulled up opposite the cartshed.

'They're going to remove the evidence,' thought Laura. 'Mrs. Croc. knew it, and that's why she wanted to stay. Now what should I do for the best?'

With Laura, deeds came an easy first and planning a fairish second. Almost before the question had presented itself, she was crawling towards the gap in the hedge where the gate was, and then, rising to her feet, switch in hand, was strolling carelessly down the hill towards the farm.

It was soon certain that her presence had been perceived, for, at the bottom of the hill, where the ploughland gave way to the farmyard, stood a nonchalant man with a piece of grass in his mouth who stepped out in front of her and said:

'No way through here, miss. Back the way you come, if you don't mind.'

'Oh, rot!' said Laura boldly. 'I've been this way dozens of times.' Without further argument she walked on. The man jumped ahead of her.

'I said you can't come this way!' he said, speaking sharply.

'But why not?' asked Laura, stopping. 'Has the farm changed hands or something? Nobody stopped me before.'

'Well, I'm stopping you now,' said the man. Laura shrugged and turned away. Mrs. Bradley, she sadly decided, would have thought of a dozen ways of dealing successfully with this sort of thing. She herself could think of nothing except the possibility of turning round suddenly and poking the man in the eye with the switch she had cut from the hedge. But that, although desirable from one point of view (for she disliked the man very much, and resented his victory over her), would scarcely, in the long run, have helped her very much, and this she realized.

She thought fast when once she had turned about, and then, as though she were hurrying from sheer bad temper, she tore up the hill at top speed. When she reached the boundaries of her hedge she still stalked on. When she knew that the man could no longer see her, she swung off in a slant and followed the line of the hedge to where the pasture ended and the dark woods met the arable land beyond. There she slid into cover like an wolf, and paused to survey the landscape.

She was on the edge of the circular wood beyond the farm-yard, and had soon descended past the disused Army hut and into the winding lane. She turned towards the farm-buildings, but was in time to retreat into the wood and see the small lorry drive away. It had to pass her, and, as it slowed at the bend (for the lane was extremely narrow), she was able to ascertain, from her position among the thick trees, that only one man was in it. Automatically she registered the number on the back, and then she came into the road and began to run.

What her intention was she scarcely knew. Instinctively she felt that she had to find out whither the lorry was bound, and whether the head and hands had been put aboard it.

By the time she had rounded the bend the lorry had gone. She toiled on until she came to the house with the four dead trees. The telegraph wires to the house gave her inspiration.

She went in at the first entrance she came to, and knocked on the door. The teak-countenanced Sorensen opened it. He scowled when he saw her, and said very briefly:

'No admittance!'

'I know! I know!' said Laura hurriedly. 'But I've got to use your telephone. May I come in? Where is it?'

To her surprise, the man made way for her at once, and then, overtaking her, guided her along the passage and opened the door of the office. Laura went in, found the room empty, seized the telephone, called up the police in Cuchester and gave the number of the lorry. The sound of the key being turned in the lock of the door did not perturb her.

'To do any real good, they ought to have cut the telephone wires,' she thought. 'Anyway, I'm on the ground floor.'

She rang up the police again, and informed them that she was a prisoner at Cottam's. Then she hung up, and walked across to the window. Outside was young Sisyphus Cassius with a short, thick, ugly cosh in his hand. He swung it and grinned nastily at her. He had not, it was clear, forgotten the morning on the beach, in spite of his attempt to redeem himself. Laura opened the window.

'I wouldn't risk it,' said Ivor. 'The film people are all on location. Had early breakfast and went off by lorry and in cars, all the whole boiling of them. There's nobody here but you and me and the fellow who let you in, and he won't interfere. My dad has him where he wants him.'

'You wretched little thug!' said Laura. She would have said more, but at that moment the door opened and Sorensen put in his head.

'I wouldn't give him much chance to use the cosh,' he said, almost kindly. 'The police might as well find you all in one piece, don't you think?'

'Agreed,' said Laura. She sauntered away from the window. Sorensen shut the door in her face and locked it from the outside, and she heard him walk away. Laura looked round the room for a weapon, and suddenly found herself face to face with her own portrait, which was hanging on the wall beside the fireplace. She studied it with great interest, for she realized, almost immediately, that this was not the portrait for which she had sat, but a very inferior copy.

Laura, although headstrong and rash, was highly intelligent. She could put two and two together as fast and as accurately as most people, and she put two and two together now. That David Battle was in some way associated with the men who had a morbid interest in the Nine Stones had been a tenable theory for some time past. That there was some connection between these men and the house with the four dead trees was an equally acceptable hypothesis. That the art of painting was inextricably bound up with the mysterious disappearances of three men could be argued with some success. That the man who had ordered the pulling out of the leaning stone was capable, if not of murder, at least of deeds in cold blood which Laura still shuddered to remember, had been proved by his strange and horrible removal of the head and hands of the man whom the vengeful stone had fallen upon and killed.

'*Ergo*,' said Laura, 'there's something dashed funny about the business of copying my portrait—apart, of course, from the fact that the subject-matter is quite funny, I suppose, in itself. Now how do those frames Mrs. Bradley spotted at David Battle's fit in?'

She swung round at the sound of the door being opened again. This time, to her great surprise, Sorensen said (and still in his former friendly tones):

'You'd better run along now; we're done with you for a bit.'

'Thank you,' Laura replied. She followed him out of the room, and was meditating whether it would be possible (and, if possible, whether it would also be useful) to leap on his neck from the back as they walked in Indian file down the passage, when he forestalled any experiments on her part by swinging round on her and blocking up the passage with his heavy frame, as he said:

'Now then, no nonsense!' To Laura, conversant as she was with Mrs. Bradley's theories of unrehearsed behaviour, this remark was a sign of fear. She looked the man in the eye.

'Now then, no hysterics,' she said. 'I'm going quietly, aren't I?' Sorensen did not reply. He merely turned quickly and led the way towards the side door.

'Get out!' he said. 'And as quick as ever you can.'

'Why?' enquired Laura. 'Surely you're not afraid of the police?'

'Get out!' he repeated stubbornly. 'We did not ask you to come.' Laura did not wait to be told a third time, but, as the front door opened, she saw a shadow move upon the wall. Sorensen laughed as he slammed the door. Laura swung herself aside, and, as the cosh ascended, ready to be brought down across her skull, she turned and caught young Cassius a full-arm back-hander across the nose and mouth, and then flung herself upon him. There was the dull impact of body upon body, and the advantage lay with Laura.

She was heavier than her adversary and had the whip hand of the situation, which she had diagnosed with savage swiftness. Sisyphus went down, with her on top. Dazed and bruised, nevertheless she recovered first, and, picking up the cosh which he had dropped, she hurled it over the tops of the nearest trees.

'Now, you little beast, I'm going to scrag you properly, once and for all,' she said. She forgot Sorensen, still in the house. Her blood was up. She fell upon the hapless Sisyphus, punched him hard in the wind, and, as he sagged, she smacked her hand hard across his eyes. A boxing brother had taught her, and a natural gift for in-fighting helped out the teaching. It was not a pretty spectacle which she left blubbering on the unweeded gravel path.

'You filthy little beast!' she said.

As she sped through the gate she heard a curdled, ancient laughter, and realized that the old man with the barrow (in which he was now taking his ease) had been a delighted spectator of Ivor Cassius' (or Concaverty's) downfall.

'So what?' thought Laura, trotting happily back along the road. 'Whose side are *you* on, Gunga Din?'

Chapter Twenty-One

★

'The wolf and the wild boar were first on the ground: and when they spied their enemies coming, and saw the cat's long tail standing straight in the air, they thought she was carrying a sword.'
Ibid. (*Old Sultan*)

T HE packing-cases full of pictures presented a difficult problem. The young men discussed its solution and came to the conclusion that the best plan was to rush the packing-cases up the ramp to the garage and get them into the village street. There they could be guarded (at the point of the revolver if necessary) until transport could be arranged for them to Cuchester, where the whole matter must be left to the police.

'And I only hope we haven't committed a felony,' said Denis, grinning. 'Now, who's doing the haulage work, and who's covering our retreat?'

'Gerry is probably the best shot,' said O'Hara, 'unless it's you, Bradley?'

'Lord, no. Come on, then, George,' said Denis. 'O'Hara, you fight a rearguard action, if necessary, with the other gun.'

'Queer they hadn't the guns in their hands when they came down after us,' said Gascoigne. 'I suppose they thought we'd run straight into the party from the motor boat, and they might hit one of their own side if they fired.'

It was dawn by the time they reached the pull-in yard with the packing-cases, and at sight of the empty lorry Denis suggested that they might as well load the packing-cases on to it and drive them into Cuchester straight away.

'The lorry must have brought them here,' he argued, 'so I don't see why it shouldn't take them back.' This simple solution pleased everybody, and was about to be put into effect when into the yard ran three men.

'Hello! Re'enter the spivs!' said O'Hara. Gascoigne also recognized the newcomers, and, taking the gun in his hand, he waved it in ironic greeting. The spivs betrayed no surprise and no resentment.

'Hey! Going towards London?' yelled the foremost. 'Give us a lift, will you, boys?'

'Cuchester!' shouted Denis. George let in his clutch, and the lorry moved slowly forward towards the entrance.

'That'll do fine!' yelled the second of the men, moving out of the way as the lorry came out at the opening. The three men then hung on and tried to climb on to the tailboard, but Denis delicately stamped on the fingers of one, a Rugger shove in the chest from the large-palmed O'Hara settled the fate of the second, and a smack across the eyes from Gascoigne foiled the venturous tactics of the third. The last the lorry pirates saw of the wasp-waisted visitors was one on his back in the dust, another dabbing his nose with a bright silk handkerchief and the stamped-on one shaking be-ringed fists with histrionic gestures of hate and fury at the tailboard from which he had been dislodged.

'I shouldn't have told them Cuchester,' said Denis. 'I don't think they have any connection whatever with the other lot, but we've annoyed them now, and they'll give away our destination to anybody who happens to ask for it.'

The road from Slepe Rock to Cuchester was winding, hilly and lonely, and it was among what seemed the first created countryside that George left the road he was following and turned off down a lane which looked as though it ended in a river. Just before it reached the water, however, an ancient cattle-road, deep with hoof-marks and oleaginous with mire, turned off round the flank of a hill, and in this surprising spot the lorry drew up.

'How come, George?' enquired Denis, who, after the contest with the spivs, had seated himself beside the driver whilst the Irishmen, nursing their guns, lay bumpily asprawl among the cargo. 'This ain't the way to Cuchester!'

'No, sir,' George replied, unearthing and unfolding a map. 'But to the best of my knowledge and belief, my tank's nearly dry, and it's better to remain in hiding than to break down in a lonely spot on a motor-road. Those fellows won't let us get away with these packing-cases without a struggle, and, with your permission, I'm going back to the road to see their car go by. Then I can foot-slog it after them into Cuchester and bring out the police to this lorry.'

'And, from all points of view, not at all a bad scheme,' said Denis. 'You mean that even if we'd had the petrol we'd hardly have outdistanced them to Cuchester?'

'Well, it's hard to determine that, sir, but the decision—mercifully, perhaps, as you suggest—is out of our hands. I will return and let you know when they pass, sir, before I commence my walk.'

'Well, look here,' exclaimed Denis, 'let *me* walk! Dash it, I'm younger than you!'

'True, sir,' said George impassively, 'but, if I may say so, the known tendency of the police to view with suspicion the humoristic tendencies of young College gentlemen, sir, leads me to presuppose that my story might be received at the Cuchester police station with more credulence and with less embarrassment to the narrator than your own, sir.'

Denis was compelled to agree with this reasonable and tactfully-worded exposition, and said reluctantly:

'You think the police would imagine I was pulling their legs, eh? Yes, there's something in that. All right, carry on, George, and God bless you!'

George had a further reason for selecting himself as victim. He had a shrewd suspicion that the mealy-mouthed and rather impressive Mr. Cassius, with his air of breeding, his respectable grey hairs and his impeccable clothing and manners, might, if he reached the Cuchester police station first—as, with a fast car, he was almost bound to do, once the angry spivs had mentioned the destination of the lorry—he *might*, thought George (stepping out with an infantryman's marching ryhthm) have lodged a complaint with the police of such a nature that whoever came in behind him with news of the lorry would inevitably find himself held for police questioning.

George had that old-fashioned conception of a wage-earner's

loyalty to an employer which socialism has done so well, no doubt, to deflect, emasculate and destroy. He saw it as his plain duty to provide the police with their victim in the form of his own person rather than in that of Mrs. Bradley's nephew, and was cheerfully prepared to be detained at, and, if necessary, incarcerated in, Cuchester police station. *Noblesse oblige* was not George's family motto, but it was his philosophy where his employer was concerned.

Before he commenced his preliminary task, that of watching for a car containing Mr. Cassius (or any other of the men who had been associated so far with the enquiry) to go by, George cut from among the reeds by the water's edge a fan of leaves, flowers and stems with which, when he returned to the junction of the main road with the turning he had taken, he could sweep away the traces of the lorry's wheels, for where the lane left the Cuchester road there was a sandy surface, and this continued round the first of the bends. With the tracks in the muddy cattle walk he could do nothing, but this did not matter so long as the passing car went straight on past the turning without the occupants realizing that the lorry was no longer ahead of them. Even if Mr. Cassius-Concaverty stopped to work out the simple mathematical evidence of time, distance and pace it was likely, George thought, that he would believe that the spivs had been mistaken in the exact minute when the lorry had been driven out of the yard. The chances were that Mr. Cassius, intent upon retrieving his pictures before it was too late, would not enter into any calculations at all, but would drive hell-for-leather after the spoil. This was exactly what he did.

Pleased with this proof of a criminal's psychology, George returned to the lorry, acquainted the young men with the news that the car had passed the turning, and then set out for Cuchester. Denis, Gascoigne and O'Hara took out pipes and indulged in undergraduate speculations upon art, life, sex, politics, ratting in barns, trout-fishing, salmon-fishing, music-hall stars they wished they had seen, Ellen Terry, George Bernard Shaw, religion, the Norfolk Broads, and other subjects upon which it was equally possible for all to talk at once and none to listen.

By the time they had exploited these themes, the police arrived and took them and the lorry in charge. Mr. Cassius, it seemed, had claimed his own, but, pending further enquiries, had not yet been permitted to take the pictures away.

Mrs. Bradley performed her errand of reporting to the police at Welsea Beaches, and then she telephoned the Chief Constable, waking him, to his peevish annoyance, from his light, pleasant sleep of the early morning.

'You ought to be up and about,' said Mrs. Bradley firmly. 'Now get out of bed at once, and come and see me. I've all sorts of things to tell you, and your Superintendent at Welsea will have things all his own way if you don't come along and begin to order him about.'

'But what mare's-nest have you got for us this time?'

'A dead body, of course. Two, as a matter of fact, only one was murdered and the other was killed accidentally. Still, you ought to be on the spot. The Druids have danced.'

Upon this infuriatingly mysterious information she hung up and caught the next bus back to Upper Deepening. There was an excellent early morning service of country buses between Welsea and the villages that way, because of a large factory two miles the other side of Cuchester which had been transferred there at the beginning of the war and had not, so far, returned to its base.

Laura's adventures had taken less time than Mrs. Bradley's travels and telephoning, and she was already back in position behind the hedge before her employer arrived. She gave an account of herself and was warmly congratulated.

'I thought you'd be mad,' said Laura candidly. 'I felt an awful idiot, getting boxed up at Cottam's like that. Still, all's well that ends well, I suppose. Do you think the police have got that little van by now?'

'Do you imagine that you would have been allowed to telephone the numbers on its plates if the driver had not intended to change them, child?'

'Oh!' said Laura, considerably dashed by this hypothesis. 'So I've done no good after all!'

'You have relieved your feelings about little Cassius-Concaverty,' Mrs. Bradley pointed out. 'Unsatisfied longings may easily lead to a state of trauma. This you will now escape.'

'I certainly gave the little thug a pasting,' agreed Laura, with satisfaction. 'Still, it hasn't helped the enquiry.'

'It has not hindered it, child. And we should not have been able to stop the lorry, in any case. I confess that I had not thought they would need to remove the identifiable portions of the dead man quite so soon. It sounds as though there have been deep doings at Slepe Rock, and thither I think we should repair as soon as we have breakfasted.'

'Anything you like. Come on, then. Dead men or no dead men, I could eat a horse.'

'What I like about you,' said Mrs. Bradley, 'is your genius for putting first things first.'

They got back to Welsea half an hour after the arrival of the Chief Constable, and discovered him in a fine mixed state of anxiety and fury.

'Where on earth have you been, Adela?' he demanded. 'I thought you were here! You might have been murdered yourself, for all I knew!'

'For all you know, I might be yet,' retorted Mrs. Bradley. 'Come and have breakfast with us, and I'll tell you all you want to know.'

By the time the meal and the recital were concluded, the Chief Constable's ill-humour had given place to surprise and interest.

'Faked pictures, you say? And possibly some stolen Old Masters? We can check up on all that, of course. I'll get an expert from the National Gallery at once. But the deaths! The deaths! How do you know it is Allwright?'

'I don't. I'm relying on you to prove it. It seems to me that it must be, and I think we've got the body for you to see.'

'Really! Good heavens! Where is it?'

'I haven't the faintest idea.'

'Oh, good heavens, Adela! Don't play the fool! *Where is it?*'

'I tell you that I don't know. I gave it to my nephew.'

'Now, look here . . .' said the Chief Constable dangerously.

'But I *did!* He went off with it, he and George, and, until I contact them again, I don't know where they've hidden it. But please don't worry. You shall have it.'

'Then where is Denis now?'

'He's gone to Slepe,' said Mrs. Bradley, with an innocent expression.

'Gone to *sleep?*'

'Well, I'm very much afraid so, which means, of course, that we shall have to go and find him. I do know that he was going to Slepe, but I shouldn't think he took the body with him. Still, there's another body you *could* see. That's the one that was killed accidentally . . . unless you think the Druids did it on purpose, which would not surprise me in the least.'

'That I should think it?'

'That it should happen. We still know far too little about the religious beliefs of pre-history, don't you feel?'

The Chief Constable, in hasty rather than in well-chosen words, consigned the religious beliefs of pre-history to a religious belief of the mediæval Church. He got up from table as soon as Mrs. Bradley rose, and stamped about in the hotel vestibule whilst she and her secretary prepared themselves for an excursion less exacting than the one which they had undertaken over-night.

'So!' said the Chief Constable, brought face to face, although hardly literally, with the headless, handless corpse. Laura, who did not want to see it, remained at a safe distance. 'Now what's all this about, I wonder?'

'I should think that the man was a local person, or, at any rate, easily recognizable locally,' said Mrs. Bradley.

'Ah! His death would lead us to the rest of the gang? Yes, I see. Yes, that must be it. Horrid fellers!' said the Chief Constable, turning away. 'You've told the Welsea police, you say? Well, they ought to have been here by now!'

As though these words were their cue, the Welsea police, in the person of their Superintendent, a sergeant ‧and four constables, appeared at this point over the brow of the hill complete with haulage tackle for removing the stone from the body.

'Got the doctor coming right away, sir,' said the Superintendent, in reply to a question from the Chief Constable. 'An accident, so we understand.'

'Yes. Mrs. Bradley here, who gave you the information, is a material witness,' said the Chief Constable. 'Well, you might as well carry on, Ellis. Not that the doctor can do anything. Still, you'd better carry on according to pattern. Now, Beatrice what about this nephew of yours and the other body you promised me? Ellis, I think you'd better put Fielding on to all that.'

'I beg pardon, sir,' said the Superintendent, 'but we've had a message through from Cuchester to know if we can find anybody to identify a certain Mr. Denis Bradley who's being held there, with another three men and a stolen lorry full of crates of pictures, pending a complaint from a Mr. Cassius that the pictures belong to him and that he claims them.'

'So they got them!' said Laura, who had heard the Superintendent's remarks from where she was standing in the ditch which surrounded the stone circle. 'Good old Denis! And good old Mike! And good old Gerry! And good old George! Whoopee!'

'Laura! Behave!' said Mrs. Bradley urgently. 'Don't incriminate us!'

'Come, come!' said the Chief Constable ill-temperedly.

'Yes, let us all come,' Mrs. Bradley agreed. 'It is more than time. I don't suppose those boys or my poor George have had any breakfast.'

Mr. Cassius was full of his woes, and tackled the Chief Constable as soon as the latter arrived at Cuchester police station.

'I recognize these two men!' he said, waving .towards Gascoigne and O'Hara. 'They've been dogging me for this very purpose! They even had the colossal impudence to put up at the same hotel at Slepe Rock.'

'There is only the one hotel at Slepe Rock,' Mrs. Bradley soothingly pointed out. 'They could hardly have used any other.'

'They've stolen my property, anyway, and I'll prosecute to the top of my bent!' said Mr. Cassius. 'You know, Sir Crimmond, it's a most disgraceful thing if a man of my standing cannot claim back his own property without being detained here like this by your policemen! I've a good mind to have a question asked in the House!'

'Perhaps I'd better hear what these fellows have to say, Mr. Cassius,' observed the Chief Constable. 'By the way, have you changed your name since you let Cottam's to the Gonn-Brown film company for the summer?'

'Changed my name? Certainly not!' Mr. Cassius replied with spirit. 'Cassius happens to be my business name, that is all. I used it in making myself known to your policemen in order to establish my title to those pictures. I deal in pictures, and I trade under the name of Cassius. My real name, as you perfectly well know, is Rufus Concaverty.'

'Ah,' said the Chief Constable. This, it seemed, was too non-committal a rejoinder to suit the claimant to the pictures.

'I dare those men to tell you how they came by my property,' he said. 'If they do dare, you will hear a story of assault and battery which will shake your faith in the public school system, Sir Crimmond.'

'Well, hardly. You see, I'm a product of it myself,' said the Chief Constable, with most unusual mildness. Ill-tempered always in his affectionate dealings with Mrs. Bradley, he was smoothness itself to Mr. Cassius, whom, it was plain, he disliked very much indeed. "Now, let's hear what you have to say for yourselves,' he added, looking at the three young men and George.

'If I might venture, sir?' said George.

'Yes, of course, man. You're the oldest. Carry on,' said Sir Crimmond, who knew George well, and respected him.

'Thank you, sir. The matter fell out as follows:'

'Take a note, Superintendent,' said the Chief Constable to that officer, who, supported by the sergeant, was burning to get in a word.

Oh, we have the whole story, sir,' said the Superintendent.

'Naturally.' ('What the hell do you think we've been doing?'
he added under his breath.)

'Never mind. You can check it against what they're going
to tell us now,' observed Sir Crimmond.

'Take a note, sergeant,' said the Superintendent angrily.
'He can write shorthand, sir,' he added, to cover himself
against any act of disobedience.

'All right. Now, George—er—now you,' said the Chief
Constable.

'George, sir?' said the Superintendent disagreeably.

'Proceeding, as per instructions, to drive Mr. Denis to Slepe
Rock, sir,' George began, ignoring the fact that the Chief
Constable had been addressed.

'What, at that time of night!' said Cassius.

'I did not mention that it was at night,' said George. 'Might
I have leave, sir,' he added, with earnest dignity, to the Chief
Constable, 'to give my account without any but the official
interruptions?'

'Certainly,' the Chief Constable replied. 'Mr. Cassius, you
will not improve your case if you do not allow this man to
speak. You may question his story afterwards.'

'I was proceeding according to schedule,' continued George,
'when I heard a party or parties by the nine stones they call
the Druids. Actuated by curiosity, I became aware that there
was something amiss, and, on looking into the matter, I
discovered that a person unknown to me had been killed by
reason of one of the stones tumbling down on top of him. The
removal of the head and hands of the defunct party by some
of the interested persons led me to believe that a crime of some
magnitude had been in progress . . .'

'*What!*' shrieked Cassius. 'You dare to stand there telling the
police those lies!'

'But they're not lies,' said the Chief Constable smoothly.
'I've seen the body myself. *Somebody* didn't intend that the
corpse should be identified. That is abundantly clear. The
police have the corpse at the mortuary by now, I imagine.
I think, Mr. Cassius, that you had better be very careful.'

Cassius for the first time looked unsure of himself. His eyes glanced towards the door, as though he half-thought of making a dash from the room. The heavy young constable standing near it met his glance with such coldness, however, that he thought better of the impulse, if he had had it, and merely asked:

'Well, but what's all this to do with my stolen pictures?'

'All in good time, sir,' said George, with a snake-like benevolence worthy of his employer herself. 'And if I might *not* be interrupted . . .?'

'Look here, Cassius, you'll have to be taken away to another room if you can't let the fellow finish,' observed the Chief Constable. 'Dash it, we shall be all day at this rate. And you, George—er—get a move on.'

'Driving Mr. Denis on to Slepe Rock, the occurrences aforementioned being no business of ours, sir, until we were in a position to report them to the police,' continued George, 'we decided we had need of a garage. Being loth to knock up the hotel people at so late an hour—for you must understand, sir, that we did not get to Slepe Rock until after midnight—we essayed the garage attached to, and/or erected upon, the yard where the lorries and motor coaches pull in during the daytime.'

'Yes, yes, man! Get on!'

'We knocked at the door of the shack and were met by a man with a revolver who chased us towards the garage, the doors of which were unlocked. To escape our assailant—presumably a man *non compos mentis*—we leapt into the inspection pit and proceeded to descend a flight of steps to a kind of cellar beneath it. In the cellar, which debouches on to a cave with a seaward entrance, we came upon these packing-cases which Mr. Cassius claims to be his property. And if Mr. Cassius will explain how they came to be down there, and why he has gunmen to guard them, then I am willing to be questioned by him as to the truth or otherwise of my story; and if not, not,' said George with finality; adding, as a courteous afterthought, 'by your leave, Sir Crimmond, sir.'

'You mean you haven't told the truth?' thundered the Chief Constable.

'I mean I have told the truth in a slightly camouflaged form, sir,' George replied. 'It would hardly do to put all our cards on the table, since it seems likely that Mr. Cassius will be charged with murder before he's through.'

'*Murder!*' said Cassius, curling his lip. 'Don't you dare to use such a word in connection with me!' But his face had gone greasy and his eyes looked anywhere but at George. 'What in hell are you talking about?'

'He is talking about Mr. Allwright,' said Mrs. Bradley. 'I think I'd like to take up the story myself.' And she recounted to the dry-lipped Cassius the things she had seen and heard at the Stone Circle of the Druids.

'Do you deny that your collection of pictures consists partly of stolen property and partly of clever fakes?' she concluded.

Cassius had nothing to say for more than a minute.

'You'll never pin murder on me,' he muttered at last. 'And those pictures are my property. And the fellow's death was an accident. If you saw it, you know that as well as I do.'

'You'd better caution this man and arrest him, Superintendent,' said the Chief Constable. 'There's obviously something behind all this, and it won't do for us to let him slip through our fingers.'

'You can't arrest me! What for? I'll sue you for this!' shouted Cassius, struggling under the iron hand of the Superintendent which was now upon his shoulder.

'George,' said Mrs. Bradley, some hours later, 'where did you learn the art which conceals art?'

'At Army courts-martial, madam,' replied the imperturbable man.

'*You*, George? Court-martialled? I have never heard anything of this!'

'Yes, madam. Once. I have also been called as a witness, but only once have I had to play the principal rôle.'

'But, George! I've never been so much intrigued since Henri was run in at Bow Street for biting an unknown woman on the shoulder on Peace Night! What were you court-martialled for?—or can't you discuss the subject?'

'I called my officer a bloody monkey, madam.'

'You—oh, George, *no!* Whatever had he done to deserve it?'

'He had called me a something basket, madam.'

'And what had *you* done to deserve that?'

'I had no-balled him three times running in an inter-Company cricket match, madam, a feat of umpiring which he did not appreciate.'

'And how many days C.B. did you get for it, George? I can't imagine you incarcerated for insolence.'

'I was discharged, madam, without a stain on my character.'

'Good heavens, George! Discharged! For . . .'

'I upheld a son's right to defend the good name of his mother, and won the day. The presiding officer had just been apprised of the birth of his first child, a boy, madam. I was aware of this fact, and prepared my defence accordingly.'

'Strategy, George, with a vengeance!'

'One should always reconnoitre the terrain, madam, before deciding upon one's tactics.'

'Well, old Cassius-Concaverty won't get a chance to reconnoitre much terrain,' said Laura, who had just come in. 'How are you going to pin the murder on him, Mrs. Bradley?'

'Mrs. Croc. to you,' said the saurian, sunnily. 'And the answer to that is that I haven't the faintest idea. Besides, our first task must be to have the two Battles arrested as well. They are sharers in Concaverty's guilt, although to what extent I cannot tell at the moment.'

'But we don't even know for certain that the older Battle is still alive!'

'We must get the younger Battle to swear to him when we have caught him. I have hopes that that can be managed.'

'Not if they're in this together! He wouldn't incriminate himself.'

'I am under the impression, child, that he would even go so far as to hang himself if he could get his father hanged, too.'

'But what makes you think——?'

'I will tell you all about it. I shan't need the car after tea, George. Take the evening off and have too much to drink. I feel I've missed the cream of you. Court-martialled for insolence! Dear, dear! And why couldn't you give your name to the Superintendent? Didn't you perceive how embarrassing it was for Sir Crimmond to have to keep calling you George?'

'I am sorry, madam, but I have recently changed my name, to be ratified by Deed Poll shortly, and I have not yet accustomed myself to the sound in public of the new one.'

'And what *is* the new one?' asked Laura, who invariably rushed in where Mrs. Bradley feared to tread.

'Cuddle-Up, miss, with a hyphen,' said George, with a wooden expression.

'*What!*' said Mrs. Bradley and Laura, speaking in unison.

'Yes, madam. On account of the Sex. They pursue me. I have been badgered once too often. Don't, please, misunderstand me, miss,' he added, turning to Laura, 'but the fact is that young women are apt to think twice before making up their minds to be called Mrs. George Cuddle-Up. It makes for awkwardness.'

'True,' Mrs. Bradley agreed, not daring to look at Laura who was showing signs of incipient hysteria. 'But how will you explain to the authorities why you wish to change to such a name? I should think they are certain to ask.'

'On the basis of being left a legacy, madam. Not for nothing did Mr. Milne write *Wurzel-Flummery.*'

'But, George, you chump, that defeats your argument!' shouted Laura. 'The name *Wurzel-Flummery* did *not* act as a deterrent! And the legacy will attract the girls!'

'And, George,' said Mrs. Bradley, 'pause and consider. What will you do when you leave my employment and seek another situation? Your expectation of life is considerably greater than my own. Have you thought that not only a wife but also another employer may be of the opinion that the name Cuddle-Up is not the sort of thing to call after a man in public?'

'I confess, madam, that the thought had not crossed my mind,' said George, looking slightly less austere.

'Then give it a chance, George, to do so. Besides (as we are already upon what presents itself to me as a morbid subject), think what it will look like on a tomb!—that is, if any self-respecting cemetery will allow it to be so perpetuated!'

Chapter Twenty-Two

★

'He asked the chamberlain why the wind had murmured so in the night.'

Ibid. (*The Lady and the Lion*)

I ADMIT I'm as dumb as a brick, but I can't see how it all comes about,' said Laura. 'What was your pointer to Cassius? You tumbled to him before Mike recognized his voice as the Con of the murder.'

'I think I was struck by the behaviour of the boy Ivor.'

'When *I* was struck by the pebbles? Only, I don't think he hit me. What was the point of it, I wonder? Why should he attack a perfect stranger? Because I *was* a stranger to him then.'

'Perhaps not perfect, though, child. I think, of course, that Ivor is Cassius' son.'

'Then why does he call him his ward?'

'An interesting question. I don't know the answer. I am inclined to think, however, that he is not particularly proud of the lubberly boy. And that suggests a criminal characteristic, does it not?—that of a vanity so profound that he prefers not to acknowledge a son who does not do him credit.'

'And how did you decide that the older Battle was not dead?'

'That was a shot in the dark, as I think I have already made plain. The bearing of the woman—we may call her Mrs. Battle, for there is no doubt of her name—on the occasion of our visiting Newcombe Soulbury struck me then as suggestive and peculiar. Besides, as it turned out, either she or David Battle must have been lying. David denied any knowledge of her, you remember, whereas she seemed to know a very great deal about *him*.'

'Is she his mother, do you think?'

'Oh, no. I am certain she is the older Battle's second wife. I think David genuinely resented the life his father led his mother, but does not hate his father for that alone. The true hatred is rooted in the fact that his father, having taught him to paint, developed his talent and then prostituted it.'

'Ah! Made him paint phoney pictures and pass them off as Old Masters!' said Laura, with deep comprehension. 'Whereas David wanted to be an artist in the true sense.'

'Instead of which, he had to learn the art which conceals art, like George,' said Mrs. Bradley. 'One of the chief sources of income to this crew of thieves and double-dealers lay in painting over the surface of genuine Old Masters so as to be able to ship them out of the country. These superimposed pictures (not bad in themselves, for, after all, they had to employ artists to do them) bore no resemblance in subject-matter or in treatment to the originals. You remember the picture bought for ten shillings a year or so ago, and exhibited later at the Antique Dealers Fair at Grosvenor House?——'

'With the contemporary portrait of Henry VIII underneath the top layer? Gosh, yes! said Laura, with great interest. 'Well, but how does Toro come into it? Was he one of them?'

'Mr. Allwright was first suborned and then victimized, child, I fancy, but that remains to be proved. We also have to discover the whereabouts of the older Battle.'

'Now the game's up, David' will give him away, if he hates him as much as you say,' pronounced Laura, with confidence. Mrs. Bradley shook her head.

'I know I said he would risk being hanged to do so, but I've changed my mind. David's is not a strong character, and he is himself too deeply implicated to be in a position to give anybody away.'

'But he doesn't know yet that he's suspected, unless Cassius can get a message through to him.'

'Which Cassius, I think, would be very foolish to attempt. What charge will be preferred against Cassius himself in the matter of the pictures I do not know. The police have a good deal of work to do there, and may even have to grant him bail while they do it. But——'

'But to pin the murder, or any complicity in the murder, on him at present is a vastly different matter,' said Laura. 'I get it. In fact, as I see it, it won't be possible, you know, to prove anything much against him, even in the matter of the pictures. I should think he's a downy old bird, and not very likely to walk into any traps. Who *is* there who might blow the gaff on him?'

'I don't imagine that there is anybody, child. He was not even the person who cut off the head and hands of the dead man up at the Druids' Circle. That was the older Battle. One could tell by his voice, which we heard, you remember, on the dig.'

'Pity Mike wasn't there. He'd have jumped on him at once. Still, there may be another chance of that. Oh, well! Here's hoping!'

'And yet, you know,' said O'Hara, when he also discussed the case with Mrs. Bradley, 'I feel we ought to be able to get those fellows for Toro's death. I mean, by that, that they've made a good many mistakes. Surely we can trip them up on one of them!'

'What mistakes would you say they have made?' Mrs. Bradley enquired.

'To begin with, there was the shocking error of mistaking me for somebody else on the day of that run. By the way, I've never seen the bloke in that car since. You know—the one who misdirected me.'

'I've been wondering about that, child, but I cannot believe that he was merely a genuine busybody who believed he was doing a good turn. If he was, the police will trace him and get him to tell his story. I did have one other thought about him. How did he speak? What kind of voice had he?'

'He hadn't an American accent,' replied the intelligent O'Hara. 'I suppose their market for those pictures was on the other side of the pond?'

'I should think so. I have a friend at the National Gallery and he is going to make some enquiries, privately, of the experts in Boston, New York and Philadelphia, to find out whether they have any suspicions that faked or stolen pictures have been making their way over there.'

'I should say that's a pretty long shot, you know. They probably won't have any information,' said Gascoigne, who was present with his cousin. 'Some of the private collectors are such brutes that they'd buy what they thought was good stuff and not let the reputable people—the expert dealers and the museum staffs—have a sniff at anything that happened to come their way, especially if they had reason to believe it might have been stolen.'

'Yes, if they know the source is tainted they'd be hardly likely to broadcast the news,' agreed Laura. 'But Mike's certainly right in thinking that this crew made a record blunder when they used him to help them carry a corpse. Why, but for that, we'd never have known anything at all about the business from first to last. Dashed odd, when you come to think of it. What do *you* say, Mrs. Croc.? That's always been the queerest thing in the case, *I* think.'

'I agree,' said Mrs. Bradley. 'Still, murder will out, you know.'

'I wish this one would,' said Laura. 'I want to go to the ballet at Covent Garden, and I can't do that, stuck here, with murderers and picture-fakers all round me.'

'But go, child, go! Take a fortnight's holiday and enjoy yourself! Why not?'

'Because I couldn't bear to miss the finish of this. Having had all the fun so far, I'd be a mutt to fade out of the rest of it. It was just a passing whiff of the vapours, that's all.'

' "Uncertain, coy and hard to please!" ' said Gascoigne, accusingly. 'Go on, Mike. Further errors?'

'Well, the woman—Mrs. Battle?—at Newcombe Soulbury seems to have acted like a pretty far-gone lunatic. Fancy her giving *you* a letter to post which was addressed to Cassius.'

'Ah, but she had no idea that we should go to Slepe Rock and contact this Cassius,' said Laura.

'She may have been justified in the supposition,' Mrs. Bradley observed. 'Either she had forgotten, or else she was not aware of the fact that a man had disappeared from Slepe Rock, just as a man had disappeared from Newcombe Soulbury.'

'Besides, she didn't know we were investigating disappearances, did she?' Laura demanded.

'That may be true,' said O'Hara. 'Well, another mistake I think they made was to allow this Mrs. Battle to move about. She was at the farm, where I first saw her; she was at the cottage at Newcombe Soulbury when Mrs. Bradley met her; then she was at the house with the four dead trees—Cottam's you know—when Laura, Gerry and I went along there——'

'I'm sorry the four dead trees didn't work out right,' said Laura. 'They ought to have been significant, but they aren't.'

'We don't know that they aren't,' said Gascoigne. 'I've been thinking things over, and it seems to me that they *do* represent four dead people.'

'I think so, too,' said O'Hara.

'You can't count the man that the stone fell on,' Laura pointed out. 'That was sheer accident. Ah, and by the way, that reminds me! *Why* couldn't they risk having that man identified? What was there about *him* that would have incriminated *them?*'

'That is a most fascinating question, and it will not be answered until the police track down the head and hands, child.'

'But will they ever do that?'

'If they do not, we must. I say that in no civic spirit. I want to know the answer to your question. Why should that man's dead body have been so dangerous? I *think* I know the answer, but Michael is the only person who can prove it.'

'But how do you mean that the four dead trees *do* represent four dead people?' demanded Laura of O'Hara, ignoring Mrs. Bradley's interesting statements.

'Well,' said O'Hara, hesitating a little and glancing at Mrs. Bradley, 'it struck me—I expect I'm wrong, mind you, and it may not be what Gerry means—but it did strike me that the deaths that really ought to be investigated are those of the drowned couple in the yacht. I mean that we've allowed for the disappearance of the fellow who owned the cottage—now the garage at the pull-in—but nothing has been said about the young couple who got drowned in their yacht; and yet it was just as important for these picture merchants that those two should "disappear" as that the previous bloke should have been got out of the cottage so that they could have it. If that couple inherited or bought it, the smugglers were no better off.'

'Oh, dash!' said Laura, annoyed. 'If you're right, that destroys the nine-year cycle.'

'The four dead trees spoil the number nine, anyway,' said Gascoigne. 'And now we see whom they represent, if they represent people at all.'

'I'd like to know who's at the bottom of all that symbolism said O'Hara.

'Young David Battle,' said Mrs. Bradley positively. Her audience looked at her with enquiry and interest in their eyes.

'How come?' asked O'Hara gently.

'It is a theory at present,' Mrs. Bradley replied, 'but I have little doubt of its truth. David has a warped and terrified mind, and I daresay it was some sort of comfort to him to write his father's guilt in some such way, even though no one, except our intelligent Laura, whose mind is powerful and not warped, might ever read what was written.'

'But Mike read it, too, when he saw the four dead trees, and so the four dead trees,' said Laura, looking happy again, '*do* represent dead people. They represent the poet who disappeared from Slepe Rock, the yachting couple, and, now, Toro. Tell me,' she continued, looking at her employer, 'how the business of my two portraits fits in, and how you tumbled to the picture-smuggling racket.'

'The second question first: my attention was attracted to a remarkable imitation of an Old Crome——'

'Do you mean a *copy* of an Old Crome?' asked O'Hara.

'No, child. That is the point. The subject of this particular picture is not one which Old Crome could have painted. I happened to recognize the subject, which chances to be a bit of the Isle of Wight, and Old Crome, so far as we know, never stayed there, but spent the greater part of his life in his native Norwich. I imagine that the picture was not painted by Battle with any intent to deceive, as, although it portrays a pastoral landscape with no view of the sea, Battle would have been the first to realize that the master would not have visited the island and therefore could not have chosen the subject. I am no expert, of course, but I have a fair knowledge of English painting of the eighteenth and early nineteenth centuries, and to me the imitation of style was unmistakeable. But, as I say, I think it was painted as a *tour de force*, and not with any intention of trying to deceive buyers into believing that it was a genuine Old Crome. I say this because it is evident that the artist has forgotten the picture. If it had been painted to defraud, he would have got it back from the dealer long before this, I fancy.'

'You mean, then,' said Laura, 'that somebody—Cassius, I suppose—discovered that Battle could do that sort of thing, and persuaded him to come into partnership?'

'That is what I believe must have happened. David Battle, acting on the principle of publishing his father's disgraceful flouting of the Muses, kept a couple of genuine seventeenth-century picture frames on view in his rooms, so that whoever ran might read, and those frames and the Old Crome fake put me on to the track of the frauds. The discovery of the cave clinched the matter, so far as I was concerned.'

'But the murder of Toro?' asked O'Hara.

'That was rather interesting. As soon as a connection was established between your big man at the farm and Cassius-Concaverty, it seemed likely that, if the fat man had been murdered, then Cassius was involved in the murder. Somewhere, throughout all this, Cassius has been hoist by his own petard—his greed for money. He received a lucrative offer from the Gonn-Brown film company for the use of his house, Cottam's, during the summer, and could not bear to turn down the offer. But for that, we should never have known anything about the business, I feel. And when Michael and Gerald talk of mistakes, I am inclined to suggest to them that the greedy and unnecessary letting of Cottam's was the greatest mistake this man made.'

'And now where does Firman come in?' demanded Gascoigne.

'That is for you and Michael to discover. I rely on you to

find out where Mr. Firman was, and what he did, on the Saturday you had your now famous run. We know that he is David Battle's cousin, and that fact alone throws suspicion on him, of course. One other thing: remember that the older Battle is still at large, and that it is most unlikely that a gambler like Cassius will turn King's Evidence. Battle is a very dangerous and quite unscrupulous man, and has nothing further to lose if once he suspects that we know he murdered Allwright.'

'Keep your weather eye lifting,' said Laura to O'Hara. 'I hope you've taken it in.'

'You, too,' said her employer seriously. 'You are in just as much danger as the young men.'

'Ditto, ditto, Brother Schmitt,' said the irrepressible Laura.

Pleased with their commission, O'Hara and Gascoigne decided to take the war to the enemy's camp, and visit the house of Firman's uncle. Here they learned that Firman had returned to his lodgings in London, but was expected to take part in the Club run on the following Saturday. They did not see the uncle, who, it seemed, was a permanent invalid, but obtained their information from the housekeeper.

'Lets us out until Saturday,' said Gascoigne. 'What about a day or two on the river?'

Both young men were enthusiastic although rather in-experienced anglers, and Gascoigne's aunt had married a man who owned a reasonably delectable stretch of water. The fishing project was doomed, however, by the announcement of an inquest upon the contents of the iron box from the Druids' Circle.

'We'd better look in on that,' said O'Hara. 'Can't leave Laura and the old lady to cope.'

So Thursday in that week, which was to have been dedicated to trout, found them in the coroner's court at Cuchester 'to keep an eye on the ball,' as Laura expressed it later. The proceedings, however, were purely formal. That the iron box contained human remains was undisputed. Whose remains they were was a matter which seemed likely to remain undecided.

Mrs. Bradley and Laura told their story, which was newspaper headlines next day, and the matter was adjourned for the police to make further enquiries.

'David Battle's the man to identify that body,' said Laura positively. Mrs. Bradley did not contradict her. 'What's more,' added Laura, on a vigorous note, 'I've just had a marvellous idea!'

Mrs. Bradley, like her chauffeur George on a similar but previous occasion, flinched slightly and began to protest.

'No, but really I have!' said Laura. 'An idea in a million! The only thing is—do you think David Battle is a suicide type?'

'It is more than possible, child, but, without attending him professionally, and putting him under the "free association" treatment, I could not commit myself to a definite opinion, you know.'

'Well, is it worth the risk?'

'For you to put your idea into practice? It may be. Until I know the idea, I cannot say.'

'I don't want to put the responsibility on you,' said Laura generously. 'So I think I'll just charge ahead, unless you forbid me. I'm sure it will get us what we want. Sort of Nemesis, you know.'

'If he did commit suicide, it would perhaps be the best way out for the unfortunate boy,' said Mrs. Bradley, pronouncing these sentimental words dispassionately.

'Good enough!' said Laura. 'Then I'm going to get busy right away!'

She went to the art-dealer's shop in Cuchester from which Mrs. Bradley had purchased the Toro, and at which she had seen the imitation by the older Battle of an Old Crome, and purchased a cheap copy of a very well-known picture. Then she said to the art-dealer:

'My friend bought a picture here, a week or so ago, by Toro. Who was Toro, please?'

'A local artist. He used to live at a place called Easey,' the man replied.

'What was he like?'

'Like? Oh, like a good many painters, I suppose—moody, irritable, noisy, quarrelsome when he was drunk, certain of his own genius——'

'And what did he look like? Did he ever do any self-portraits? Most artists seem to,' said Laura, playing the garrulous innocent but almost holding her breath for the reply. 'I mean, did you ever see him? Did he bring his paintings here himself?'

'Oh, yes, at one time. He was very badly off, I believe, and used to peddle his pictures round the countryside to all the big houses. He brought one or two canvases to me, but I think he made most of his money by pitching a hard-luck story and selling his stuff on the instalment system when he couldn't get a ready-money settlement. He was a very fat man. Even when he was still in his twenties he must have weighed sixteen stone. I used to tell him to give up painting and go in for professional boxing. But he used to hold up his clenched fists, and say, "But my hands, man! My God-given hands!" I don't think they were, mind you,' the dealer continued. 'Not in the sense that he meant. He was a talented fellow, in a way, but he was not one of those artists whose pictures are hoarded by my trade against future fame. Not much of a draughtsman, either. Personally, I like to see a picture well drawn, and in perspective, and that sort of thing. I've not much use for the Impressionists. Lazy dev—— people, I call them.'

Laura was too good a detective, she flattered herself, to leave the subject at Toro. She wandered round the shop, asking various questions, and then, at the entrance of another customer, took her leave and said that she had had a very interesting morning.

She packed her picture carefully when she got back to the hotel, acquiring paper and string from her friend the porter. Then she wrote a short note to David Battle, and despatched both parcel and letter from the Welsea post office. The note read: *Come clean. The game's up. Laura Menzies.* The picture was that entitled: *When Did You Last See Your Father?*

Chapter Twenty-Three

★

'"Unlucky wretch that I am!" cried he.—"Not wretch enough yet!" said the sparrow.'

Ibid. (*The Dog and the Sparrow*)

'So far, so good,' said Mrs. Bradley. 'And I confess, child, that your seemingly artless enquiries have produced better results than I myself could have hoped for, had I gone to the art-dealer again.'

Laura glanced suspiciously at her employer, but Mrs. Bradley's remarks appeared to be made sincerely.

'Oh, well, I don't know,' she said modestly. 'Only, it seems to be Toro all right. The remains in that iron box, I mean. Is it true that there isn't enough left to identify?'

'The body *could* be identified,' said Mrs. Bradley judicially. 'The question is to find someone able to recognize certain features, notably a fracture near the elbow of the right arm. Such a fracture may have caused permanent stiffness of the arm, and, in this case, I should say, had almost certainly done so, because adhesions had formed.'

'But that means a motive for the murder!' cried Laura. 'Don't you see? He wasn't any good to them any more, and so they killed him.'

'I know that, but I am hoping to find an even more convincing motive, child, and I think I am on the track of it.'

'Such as?' asked Laura, eagerly.

'Such as blackmail,' Mrs. Bradley replied. 'The fracture is an old one—possibly several years old. This is only theory, I know, but it seems to me that once Allwright became unemployable as a painter (as you suggest) then the probability is that he blackmailed Cassius and Battle in order to make a living.'

'Could he do that without the risk of giving himself away?'

'It is possible. He seems to have been an enterprising man in a dishonest way, and I should say that there is nothing to prove that he realized that he was working with a gang of criminals. He would have argued, I imagine (if the police had been brought in), that he had worked on commission as a copyist, or something of that sort, and was in ignorance of the real nature of the trade in which he was employed. I think a good lawyer would be able to convince a jury about that, too.'

'One thing,' said Laura, 'that has puzzled me a bit. Why did they want another artist when they already had the two Battles? It seems to me that every extra person they took into partnership was another nail in their coffins, if it ever came to the police being brought in. They couldn't be sure that none of their assistants would confess, if it came to the point.'

'I think it was a question of providing various styles of painting, child, that's all.'

'Ah, yes. Various styles. Of course! It wouldn't do for all the fakes to look alike. I can quite see that. So they murdered Toro because he was blackmailing them, did they? A lovely lot, aren't they, him included! I do hope we get them where we want them! I wonder how Mike and Gerry are going to get on with Firman?'

Mrs. Bradley wondered this, too, and her thoughts were not unduly optimistic. She doubted whether Firman had been more than a pawn on the maze-like board of play among Battle, Battle, Allwright and Cassius. Little, she believed, could be learned from him respecting the major operations of the criminals, simply because she did not think he knew enough to be dangerous. The likeliest thing was that Firman had found out from his relatives, the Battles, that there was an easy way of making money if one did occasional simple, slightly shady little jobs and kept one's mouth shut, and the most that Gascoigne and O'Hara could hope for, in her opinion, was that a truthful account of Firman's movements on the day of the murder of Allwright would lead the police in the direction of the murderers.

One thing perturbed her, however. As she had foreseen, the police, unable to charge Cassius with any crime for which he could not demand bail, had been compelled to release him. The work of cleaning and recognizing the pictures (if any) which had been stolen, and the even slower task of discovering to whom and when the faked pictures already exported had been sold, and under what conditions, made it impossible to charge the man with any indictable offence, or to hold him until the necessarily lengthy and tiresome enquiries had been concluded. Still, all questions concerning the pictures were now out of Mrs. Bradley's hands.

Once there was any proof of murder against Cassius, however, a very different aspect presented itself. Cassius could be arrested, cautioned and charged. But there was many a slip, she decided. David Battle and Firman, between them or separately, might be prepared to furnish the evidence that was needed, but the chance that they would do so was a slender one; all the more slender because it was extremely doubtful whether Cassius had had any hand in actual murder at all. It was not even Cassius who had cut the head and hands from the body pinned under the stone. That, almost certainly—but for the conditions of moonless darkness and the feeble glow of the artificial lights used that night, she would have said *quite* certainly had been the work of the bloody-minded and cruel older Battle.

Meanwhile Cassius was at liberty and might or might not communicate with the older Battle, whose identity, incidentally, still had to be proved, for although O'Hara could swear to the man he had helped at the farm, it was not beyond dispute that this man was David Battle's supposedly missing father.

Mrs. Bradley had often wondered, since the beginning of the adventure, how Battle had contrived to 'disappear' and yet go on living in a district where he must be well known. She had come to the conclusion that he no longer lived in the district, but only visited it secretly from time to time. So far there had been no sign of him except at night, so this might mean that he remained hidden during the day—at Cottam's,

possibly—and only ventured out when there was little chance
of meeting anybody who might recognize him. The nine-year
cycle thus found some explanation and ceased to be a pheno-
menon. Battle only came back to the neighbourhood to help
dispose of the pictures.

Mrs. Bradley was afraid of Battle; not on her own account,
but on behalf of young Michael O'Hara. Of all their party,
O'Hara was the only one who could swear to the man, and,
what was more important, who could swear to the man who
had advised him before he arrived at the farm. He could also
swear to the woman, and, this being so, and as Mrs. Bradley
herself could identify her as the woman who had been living
in Battle's old cottage at Newcombe Soulbury, it would not be
difficult to make out a case against her as an accessory,
particularly as she had also been seen at Cottam's by Laura
Menzies.

Once O'Hara had sworn that Battle was the man whom he
had helped at the farm, and had sworn to him as having been
concerned with the attempted removal of the iron box (or
coffin, as it must now be called, Mrs. Bradley supposed), the
police would have little difficulty in building a formidable
case. Whether their accusations would include Cassius it was
not possible to determine, because, although Cassius had also
been concerned in the attempt to remove the iron coffin, he
might be in a position to show that he knew nothing of its real
contents but had assumed them to be some of the more
valuable of the stolen pictures.

Battle's life, it seemed to the elderly lady, depended upon
young O'Hara's shut mouth; and as there is only one way of
permanently shutting a mouth, Mrs. Bradley was more
anxious than she liked to confess to Laura, and none the
happier in that O'Hara so far had not been threatened or
attacked.

When Saturday came Gascoigne and O'Hara had their
plans ready. They had been supplied with route-maps of the
afternoon's run, and had studied these diligently. They had
also compared them with the Ordnance Map, and had even,
on the Friday afternoon, walked over the course.

'And now all we want is a fair field and no spectators,' said O'Hara.

'And to be certain that Firman means to turn up,' said Gascoigne.

'He'll come,' said O'Hara confidently. 'He'll probably be gunning for me, don't you see, as ardently as I'll be gunning for him!'

'Yes, I'd thought of that,' said Gascoigne, gloomily. 'It's the one thing I don't like at all about this business. Supposing he's got a revolver?'

'What, with running togs? Be your age! How could he carry a whacking great revolver on a cross-country run and not have it spotted?'

'He could kid people he was the starter,' said Gascoigne, grinning. 'All right, I won't play grandmother, but we'll keep a weather eye lifting until we get him where we want him. I've conceived a dislike for the little ferret.'

The headquarters of the small but keen running club to which Gascoigne and O'Hara belonged was just over the Somerset border, but the club had no ground of its own and was dependent upon the local amateur football club (whose secretary happened to be one of the members) for changing-rooms and a field on which to practise.

During the winter, however, the football club's ground and changing-rooms were not available, and the members who joined in cross-country running had to make the best of things in a small public house called the *Horse and Hound* which allotted them a sitting-room and a bathroom every Saturday afternoon between September and April.

To the *Horse and Hound*, therefore, Gascoigne and O'Hara repaired, there to exchange jests with the rest of the runners and to change into dark shorts and white running vests ready for the word to be given which should set them on the track of the mysterious and (they thought) criminal Mr. Firman.

'He's turned up all right,' said O'Hara, as they stood

dancing about on the pavement outside the public house waiting for the rest of the field. 'He didn't bat an eyelid when I greeted him.'

'Probably quite a downy bird,' suggested Gascoigne. 'Wait until we catch up with him later on.'

They had decided upon the spot where they would contact Firman, and were anxious only that he should reach it.

'No use making it too close to the start,' had said Gascoigne; and O'Hara had agreed. The country they were to traverse was distant twenty miles or so from Yeovil, and the runners, changed, and with overcoats over their shorts and vests, made the first part of the journey by train.

It had been agreed between the cousins that they should separate fairly near the beginning of the course, and converge upon the quarry later. O'Hara was to shadow Firman, and Gascoigne, as the better runner, was to forge ahead for the first mile and a half and then gradually fade in again, as it were, towards the meeting-place.

The plan, as Gascoigne saw it, had this disadvantage; that if O'Hara were really a marked man, it was quite likely that the older Battle (who would have heard about the run from Firman) might have decided that the afternoon offered as good a chance as any of ambushing O'Hara and putting him out of the way without troubling Firman with this task.

He mentioned this to his cousin, but O'Hara, with a light-hearted reference to forewarning and forearming, refused to take the matter seriously.

'Let's concentrate on Firman,' said he; and before there was time to say more, the word was given, and the runners cantered off. Gascoigne and O'Hara had no scruples about finishing or not finishing the run, although it was an inter-club match, for it was considered likely that the home team would get the first half-dozen places at least, unless there were unforeseen accidents, for the visitors were a very much younger team consisting for the most part of youngsters of seventeen. In fact, it was as much to put this club on its feet as from any desire to score at their expense, that the good-natured secretary of the home team had put his men into the field.

Gascoigne was a more sensitive and a more imaginative man than his cousin. He disliked intensely the thought that O'Hara, far from being one of the hunters, might as easily be tracked down and murdered; therefore he trotted alongside another member of the team, an old Cambridge Blue who had been a good man in his day, and apprised him, as they cantered over the common which formed the first part of their route, of the course which events had taken.

'Good Lord!' said the Cambridge man. 'What fun!'

Gascoigne then bespoke his assistance, and, soon satisfied that he had a staunch ally, he lengthened his stride and went to the head of the field, and (not too obviously, he hoped) began to run at a pace which was foolishly fast if he had hoped to finish the course. O'Hara tagged on to Firman, and the Cambridge man stuck to O'Hara as he had promised. Firman was not much of a runner, and the trio was slow.

The course was a circular one, with the starting-point on the northern circumference, so that at no time during the run were the competitors at more than about four miles from their base. The route avoided roads as far as possible, and permission had been obtained for the teams to include two private parks in the course, one south and one east of the starting-point. Here and there along the course were friends of the clubs who possessed cars and motor cycles, and acted as guides and checkers-in.

Between the two private estates lay a fairly considerable wood. A long hill led up to it, and on the home side there was a stretch of sand and heather known locally as Punch Dripham. It was uneven, and contained deep hollows not dangerous unless one wandered into them in the dark, but large enough, for the most part, to hide, say, a patrol of Boy Scouts or four or five men, for the lips of these places were overhung with soft soil in which great roots of heather writhed, while in the holes themselves there were wild, labyrinthine bushes of ancient gorse and occasional clumps of bracken.

The *rendezvous* for Gascoigne and O'Hara was to be in the depths of the wood before they reached Punch Dripham, and Gascoigne, arriving, according to arrangement, well ahead of the rest of the field, plunged in amongst the undergrowth until he was about twenty yards north of the path, and thank-fully—for the pace he had set himself had been a hot one—he lay down on the bank of a small brook which flowed through the wood and waited for the signal from his cousin. The last of the checkers-in had greeted him some mile and a quarter further back along the course.

The Cambridge man, Gascoigne hoped, had been able to stick to O'Hara. He glanced at the wristwatch he was wearing, and by which he had been timing himself, and decided that he could take ten minutes' rest at least before the others arrived.

It was very quiet in the wood. It was so far from any road along which vehicles could pass that its selection as the place in which Firman should be interviewed had seemed obvious. Gascoigne dipped his hand in the brook. It was clear, and rippled pleasantly over sand. Time passed. He looked at his watch and wondered idly why the checker-in had mentioned that people were shooting on the estate. He had not heard a sound of it himself. At the end of a quarter of an hour he felt irritable; at the end of twenty minutes he was anxious.

The trouble was that he did not know what to do. If he left the wood and so missed the others, that would be unfair to them and a breaking of the agreement which had been made. On the other hand, there was always the chance that one of them had met with a mishap. O'Hara had turned his ankle on the previous run; such accidents were always liable to happen. It might even be something more serious; one of the three spiked on a fence, through trying to vault it and slipping at the take-off, perhaps; or somebody helpless with a broken leg or badly-torn muscles.

Twenty-five minutes; and Gascoigne, in an agony of indecision—a state of mind to which, with his supreme, unegotistical self-confidence, he was entirely unaccustomed—began to walk through the woods to find out whether, by any possible chance, the others had arrived without his knowledge and were in another part of the wood.

The trees gave place, at one point, to a little clearing. He found Firman's body half into a large clump of very tall, pink willow-herb. He would never have seen it but for the cloud of flies that rose with guilty haste at his approach. He would, even then, have walked on, but he could not help seeing the area of smashed, long stems and the welter of crushed, pink blossoms. The next sight, that of the gaping mouth and one wide-open, horrified, dead, glazed eye, filled him with nightmare horror. There was a hole through Firman's skull where his other eye had been, and a blackening of powder and a scorching of skin round the wound. Gascoigne had never felt so ill in his life. The fine afternoon surged blackly about him. He turned and staggered away, and then fell down in a near-faint merely from shock.

He had managed to struggle to his feet, and, pulling himself together, was wondering—his heart hammering and his mouth as dry as sand—what he had better do, when a youthful voice from a bush beside him observed on a confident note:

'You're dead! It's a *plame* we're *gaying*.'

Gascoigne jumped a couple of yards. Then out of the bush crawled a boy in the uniform of a Wolf Cub. He was an engaging-looking child with scratched knees, freckles, a green cap, a grey jersey and a broad smile.

'I bagged him, Chinstrap,' he observed.

'Yes, Mr. Handley,' responded a second voice, as its owner followed the freckled Mr. Handley on to the path. 'I don't mind if you did, sir.'

'Well, it's a fair cop, Governor Handley,' observed Gascoigne, collecting his wits. 'How do, Colonel?'

'Happy to meet you, sir,' responded the Colonel. '*Cow dew*, did you say, sir? I'll try anything.'

'Well, look here,' said Gascoigne earnestly, 'as it happens, I'm rather in a spot.'

'*Lather in a pot?* I don't think I should like it,' giggled the Colonel, entranced by his own wit. 'Did you hear that, Mr. Handley? He said "rather in a spot," and I said "lather in a pot." Not bad!'

'Oh, dry up, Chinstrap, and don't be funny,' said Mr. Handley, giving the Colonel a dig in the spine which made him wince. 'Can't you see he's serious? Are you training for anything?' he asked, looking with great interest at Gascoigne's running-vest with the Club badge on the left breast.

'No. Just a cross-country run,' said Gascoigne. 'But I'm a—a sort of a special constable in my spare time—help the police a bit, you know—and I'm on the track of a criminal and I want to get in touch with them. Where's the nearest police station? Do you know?'

'We wouldn't be Wolf Cubs long if we didn't,' said Mr. Handley, giving a realistic howl. 'Look here, we shall probably go a good deal faster than you, even if you *are* a runner. We have to keep up a wolf's pace, you know, which most grown-up people can't manage. It takes a bit of doing, I can tell you! So perhaps we had better forge ahead and you can follow at your own pace. We'll leave a *spoor*. Where do you want the police to meet you? Wouldn't you like us to help you track the criminal? We're *very* good at tracking, you know. I'm the best tracker, and Chinstrap comes second, and then——'

'You silly ass!' shrieked the Colonel. 'Of course you're not the best! Why, only last week——'

'Oh, dry up! We're on a job,' said Mr. Handley hastily.

'You're jolly good chaps,' said Gascoigne, gratefully. He had been wondering how he could manage to get rid of the two children. It was quite impossible that they could play in the wood for long without discovering the body. 'All right. You push along, then, but mind how you go. I shouldn't rush. I wouldn't have anyone of the Itma team hurt for any money.'

'*Dirt and honey*, sir?' said the irrepressible Chinstrap, smacking himself on the head, or, rather on the cap, with delight, and then ecstatically punching his friend. 'I don't think me sister would like it.'

The two little boys then neighed like horses, and began to canter away.

'What, *Crafty Clara?*' came over the air on the boyish, treble notes of Mr. Handley. 'The woman who——' Gascoigne missed the rest of it, and settled down grimly to await the arrival of the others, not certain how long it would be before help came, and speculating upon the length of time the body had been in the wood before he had arrived. He could guess who had killed Firman, but not where the murderer had gone. It was evident, though, that the checker-in had heard the shot, and this would help to fix the time of the death.

At the end of ten minutes he heard the sound he had been awaiting, the call of the cuckoo repeated four times. He came out on to the path by which he had reached the wood, and saw O'Hara alone.

'We're too late,' he said, as soon as his cousin came near. 'Somebody's shot poor Firman through the head. I've found the body.'

'We saw him kidnapped,' said O'Hara. 'That fellow—Battle, or whoever he is—swooped on him with a car just as we'd got him cut out from the rest of the field. He forced him to get in. We've been trying to find out where the car went. That's why I'm late. Is he really—I suppose you do know that he is dead?'

'He's dead all right. He was killed before I got here. I found the body. It's back there.' Gascoigne jerked his head. 'Could you swear to Battle?'

'Impossible to swear to him. For one thing, he'd got a tin hat on—you know how that alters a chap's appearance—and he had a handkerchief tied over his mouth and chin. There was nothing to see but his eyes, and I couldn't have sworn to those. I mean, not at a trial or even to the police.'

'It wasn't Cassius, I suppose?'

'It might have been. I couldn't say. Nobody could accept my identification, I'm afraid.'

'What happened, exactly?'

'Well, it isn't very easy to describe. He just drove straight up to Firman. I thought he was going to drive into him at first. So did Firman. He jumped a gorse bush and the fellow drove straight on after him. Then he took out a gun, after he had pulled up the car, called on Firman to stop, went up to him, stuck the gun in his ribs, and took him back to the car. Firman got into the car, and away they went.'

'Where were you when all this happened, then?'

'About two hundred yards behind; but we were on the

other side of a hedge, and I don't think the fellow saw us. He was in the deuce of a hurry. Neither of us did a thing. I still don't see what there was to do. The two were in the car, and the car was off, before we could grasp what had happened.'

'Did Firman seem to know the chap?'

'Oh, yes, there's not much doubt he did.'

'Well, this fellow's killed him—or somebody has.'

'Yes, well, I've sent someone to fetch the police. I'd better trot back and direct them here. I should think he's got them by now. By the way, I found a telephone, and rang up Mrs. Bradley. I thought she ought to know about the kidnapping.'

'We shall have to ring her again.' said Gascoigne gloomily. 'We *are* unlucky. It looks as though Firman knew something really important.'

'Or else that, whatever he knew, they had reason to think he'd spill it.'

Chapter Twenty-Four

★

'. . . so she said he was like a green stick that had been laid to dry over a baker's oven.'

Ibid. (*King Grisly-Beard*)

LAURA, meanwhile, had received a reply to her message and gift. She had given the address of the hotel at Welsea to David Battle in case there should be any queries about the portrait of her that he was painting, and here she was rung up on the telephone at about the time that the police, converging on two sides—for the Wolf Cubs had made haste to call the local police constable to the wood—had seen the body of Firman and had taken it, Gascoigne and O'Hara into their charge.

'Is that you, Miss Menzies?' came over the line. 'This is Battle. I say, never mind anything else, but could you sit to me again?'

'What's gone wrong?' enquired Laura.

'Nothing. Your portrait's finished. I want to paint you again.'

'Eh? Why?'

'I want to. Will you come? I want—I'm sure you won't disappoint me—I want to paint *you* this time. Not just your face and hands and clothes.'

'What, in the so-and-so?' said Laura thoughtfully. 'My young man would have a fit.' She took the instrument from her ear and stood entranced awhile at this prospect. '*What* do you say?' she enquired, becoming aware that the telephone was still bleating.

'I said you *must* let me. I'm going to call it *Atalanta* or else *Hippolyta*. I don't know yet. You've *got* to come.'

'Only correctly chaperoned, then,' said Laura. 'And by somebody with a gun,' she added darkly to herself, remembering that he was the son of Toro's murderer.

'What? Chaperoned? Oh, any darn thing you like. When can you come?'

'I'll ring up and let you know,' said Laura, with a degree of caution to which ordinarily she was a stranger.

'And, I say! You wouldn't marry me, I suppose? I feel I could do great things with you beside me, urging me on, and——'

'Waiting until you've served your seven years' stretch!' said Laura derisively. 'You forget what's coming to you, my lad, for defrauding the art-loving public! Well, I'll let you know about the rudery. I'm not promising, mind! I don't want the sack from Mrs. B.'

She hung up and went to find her employer. Mrs. Bradley, however, was no longer in the hotel. She had gone to confer with the Chief Constable on matters of public importance, and, to his annoyance, she arrived in time to prevent his enjoyment of his Saturday afternoon golf.

'Good heavens, Adela!' he protested. 'Can't you choose some more reasonable time?'

'I thought you might like to know that the dead man is almost certainly Allwright, and that you could learn a good deal about him by circulating a description of him to the banks in Cuchester. He'd become a blackmailer, and has probably paid in a good deal of money somewhere—always in cash, I should imagine. You could also gain something from an examination into the private affairs of Mr. Cassius Concaverty.'

'We've got that in hand. From the account in the name of Concaverty, about fifteen thousand pounds have been withdrawn since the beginning of December, 1946.'

'Ah! That fits nicely, doesn't it?'

'Fits with what?'

'With the medical theory that the arm in the iron coffin was injured about four years ago. Allwright would have pleaded with and begged from his employers for a bit, and then, when the war was over, he would have begun to black-mail them.'

'Yes, that all sounds feasible, doesn't it?' Sir Crimmond agreed. 'But, look here, Adela, it will keep until Monday, dash it! Fielding is in charge of the case, and he's a thoroughly competent fellow. Dash it, I want to play golf!'

'Well, you can't, unless I come with you. And if I do, I shall walk round with you and tell you all about the older Battle, and you know how you dislike to carry on conversations on the greens.'

'You're a blasted nuisance!' said the Chief Constable, glumly. 'All right. Come into the house. I shall have to telephone and put Beauchamp off.'

'You see,' said Mrs. Bradley, when this was settled, 'the trouble is that even if you do catch Battle, and charge him with murder——'

'But we can't! We haven't a ha'porth of proof! Dash it, the fellow's laughing at us!'

'I know. That is why, as I am trying to tell you, you must find some from somewhere. Somebody murdered Allwright, and you won't get any more out of Cassius. When it comes to the point, and you get the American side of it, he may talk about pictures, but he certainly won't talk about murder.'

'I know all that.'

'Of course you do. I have a fatal habit of recapitulation due to having to lecture to people who won't read books but have been brought up on a diet of films and the wireless. Well, all that I was going to suggest is this: at Cottam's there is an old man, very simple, employed on odd jobs in the garden. Why don't you get him to describe Allwright and Battle? Then, when you arrest Battle, the old man could be brought along to identify him.'

'That won't help. It isn't getting Battle identified that's going to be the trouble. It's getting young O'Hara to swear to him. O'Hara is our only reliable witness to what happened at the farm, and——'

'I know. But what *you* don't know is that——'

'Nobody is going to believe—no juryman at any rate—that

O'Hara can identify with certainty a man he saw only at night by the light of an electric torch.'

'He heard his voice, remember. Oh, I agree about the jury, but I was just going to tell you——'

Before the Chief Constable could hear the rest of the sentence, the telephone rang.

'It's Inspector Fielding, dear,' said his wife, who had taken the call. 'Will you take it in here?'

'No, no. I'll come into the lounge. You stay here and look after Adela. I daresay she'd like a cup of tea. I expect Beauchamp to ring up about a foursome to-morrow. He said, when I put him off to-day, that he'd try to fix something for to-morrow.'

'Well, how are the patients?' enquired the hostess, when she and Mrs. Bradley were left alone. 'I hear you've been spending your summer holiday getting my poor old Crimmie's goat?'

Sir Crimmond's wife was a bright-eyed woman of thirty; his second wife, in fact, and the apple of his choleric eye. Mrs. Bradley denied indignantly, first, that she had had a summer holiday, since coming to see one's grandchild christened could scarcely be called that; she added, that, until the birth of the baby, she had been lecturing in Denmark; secondly, she denied that she would ever be wicked enough to get Sir Crimmond's goat under any circumstances whatsoever unless he turned into a wife-beater.

At this point Sir Crimmond reappeared. He was red in the face and very angry.

'Damn it, Adela! Do you know what's happened now?' he demanded. 'Those confounded nit-wits have allowed another murder—*another murder!*—to be committed within my boundaries! A man called Firman has been found shot through the right eye—death instantaneous—in a wood about three miles from Beauchamp's own place, the *Towers*, at Little Beddlehampton! The county's becoming a shambles! Really it is! I've got to go and see to it, of course. You'd better come with me. You can give me your views as we go.'

'I haven't any views until we have seen the body, and until

I am sure those two boys are safe,' said Mrs. Bradley. 'Mr.
O'Hara and his cousin, Mr. Gascoigne, were out with this
man Firman in an endeavour to extract information with
regard to the other murder.'

'Upon my soul! So the two things are connected! You'd
better—— Oh, no, I remember. Yes, of course. Oh, Lord!
I hope young O'Hara's all right. An intelligent boy. His great
grandfather was the young Tim O'Hara who said to Queen
Victoria——'

A long reminiscence followed to which Mrs. Bradley,
accustomed to improbable stories about Queen Victoria,
scarcely listened. At the end of the narrative, she said:

'I was going to tell you, just before the telephone rang, that
I don't think Michael O'Hara is in any more danger now than
his cousin or Laura or myself or even Denis, and, possibly,
George.'

'Why not? I thought you said——'

'Yes, but, you see, when we were pretending to begin some
archæological excavations at the circle of the Dancing Druids,
a man came up to O'Hara and asked him why he had left the
car on the night when he helped to carry the body.'

'He did? Point-blank, like that?'

'Apparently.'

'So all of you could swear to this man?'

'Yes, but it wouldn't help very much with a jury, any more
than——'

'No,' said Sir Crimmond, thoughtfully, 'I can see that.
There are no other material witnesses except the body, which
isn't proved to be Allwright's. It would be young O'Hara's
story against this fellow's denials.'

'He might not even deny it.'

'Eh?'

'O'Hara may be able to recognize Battle—I call him Battle
because that is who it must be—but he could not possibly
identify the body he helped to carry.'

'Oh!'

'It was wrapped and swathed in such a way that no features
were distinguishable.'

'So?'

'So all that Battle, who is nothing if not a resourceful and desperate man, would need to do is to provide himself with an accident case—not difficult; the gang he and Cassius have had to employ is fairly large, and one or two of them that I myself have seen must be heavy men—and take you to hospital to see it. The "case" will have been primed with a tale——'

'But a hospital would see through a malingerer in half a minute!'

'The man wouldn't be a malingerer,' Mrs. Bradley pointed out in gentle tones. 'He would be a genuinely wounded man. Battle and Cassius would certainly see to that. In fact, I should say that such a "case" has existed since the day that Firman saw Gascoigne and O'Hara at that farm on the Sunday morning.'

'Then wouldn't he give the game away through sheer annoyance at having been victimized? This fellow they crocked, I mean.'

'Not if he has been told that his life depends upon his compliance, do you think? And, of course, he's been very well paid. The only thing is that he was not at a local hospital. Still, they will have thought of the time-factor. He will be in a hospital outside the county boundaries.'

'Then how *are* we going to get them?'

'I want you to arrest Battle's wife and his son David.'

'I can't do that!'

'It's our only chance, and you must do it at once, and not bother about a warrant.'

'I won't do it! Good Lord, what next? Gangster methods, nothing less! I'm surprised at you for suggesting such a way out!'

'Very well. It's the only solution, so far as I can see at present.'

She was silent. The Chief Constable glanced at her once or twice, but her witch-like countenance was as calm as the face of a Chinese, and her brilliant eyes were closed, displaying long black lashes against cheeks the colour of old ivory. Her ungloved, claw-like hands were gently clasped in her lap, and the September sun glinted suddenly on the jewels in her rings, giving the Chief Constable a start, as though a dagger had been flashed before his eyes.

'Well, suppose I did do it?' he said presently.

'I think that the birds might fly,' said Mrs. Bradley, opening her eyes. 'You can, I imagine, find some reason for arresting Battle and Cassius for trying to leave the country?'

'Ah,' said the Chief Constable, looking happier. 'And you think the wife and son will give us all the evidence we want?'

'Yes, and you will obtain more from the death of Firman. There is nothing very secret about that. But——'

'Don't you think that as a result of that—if they did it! We've no evidence, mind!—they will cut and run before we arrest the wife and son?'

'I don't know whether they can.'

'We can have the ports watched, just in case——'

'They won't leave from a port,' said Mrs. Bradley. 'They will leave from their smugglers' hole. They've got their own ship, remember! The one which they used to carry the pictures. But they will have to get in touch with her, and, if you act quickly, they won't have very much time.'

'Which of them did kill Firman, do you suppose?'

'Cassius, I should say.'

'But Battle—if that's who it is!—is surely the killer, from what you've told me.'

Yes, but I expect he wanted to have Cassius as deeply implicated as he is himself. Besides, although we've no evidence that Cassius is a killer, there's not much doubt that his son is a murderous little brute.'

'Yes, but——'

'I always think the *Copper Beeches* is one of the best of the Sherlock Holmes stories, and, in my own profession, you know, we learn a good deal about parents from a careful study of their children.'

'But I'm going to have a warrant, all the same,' said Sir Crimmond suddenly. 'I had to call on Beauchamp, anyway.' He lay back in his seat, looking pleased. 'What was that last "but" of yours?' he asked suddenly.

'No,' said Laura decidedly. 'I'm not going to be a decoy duck for anybody! If I sit for the bloke it's to be because he wants to paint me, and not just to keep him busy while the police come along to arrest him. You can keep me out of it.'

'I only asked! I only asked!' said Sir Crimmond, annoyed. 'What on earth a respectable young woman is thinking about to be painted like that by a fellow who is no better than a common criminal, I don't know. If you were *my* daughter——!'

Laura put out her tongue at him, and went out, humming a tune.

'Confound this new-fangled morality,' growled the irate man. 'Imagine a girl willing to be painted in the nude and yet not willing to assist the police in the execution of their duty by keeping the fellow busy until we can get along to arrest him!'

'Speeches on morality from a man who is willing to persuade a girl to act like a Judas, and yet himself won't do a simple, illegal little thing like arresting a man without a warrant, gives me food for thought,' said Mrs. Bradley. 'I am on Laura's side.'

'Oh, you women always stick together!' said the Chief Constable pettishly.

'If we did, we should have ruled the world long ago,' Mrs. Bradley retorted. 'Arrest the man, and don't keep cackling about it. But, if I were you, I'd arrest the woman first. Send your police to Newcombe Soulbury, to Cottam's and to the farm simultaneously. She's sure to be at one of them, unless they've spirited her away.'

But Mrs. Battle—a name she confessed to as soon as she saw Inspector Fielding, who came (armed with a warrant), to arrest her, had not been spirited away.

'She says she doesn't know a thing about Battle,' said the Chief Constable peevishly to Mrs. Bradley, later, 'except that he belonged to a Fascist organization and had to "disappear" as a precautionary measure. She affects to believe that it's in connection with pro-Fascist activities that we want to arrest him now, but swears she knows nothing about that side of his life. She says he's been a good husband, and that's all she cares about. She also reminded Fielding that we can't use her evidence against Battle. So that's your precious idea gone west, as I knew it would! *Now* what do you suggest?'

'That you try your luck with David Battle,' said Mrs. Bradley, unperturbed by these slurs upon her theories. But David Battle's reactions were not more helpful than those of his stepmother. He would answer any questions the police liked to ask, he would go to prison, he would be hanged if necessary, so long as he was allowed to paint Laura Menzies as *Atalanta, Hippolyta,* or, as he now thought likely, *Artemis Orthia.*

'Did he really say that?' Mrs. Bradley immediately enquired.

'What?'

'*Artemis Orthia.*'

'Yes, he did. The sergeant's shorthand is impeccable. If he wrote *Artemis Orthia,* then that's what the fellow said.'

'I'll tell Laura,' said Mrs. Bradley. 'You may find her less scrupulous this time.'

Chapter Twenty-Five

★

'After some time, however, the old fox really died; and soon afterwards a wolf came to pay his respects.'

Ibid. (*Mrs. Fox*)

'ARTEMIS ORTHIA?' said Laura. 'But wasn't she made out of a tree? Well, I take it as a mark of favour on David Battle's part that he should give me a warning of my impending demise!'

'So, you see,' said Mrs. Bradley, 'we want to know why the ice-cart came here that day.'

'Ice?' said the old man with the wheelbarrow. 'Oh, ah. Ice. I remember.' He ruminated, pulling at a small clay pipe the colour of the soil. 'Ice, says you. And proper, too. But it were them fillum folks ordered it. Wanted to make a picture of the North Pole explorers, or summat of that, so they tell me. Photography, like. The ice all throwed out in a pond they dug in the garden. Show ee? Ah, I'll show ee. It were over there where they planted them bits of pine trees.'

'And who stayed here besides the film people and Mr. Concaverty?' Mrs. Bradley enquired. 'Did you ever see anyone else?'

'Why, no, I dunno as I did.'

'No one else was a stranger to you except the film people?'

'Nobody else, without it might be some of the indoor servants. But such as them 'aven't time for the likes of me.'

'So that's that,' said the Chief Constable briefly. 'Now,

what? Or shall we go to the cave? Is that old man in the plot?

'I was right to forbid Laura to go to David Battle's studio,' said Mrs. Bradley, following her own train of thought. 'Behold the fifth dead tree.'

She went back to the old man. He had finished his pipe and was contemplating it before knocking it out against the ancient brick wall of the culvert.

'What killed the trees?' she enquired.

'Ah!' said the old man, making up his mind, and knocking the pipe out carefully. 'Got a hairpin, I wonder?'

Mrs. Bradley produced one from among her shining locks and handed it over.

'You know who killed them, I suppose?' she asked carelessly.

'Me? Oh, I knows. None better. It were that there expert they brought down. "Got to 'ave 'em dead," says Mr. Concaverty to me. "Wanted for the fillum," he says. "Can you kill 'em?" he says. "I can kill moles and that old water-rat, and chickens and pigs, and an old turkey gobbler or two. That's me," I says. "But trees! Nobody don't kill trees," I says, "without they're daft," I says. "Now if 'twere only that there old water-rat," I says . . .'

'Yes, but what did this expert look like? And how did he kill them?' enquired the Chief Constable brusquely. The old man looked at him with rheumy, intelligent, blue eyes.

'He were biggish,' he said. 'Ay, he were biggish. And he killed 'em with turps and resin, and with burnin' at the roots, and with brimstone from hell, and with curses. Ay, how he cursed them there trees!'

'So you've come!' said David Battle.

'Yes,' Laura agreed. 'But only to arrange terms.'

'Terms?'

'Sure. If I'm to sit to you for some kind of anonymous classical work, I must receive pay.'

'Pay?'

'Don't keep up this Echo on Parnassus stuff. What sort of mutt do you think I am? I have to earn my living, don't forget.'

'Yes, but . . .'

'But me no buts. What are the odds?'

'Odds?'

'Oh, Lord!'

'Now, look here,' said Battle, putting down the charcoal he had picked up and coming over to her, 'nothing was said about fees.'

'I know. I've come to say something about them now. Your rake-off from those faked pictures must have been fairly considerable. Where do *I* come in?'

'You little . . .!' said Battle, looking dangerous.

Laura, who topped him by two and a half inches, and weighed considerably more than he did, resented the adjective considerably more than the noun.

'Little nothing,' she observed coldly. 'And while we're on the subject of emoluments, just what did they pay you for blotting out that wretched Firman?'

Battle went white, and Laura, accustomed to teasing her brothers, instinctively ducked. But he made no move to attack her. He turned away and said pettishly:

'Don't be a lout. You know perfectly well I don't kill people.'

'Still got to break your duck?' said Laura pleasantly. 'Well, that's all right with me. If it comes to a toss up between us, I bet I'm as good as you are. Now, reverting to the main topic of conversation . . .'

'Will five bob an hour do? I can't afford more than that.'

'Make it seven and six, and it's a do.'

'But . . . all right, then. There's a screen over there. Get ready behind it, and then——'

'Yes, I know,' said Laura. She had to pass the screen to reach the door, and gave it a hearty shove as she went by. Apart from the fact that, as she had supposed, there was someone concealed behind it, she learned nothing from this manœuvre, and did not stay to repair her knowledge. She tore down the stairs and went straight to Cuchester police station. By the time the police got to the house, however, both David and the other bird had flown.

'So now for the cave,' said O'Hara. 'You know, Laura, you ought to be throttled for going to Battle and risking your silly young life.'

'So I shall be, when my young man comes here, and he's due back any day now,' said Laura with great contentment. 'Mrs. Croc. created a bit—unusual with her—but I still say it was worth it. I intended to bust David Battle's *bona fides*, and I did.'

'His what?' asked Gascoigne loftily. He also was very angry with Laura for placing herself in danger, a position reserved by rights for gods and men, and, apart from this lordly sally, had ignored her since their reunion.

'Suspenders to you,' said Laura vulgarly.

'Laura,' said Mrs. Bradley, later, 'cannot forgive David Battle for having the same Christian name as her fiancé. It endeared him to her at first, and the reaction is all the more severe.'

Unaware of this acute reading of her subconscious mind, Laura sent an affectionate telegram to her beloved, and prepared herself for the cave.

The company, apart from policemen, was to consist of all the protagonists in the drama except for Denis, who had been requested to turn out for his Rugby football club against Richmond. This call of the wild could scarcely be ignored, so, regretfully, he had been obliged to leave his favourite aunt to her own devices for a while and shoulder the responsibilities of manhood.

The others, as Laura gleefully expressed it, were all in the swim, and the party went by car to Slepe Rock under the cover of the darkness and the protection of the police.

'We shall depend upon you to identify these men, sir,' said Inspector Fielding to O'Hara.

'I'll do that,' the kingly youth responded. 'The thing is, what are you going to charge 'em with? Those remains in the iron box haven't been identified yet, and I don't think my identification of the fellow who kidnapped poor Firman would be accepted.'

'Well, sir,' said the Inspector, 'we are hoping to charge them with the murder of a Mr. and Mrs. Nankison, whose bodies *have* been identified.'

'Never heard of 'em.'

'Not by name, sir, perhaps. Since we got to know of the goings-on in this cave, we've been doing a bit of investigating, and the conclusion we've come to is that drowned persons— you may recollect hearing that the first owners of Slepe Cottage, as it was then called, were lost in a yachting accident —might possibly get washed up in a cave or almost anywhere, but what *doesn't* happen to them, strange to say, is that they get themselves nicely buried there, with a couple of limestone boulders to keep them down.'

'Good heavens!' said O'Hara. 'Not really? I mean, you haven't *really* found that drowned couple who inherited the house from Bulstrode?'

'And Mr. Bulstrode himself, sir, what is more,' said the Inspector with great satisfaction. 'Also a head and a pair of hands, which we should like to have identified.'

'Did Mrs. Bradley put you on to it?'

'Yes, she did, sir. And a nod was as good as a wink. The police, in their way, sir, are not entirely without imagination.'

O'Hara and Gascoigne, not unused to the interior of Bow Street after Boat-Race night, did not believe this last statement. Gascoigne chuckled, O'Hara was silent, and soon the police car, followed by that of Mrs. Bradley, crept down the long hill towards the sea, and drew up half a mile from the bay.

'Now, then,' said the inspector, 'everybody quiet, please. And no torches unless you see me use mine. You'll have to manage in the dark, the same as cats.'

'And bats and owls,' muttered Laura. But, like the others,

she followed the route in silence and in the darkness. The little party—there were a sergeant and two constables with the inspector—soon climbed the grassy slope to the top of the cliffs above the bay, and there, at a curt command, they lay and waited.

Time passed, and three of the hunters had begun to think that the quarry was not going to show up when a searchlight, playing over the bay from a point to the east of the watchers, picked out a fair-sized yacht and a couple of boats which seemed to be making towards her.

'O.K. for vision,' muttered Inspector Fielding contentedly, and took his policemen away with him. The boats, in the searchlight's beam, became a couple of frenzied insects, their oars sprouting like legs.

'Why can't we go with them?' demanded Laura, referring to the police, and feeling disappointed and affronted by the rather mean tactics of the regulars.

'Because they won't let us, and because we have other fish to fry,' replied Mrs. Bradley. She did nothing, however, for twenty minutes after she had made this statement, and her companions assumed restful attitudes, talked softly, and kept their eyes on the sea, which was again in darkness.

Suddenly Mrs. Bradley rose to her feet.

'Time for the kill, she observed. 'If you wish to be in at the death, you also may be in for a fairly long walk.'

'Not——?' exclaimed Laura suddenly.

'Yes,' said Mrs. Bradley. 'We are going to take your Ancient British trackway—all of us except for George.'

'Cuddle-Up to his intimates,' said Laura, with a deplorable giggle.

'George will take the car to Welsea, garage it, and go to bed,' said George's thoughtful employer. 'There is no need for him to spend the night out.'

'I beg your pardon, madam,' said George, extremely coldly. Mrs. Bradley knew better than to argue with him, and replied with great cordiality:

'Very well, George, but you may have to lurch, belch **and** bellow, when the time comes.'

'Very good, madam. I have often played the part of an inebriate at domestic festivals in order to amuse my mother's guests, and shall not be at a loss,' replied George sublimely.

The party, guided by Laura, took the three-thousand-year-old track across the hills. Laura remembered it chiefly as a thyme-scented open vastness of sky and scudding clouds, the distances broken by green and treeless contours on which the round barrows stood out like the old, healed wounds on an oak; but now there was nothing to see except the faint gleam of torches on the ground, and Laura, working by compass, divination and what she privately regarded as her personal luck, but which included a *flair* for direction inherited from a long line of Highland moor-and-mountain men, led the party up the first long gradual slope and down the second steep one, past the small circle of standing stones and up to the ancient camp.

'All right, so far,' she said, getting up from a tumble into the camp's grassy ditch. 'There's a wood comes next, as I remember it.'

'And in that wood, where often you and I upon faint primrose beds were wont to lie, we will ambush the villains Cassius and Battle,' said Mrs. Bradley.

'You seem very sure about this,' said O'Hara suddenly. Mrs. Bradley wasted upon the upland darkness a horrible and satisfied leer.

'I don't know how to find my way into the wood,' said Laura, halting upon its outskirts. 'If it were daylight, we could skirt it and see the three barrows beyond, but——'

'Three barrows and three dead men,' said O'Hara, with Irish omniscience.

'Then here we stay,' said Mrs. Bradley. 'We don't need to go in among the trees.'

The night was chilly, and the woods were wet. The party remained upon the outskirts, where Laura remembered fallen tree-trunks. They took these for seats, and waited in patient silence broken only by the striking of a match as the young men lit their pipes.

Mrs. Bradley, whose amiable custom it was to devote her sweets to her young friends, had come with sundry pieces of chocolate. These, and some slices of bread, sustained the party, and a nip all round from her flask helped to keep out the chills and the damp.

At two in the morning, by Laura's luminous watch, a light appeared among the trees on the edge of the wood, and there was the sound of voices. At a nudge from Mrs. Bradley, Gascoigne got to his feet, switched on his torch, and, loudly swearing, began to grope his way towards the direction from which the voices came.

'Me, too?' muttered O'Hara, under cover of his cousin's noisy progress.

'No, child. Listen. We must find out first whether these are the right people.'

'Yes, of course.' He relaxed again and listened. Gascoigne had waylaid the newcomers.

'That's the man!' murmured O'Hara, recognizing the voice of the older Battle.

'Then up and at him!' Mrs. Bradley commanded. 'Never mind the rules——'

'Just knock 'em cold,' said Laura, going into battle with her usual single-minded enthusiasm.

'All three of 'em!' yelled Gascoigne, from the van of the engagement. The enemy, taken entirely by surprise and out-numbered six to one (for a posse of policemen, to Laura's fury, got up suddenly like partridges from the ground) formed an easy prey. They were Cassius and the two Battles. Cassius' son, the lubberly Ivor Sisyphus, was found next morning hiding in the wood.

'And now,' said the voice of Laura's fiancé, David Gavin, who had accompanied the police from Welsea, where he had expected to find Laura that evening, 'what's all this about?'

'If only we could go to bed together,' said Laura rapturously, from her seat on Mr. Cassius-Concaverty's head, 'I'd have plenty of time to tell you.'

'I doubt it,' said her swain, 'but we could try.'

An unpleasant task awaited O'Hara next day. Mrs. Bradley had concluded that the head and hands, which had been dug up from the floor of the cave with the bodies of Bulstrode and the drowned couple, must belong to the man who had misdirected O'Hara (mistaking him for Firman) on the day of the Club hare and hounds.

O'Hara's confirmation of her theory clinched the case against the Battles and Cassius.

'I'm afraid of the Druids,' said Laura. 'I shall never go near them again.' The young men were not of this opinion.

'It's remarkably interesting, you know,' said O'Hara. 'They're called the Dancing Druids, and one of them *did* dance. You can't get away from that. It's having buried that fellow's head and hands with the other bodies which has finally done down those murderers.'

It was left to the Chief Constable, however, to say the last word about dancing. It was addressed, moreover, to Mrs. Bradley.

'You've got something—I don't know what to call it, you know, Beatrice,' he said. 'But you always make me think of that fellow—Dante, was it?—"*and then a star danced, and under it you were born.*" '

'Don't make love to her in front of my face,' said his wife.